Endgame

DENISE ROBERTSON

Endgame

Published in the United Kingdom in 2011 by Little Books Ltd,
Notting Hill, London W11 3QW

10 9 8 7 6 5 4 3 2 1

A CIP catalogue record for this book is available from the British Library.

ISBN 978 1 906264 18 5

Every effort has been taken in the preparation of this book. The publisher or
editors cannot accept any liability for any consequences arising from the usage
thereof, or the information contained therein. Every effort has been made to trace
the owners of copyright. If any rights have been unwittingly infringed any correc-
tions will be made to future reprints.

Printed and bound by CPI Bookmarque, Croydon.

Endgame

Chapter One

FOR A MOMENT THE STILL-UNFAMILIAR bedroom was a shock, but then Ben's eyes adjusted to the morning light filtering through the curtains, and he took in his new abode. He had moved into the already furnished flat months ago. It was not large but the rooms had high ceilings, and at least it was his territory. Living with his sister and her family after he had walked out on his wife had been comforting at first, but then he had needed his own space.

He allowed himself a moment to remember his old house. The house he had shared with Diana for nearly seven years. The house he had bought to celebrate his marriage, and his elevation to the chairmanship of Webcon. Little more than six months ago he had been the man with everything – beautiful wife, top job, and money galore. Now he had no marriage, no wife, and no reason to get out of bed. He still had money, but, once there was enough of it, money was cold comfort.

He shifted on the pillows, musing about how, in a comparatively short time, his life had turned upside down. It had begun that day he was called to his grandmother's house. He had known his marriage was under threat, had known that predators were circling his company, but somehow he had managed to push those things to the back of his mind. 'I was going through the motions,' he thought. 'Trying not to think the unthinkable.'

Diana had been there in the bed beside him, as desirable as ever. A day at the office lay ahead of him, post neatly opened on the desk, coffee or tea on hand, as befitted the chairman of a mighty company. And then the phone had rung and his grandmother's nurse had spoken. 'She wants to see you, Ben. Now. She hasn't slept at all.'

He had dressed and gone round straight away, expecting to find some minor upset over the running of the house. 'What's the mystery?' he had said light-heartedly when he bent to kiss her cheek. Remembering now, he realised she had shrunk from his kiss. He should have known then that something momentous was happening.

'It's difficult,' she had said. 'It's difficult.'

Ben had felt irritated, thinking of the problems waiting for him at the office – but when she began to speak his tongue had dried in his mouth. Remembering it all now, he threw back the covers and swung his legs to the floor. What the hell was he doing, going over old ground again? He ought to be thinking ahead.

As he buttered toast and watched bacon curl in the microwave, he thought about Max. God, he missed a dog about the place. The first thing he would do when he found a house to buy would be to collect the labrador. At least he had managed to retrieve the dog from the wreckage of his marriage. He had made it a condition of easing his wife's way to his money, and it had been cheap at the price.

He leafed through the newspaper as he ate. Endless speculation about the Coalition, a pop star and a footballer caught up in scandal, and dire warnings about the staple food that all the time you'd been eating it had been gnawing at your vitals.

Britain 2010. But voicing the date to himself made him think: 2010, 70 years since World War Two had devastated lives, and ultimately had an impact on his own.

'I'm going to tell you something shameful.' His grandmother's voice had been shaky at first, but had strengthened as she went on, as though telling the tale was relieving her of a burden. 'It's something I did . . . we did, your grandfather and I . . . a long time ago. I don't want to die with it on my conscience, Ben – without making amends of some sort. But I need you to help me.'

Thoughts of dementia had fluttered through his mind then. If only it had been that simple.

'You've grown up with Webcon as a big and profitable business. But it wasn't always like that. Brewis and Webster, it used to be called. Jack Brewis, the other partner, was a joiner. He did the work and your Grandfather Webster ran the office and looked after the money. And then the war came. Jack Brewis was in the Territorial Army and they called him up in 1939. He had three children but he still wanted to go and fight. His wife was called Mollie. Your grandfather and I had just been married, and because of his limp he wasn't called up.

'The small business should have folded when Jack went off, but your grandfather wouldn't let it.' She had seen the puzzlement on Ben's face then, and put out a hand to console him. 'I'm sorry, darling, but I have to tell you all this, before it's too late.'

Ben had muttered something, but she seemed not to hear, so intent was she on the telling. 'The air raids began in 1940. Mollie took fright for the children and Jack wanted them out of London. So in the August of 1940, Mollie took them to Yorkshire. She told me a billeting officer went with them from door to door, begging people to take them in. The raids were heavy until November, but then they stopped bombing London and started on Coventry. I think that was what brought her back to London that day. She thought it might be over.'

Where was this leading, Ben had wondered, still impatient to get to the office. But he hadn't liked to interrupt.

'A telegram came, saying that Jack Brewis had been killed. Your grandfather had to get on a train, and go and tell Mollie.'

Outside the window, now, a police siren wailed. It was a welcome relief to Ben's thoughts, and he pushed back his chair and went to the window. Outside London was teeming with life, people coming and going, all of them with a purpose. 'I need a purpose,' Ben thought. But what did he want to do with his life? He stayed at the window, his thoughts going back to that Hampstead bedroom.

'How old were the children?' he had asked his grandmother, and winced when she told him the oldest hadn't yet turned nine. And then she had dropped her bombshell. 'When she came back to London, leaving the children behind in Yorkshire, Mollie made me promise. "Promise you will take care of my kids, Gwen, if the worst comes to the worst," she said. And then she went. She wanted to make sure their house was still safe – it had been in the papers about empty houses being broken into. She'd been gone about an hour when I heard the German planes – 400 people were killed in that raid, and Mollie was one of them.'

The sound of the ticking clock had seemed to grow louder in the room, and his grandmother's pale-blue eyes had filled with tears. 'I let her down, Ben. But worse than that, we also robbed her children.' She had told him then of his grandfather's annexation of the business, the covering up of the three children's financial rights, and their shuffling off as orphans for adoption. His grandfather had gone on to build a huge and prosperous business, using the Brewis family's share of the capital, and the children had disappeared from view.

'I want you to find them, Ben. I'm going to leave them all my shares in Webcon. I have to put things right before I die. Find them for me, because if you don't I can't rest.'

And so it had begun – the quest to find three children vanished into a vast population nearly 70 years before. Was his absorption in that task what had destroyed his marriage and lost him his job? But even as he thought it he discarded the idea. 'Your wife was screwing your chief accountant. That was what destroyed your marriage,' he told himself. 'And Webcon was a plum ripe for picking, something you couldn't have prevented even if you'd tried.'

At least he had found the children, locating them one by one. And he had found a friend in Barbara, the daughter of one of the children. That was a plus. But while he had been fulfilling his promise to his grandmother, both his marriage and his role at Webcon had crumbled. He closed his eyes against the pain of remembering Diana's words at his grandmother's funeral. She had walked towards him as soon as the thrust of consoling friends had dwindled. 'We need to talk, Ben. I've filed for divorce . . .'

He had interrupted her: 'In case you hadn't noticed, this is a wake.' But his admonition hadn't deterred her.

'I'm sorry your grandmother's dead. But I'm saying we need to sort things out.'

He had winced inwardly at the greed he could see in her eyes. 'You mean you want your pound of flesh?'

Her head had come up in defiance then. 'If you want to say that, yes. I want what's mine. And I hope you've dropped that ridiculous orphan hunt. They won't get a penny of my money.'

'Bitch!' he had thought, but all he had said aloud was, 'I want the dog. Max is mine.'

Thinking of Max now gave him the impetus he needed to make for the shower. This flat was fine for the moment, but no place for a dog. He would need a house, and sooner would be better than later.

* * *

Barbara Tulloch regarded her face in the steaming mirror. Not bad, considering she had been up half the night reading the case notes. 'I want this case,' she thought fiercely. 'I deserve it.'

But the truth was that if she got it, her first murder case, it would be for one reason only: that Henry Maddox didn't want it, because it was unwinnable. Henry didn't do failure. Before asking her to read up the papers, he would have studied every possible loophole, clean or dirty. Henry was the living personification of the old legal joke: 'Ethics is a county to the east of London.' If he was prepared to pass the case to her, there'd be no loopholes to help the defence.

She rubbed a space in the steam on the mirror and grimaced into it.

'Mug,' she said aloud, and then reached for her toothbrush.

'You can do it,' Ben had said when she told him. She had pulled a face but he had pooh-poohed her doubts. 'Look,' he had said at last, 'isn't the fact that you and I are friends the absolute proof that nothing is impossible?' And she had had to agree. It was almost impossible to believe that real friendship could have come out of the hostility she had felt towards him at the first time they met.

'He's called Webster,' her grandfather had said. 'Ben Webster. He's been searching for your father . . . something to do with his grandmother being ill and wanting to trace three adopted children, of which your daddy was one.'

Alarm bells had rung in Barbara's mind then. Her grandfather wasn't rich, but he had savings, and the world was full of shysters anxious to prey on the elderly. But Ben had been no shyster; he had come bearing gifts. When the Webcon affair was settled and his grandmother's will probated, she would be richer by a sum that still made her heart skip a beat.

She pursed her lips in a soundless whistle and got on with getting dressed. If there was such a thing as an unwinnable case, it wasn't going to be one of hers.

*   *   *

Dolly moved the telephone to her other ear, and waited for a human voice on the other end. It had better bloody come after she'd gone through the half-dozen options to get it.

'Can I help you?' The voice was Cockney and bored, but at least she could understand it, which was more than happened on every phone call.

'I've got your advert here. For river cruises. I don't want to book up – not yet – but I'd like to see the brochure. Europe. None of those far-off places with crocodiles. The name's Graham. Mrs Dorothy Graham, Buena Vista... that's B-U-E-N-A Vista . . . you've got it, good. Arundel Drive, Chigwell, Essex.'

When she had given the postcode she put down the receiver and then immediately picked it up and dialled again.

'Maggie, I hope you have suitcases? That cruise we talked about . . . I've sent off for the details.'

At the other end of the line her newly discovered sister Maggie was humming and hahing about expense.

'Don't be silly,' Dolly said. 'We're coming into money, you know that. And even if we weren't, I've got enough for a river cruise. It's not the *Queen Mary*. Now, I've got to go because Tootsie needs letting out. I'll keep you up to date with progress.'

She was smiling as she put down the phone and crossed to sit beside the Bichon Frise curled in a corner of the sofa. 'I'm going on holiday with my sister, Tootsie. Fancy that. Our Maggie. I hardly know her yet, but I expect we'll get on. It'll be kennels for you, I'm afraid, but you know I'll tell them about your chicken . . . and your prawns on Fridays. So there's no need to fret.'

* * *

Maggie Riley sat regarding the phone long after she had put it down. Dolly was a whirlwind, and no mistake. 'I hardly know anything about her,' Maggie thought, fear suddenly clutching at her chest. It was too soon for them to go on holidays together, or things like that. They needed time to get to know one another again. However close they had been as children, they were grown women now, who had been apart for most of their lives.

'We're old women,' she corrected herself. It was 68 years since the man and woman had come in the car and taken Dolly away. She had screamed for her mother and for Maggie, but the man had held her fast and said, 'Now, now. Let's be sensible.' He had turned to the WVS woman then and said, 'Get it over. You explain,' and carried Dolly, kicking and screaming, out to the car.

'I can look after her,' Maggie had said. 'And Mrs Webster is coming for us. She promised.' But in her heart she had known Mrs Webster would not come. They were orphans now, and there was nothing an eight-year-old could do against a man and a woman in a car.

A week later, Billy had been taken, but he had been too little to cry for her, or even for the mother he was already forgetting. 'It's for the best,' they had said, and this time the man in the car had been a vicar, which everyone seemed to think was a good thing. 'Dolly and Billy will have better lives, Maggie. They've both gone to good homes, homes with every advantage.' She herself was too old for anyone to want to adopt her, besides which she wasn't pretty like Dolly, so it had been Northfield Children's Home for her, and then a life in service.

But then old Mrs Webster, the Mrs Webster who should have come for them but never did, had left them a fortune, and Ben Webster had found her, and found Dolly for her – Billy too, although by then he was dead and in his grave. But there was his daughter, Barbara, and she was a lovely girl. A sister and a niece and a lot of money had dropped into her lap out of the blue – so why did she feel so afraid?

Maggie sat for a long time before she got up to fetch the brandy from the cupboard where she kept her pills, and poured herself a calming tot.

* * *

'Well, what do you think?'

Henry leaned back in his leather chair and regarded her over his spectacles. Barbara tried not to sound too keen. 'It seems open and shut, to me: he did it. But with the right jury, who knows?'

As she had expected, Henry was playing out a little charade. 'I'm not sure it's right for your first capital case. As you say, a guilty verdict's almost certain. I'd do it myself if it wasn't for the wretched Milliner business, which could drag on for months.'

'You lying bastard!' Barbara thought. Henry wouldn't touch a sure-fire failure like this one with the proverbial barge pole. But she played along.

'Well, someone's got to do it, so I don't mind taking it on.'

'If you're sure, then – on your own head be it. And it goes without saying, anytime you want to consult. . .'

Behind him the oak panelling gleamed in the noontide sun, and Barbara schooled her face not to beam in harmony. 'Of course,' she said. 'I know you'll be there for me, but for now I'll plough on. I'll see the defendant tomorrow, and decide whether or not he'll make a witness.' She waited until she was in the outer office before she high-fived the air to demonstrate jubilation.

*   *   *

As Ben had expected, Barbara's phone was only taking messages. 'Hope today goes well,' he told the answering machine. 'I'm free for a drink tonight, if you want to talk. Ring me.'

As he threaded the car through the city towards his sister's house, he tried to make some plans. The trouble was that so many things were still in limbo: his divorce, probate of his grandmother's will, and the take-over of Webcon, which was still not settled. 'I need a new direction,' he thought. 'But not in construction. Webcon was wished on me at birth. I was reasonably competent, but I was never cut out for it.'

But that brought an even more disconcerting thought. What was he cut out for? 'I'm 34 years old, and I haven't a clue what to do with the rest of my life.'

*   *   *

Dolly had smoked salmon and potato salad for her evening meal, and Tootsie had a little salmon to complement his chopped chicken. She felt mildly excited about taking a cruise. The brochure would be here by the end of the week and she could ponder the options. It would be up to her to choose. From what she could make out, Maggie had had holidays when her husband was alive, but nothing ambitious. 'Compared to her I'm a seasoned traveller,' Dolly thought, and once more blessed the long-dead Eddie, who had transformed her life.

She would look after Maggie. She had spent a lifetime trying to blot out the memory of when they had all been together as a family, but now it was flooding back. She couldn't remember the faces of either of her parents, but she could remember Maggie's determined little face as she battled to keep them together. Three of them in the bed, Billy in between the girls, and peeing over them most nights.

And then the man and woman had dragged her away in spite of Maggie's protestations, and some while later she had descended into hell. She closed her eyes against the memories of the men bearing down on her. '*Is that good? Is that good?*' And she had clenched her teeth against her own disgust and said, '*Yes, yes,*' because that was what they wanted to hear. She would never tell Maggie any of that, no matter how close they got. 'Never look back,' Eddie had said to her, and it had been good advice.

She looked at the dog. 'Shall we have a little night-cap, Tootsie? And then we'll see what's on the telly and put our feet up.' The dog's coat was warm and soft beneath her fingers and she was going on a river cruise. Life wasn't all bad. Not now.

*   *   *

Ben saw Barbara as she came through the pub door, shaking raindrops from her red hair. Her face was pale as usual, but her eyes were shining. 'You've taken the case,' he said, a statement, not a question. She was sliding into the seat opposite and reaching for the gin and tonic he had waiting for her.

'Yes. I can't win it, but it'll be an experience.'

Ben raised his glass. 'To progress,' he said. 'If not victory, progress.'

They drank and for a moment there was silence. 'What about you?' she said at last.

He shrugged. 'I don't know what I'm going to do.

Suggestions?'

'You know what I suggested . . . that you find Maggie's baby. I'll help, and you can use an agency. You found the three children . . . what's one more?'

It wasn't what he wanted to hear. Maggie's baby had been born more than 60 years ago, the result of rape when she was only 15. If his grandfather had done the decent thing by those children, the rape would never have happened. But why should he feel responsible for it? 'I'm thinking about it,' he said. 'Now, do you want to eat?'

* * *

Maggie kneeled to say her prayers, as she had done ever since childhood. Her bed was warm and soft, but sleep was hard to come by these days, and a moment of prayer sometimes helped. 'Life's happening too fast,' she thought. 'It's all good, but it's too much, coming like this.'

Prayers ended, she threw back the covers and climbed into bed. If Jim had still been alive, it would be different, she thought as she settled down. Except that he had never been keen on her trying to find Dolly and Billy. As for the other baby, the one that had come out of the rape, he had never liked reference made to that. Not that he had said as much, but she had seen it in the lie of his lips.

But if it was true that she was going to be rich . . . and she would believe it when she saw it . . . she could employ someone to find her baby. Having been born in 1946, he would be 63 now, or was it 64? You could be dead by 64.

The thought was so unbearable that Maggie squeezed her eyes shut and tried to think about river cruises. But that was scary too, so she turned on her side and started to work out her Co-op order for the weekend.

Chapter Two

'Bowes! Your legal's here.'

Inside the room there was a sound of a chair being scraped back on the floor. Barbara followed Howard Breen, the accused man's solicitor, through the doorway as the prison officer stood back to allow them entry. The man on the other side of the table was 27. She knew that from the brief, but he looked younger, boyish even.

'Sit down, Terry.' The solicitor's voice was soothing but still the man flinched at his words. 'This is Miss Tulloch. She's very good and she's going to represent you.'

Barbara held out her hand, and after a moment the man took it. His hand was cold and clammy. 'He's afraid,' Barbara thought. That would make things easier. No one was harder to represent than a cocky defendant. Juries hated them.

'I've read the brief,' she said, when they were all seated. 'But now I'd like you to tell it all again, from your point of view.'

He was looking to the solicitor for reassurance. 'He doesn't trust me yet,' Barbara thought. The solicitor was nodding encouragement, and at last and haltingly, Terry Bowes began.

'I wanted to tell her I'd got the job . . .'

Barbara held up a hand. 'I know, but can you go back to the

very beginning. Where you met Julie Carter, and when?' Again the fleeting glance to the solicitor, but when Terry spoke his voice was stronger than before.

'I did a job for her, at her salon. Just a few repairs. But she was really nice about it, so I said forget the bill. She said she'd buy me a drink . . .' He was almost smiling at the memory.

'Julie was older than you?'

He nodded. 'Yes, but you'd never have known it. She was . . . well, people used to think she was some kind of star.'

Barbara smiled at him. 'I've seen the pictures of her. She was glamorous.'

'It wasn't just that, the make-up and everything. I mean, that was her job – looking good. But she was just as beautiful without it. "Slap" she used to call it. "Can't be seen without me slap."'

Barbara felt a twinge of unease. 'I'm not sure he did it,' she thought, and then remembered the weight of evidence against him.

* * *

'Ben!' Peter Hammond was half-rising to his feet behind the restaurant table.

'Sorry to be a bit late,' Ben said, but Peter was already pouring him a glass of red and handing him the menu.

'Don't give it a thought. Now hurry up and choose – they say the fish is good. We've got a lot to talk about.'

Ben felt himself relax. He really liked Hammond, and had been glad of the invitation to lunch. Their friendship had grown over the years in which they'd worked together at Webcon, and he would be sorry to lose it. Peter was one of the few things he would miss about the office, now that Madge had left it.

He chose a seafood pancake to start, and griddled kidneys

with spinach purée and new potatoes.

'How's the flat?' Peter asked. 'I hear Diana's still at the house.'

'So I believe.' Ben was reluctant to discuss his marriage, but there was little point in dissembling with Peter. Diana had cuckolded him with a member of his own staff, which must have been the talk of the office long before he knew himself. He raised his gaze and looked squarely at his former colleague. 'What's Pyke doing?'

Neil Pyke had been Diana's lover – still was, as far as Ben knew. Ben had suspended him as chief accountant when he discovered it. But Pyke had also been hand-in-glove with Headey's, the company that was taking over Webcon, so no doubt he was back in place by now.

'I'm not sure what friend Pyke is up to,' Hammond said carefully. 'He's working out of Headey's, so I'm told, and he's been in twice with their head honcho. Brown-nosing as usual. Are he and Diana still together?'

'I neither know nor care,' said Ben, 'but I expect so.' Around them the restaurant buzzed with conversation. 'We don't talk much, except about money. She's very keen to get her rights.'

'Bloody awful,' Hammond said ruefully. 'Still, you've got the right attitude, letting it go over your head. It's an unfair world, and the sooner we men accept that the better. To get down to important matters . . . not that . . .' He floundered, suddenly realising that he had dismissed Ben's marriage as unimportant.

'I know what you mean, Peter. What were you going to say?

Hammond didn't answer until their first course was placed before them and they were beginning to eat.

'The recession is biting far harder than Headey's expected. Webcon is land-rich, but what good is land, even with planning permission, when contracts are being cancelled right and left? Those US firms that were coming into Canary Wharf – they're all on hold, or off altogether. The industry is holding its breath.'

The excellent pancake suddenly turned to ashes in Ben's mouth. If Webcon went down, what would happen to Adele, to the aunts so newly come to a fortune? He himself would survive, and so would Barbara, he on family money, she with her profession.

'You paint a gloomy picture,' he said carefully, and was relieved when Hammond saw someone he knew across the room, and moved on to the safer territory of gossip.

* * *

Dolly poured herself a glass of sherry and eased off her shoes. She had had a salad lunch, and she could afford a few extra calories. She might even have a truffle with her sherry if she could be bothered to go in search of them. She reached for the envelope containing the river cruise brochure, and opened it up. She and Eddie had gone on cruises almost every year: the Mediterranean, the Aegean, the Atlantic. Twice they had crossed the Atlantic. But Maggie would be swallowed up in a luxury liner. A river-cruise would surely be more her style? The Rhine or the Danube, perhaps? Even the Seine? 'I could show her Paris,' Dolly thought, and then sat back, lost in wonder at the very idea.

When they were children, Maggie had always been the strong one. Dolly closed her eyes, remembering. They had lived in London, that much she could recall. The house had been dark and small, but very safe, and there had been a lot of laughter. Especially on Friday nights, when Dad got paid and came home with chocolate bars in his pockets. 'What chocolate?' he would say, wide-eyed, when Dolly asked for her bar. She had been the forward one even then. 'I ain't got no chocolate.' And then he would produce it, and her mouth would water at the sight. 'I had forgotten that,' Dolly thought. 'How could I have forgotten that?'

But Dad had gone off to war and Mam had cried. It was Maggie who had got them through. 'I was the looker,' Dolly thought, 'but Maggie got us through.' But Maggie hadn't been able to get them through when Mam was killed, and Dad already dead. 'A hero,' someone had told her, and Maggie had had to explain what a hero was.

Dolly reached for the brochure and tried to concentrate on *A Journey through Provence*, but couldn't see the print through the tears.

* * *

Barbara pushed the pint glass across the table and settled in her seat. 'I'm grateful for this, Frank.'

The man opposite her had CID written all over him but his eyes were kind. 'Well, remember – you didn't get any of this from me. No names, no pack-drill. I had my doubts about the lad, at first. The trouble is, the case against him seems watertight. Julie Carter sounds to have been a go-ahead young woman – late 30s, but she didn't look it. Anyway, she's there alone, with only one client . . . very upmarket, the client – husband's a diplomat.'

'Did Julie have other staff?'

'Two, but they'd gone early for some reason. The client has her massage or whatever, and leaves. Julie's alive and well at that stage. Five minutes later, Bowes goes in, five minutes later he comes running out – that's on the security camera of the store opposite – runs two streets, and then dials 999 to say that Julie's dead on the salon floor. No one else went in, not by the front entrance . . . there's a back entrance but it was locked at the time.'

Barbara scribbled 'Door' on an envelope in her bag. That door would bear investigation. She looked back at the detective. 'No weapon. If Bowes shot her, what did he do with the gun?'

'That's a weak spot . . . but he didn't pick up the phone in the salon to dial 999. The prosecution reckons he came outside to ditch the gun. And remember, he ran round a corner before he phoned.'

'Was a search done? Silly question, of course there was a search.'

'Fingertip. Nothing found. Was it passed to an accomplice? Did he throw it into a passing vehicle? It is the one weak link in the prosecution's case.'

'Where did he get the gun?'

'Where couldn't he have got the gun? London's full of them, if you've got the money and the contacts. The theory is he bought it on the black market.'

'He doesn't seem a typical criminal, Frank. I found myself almost liking him.'

Frank Fisher leaned towards her. 'Watch yourself. You can't go soft in this game, Miss Tulloch. Some of the worst villains look exactly like your average saint. Now, can I get you another before I go?'

* * *

'Sit down. Have you eaten? I expect you're living hand to mouth without me there to look after you.'

'I have eaten,' said Ben, smiling at Madge, 'but only because Peter Hammond took me to lunch. I am lost without you. But I haven't come to cadge a meal, I've come to see how you are.'

Madge had been Ben's PA ever since he had become chairman of Webcon. She had served his father and his grandfather, starting as a 15-year-old in the outer office. Today she was not the prim figure she had always been at work, with not a hair out of place, but she looked good dishevelled. 'She's happy,' he thought and was glad.

'How's the flat?' she asked. She had found the flat in Margaret Street for him in the twinkling of an eye, just as she had done everything, and had made sure he had everything he needed there. It had been the last thing she did before she retired.

'It's strange. I miss the house, but that flat's exactly what I need at the moment. When I get Max . . . did I tell you I'd asked for Max? . . . I'll need a house with a garden of some sort, but that can come later. Now, tell me your plans. And how's the boyfriend?'

'Nearly as hard to manage as you, but we're getting there.' She was to marry – well, Ben supposed they would marry – Arnold Sparrow, the private detective who had located the three missing children for Ben.

'Still moving to Spain?'

'You bet. I want some sunshine, Ben. Forty-four years in a stuffy office – I deserve it. Why are you pulling a face?'

'No reason. I'm glad you're going to get some sun. I could have done with Sparrow's help again, though.'

'Not with Diana, surely? You know what she's been up to.'

'No, it's Barbara. She thinks that I . . . we. . . should find Maggie's baby for her.'

'Good. I won't forget the night she told me about that. Fifteen years old and raped on a train, more than once probably, if truth were told. A bunch of drunken servicemen on the brink of demob.'

When he had first brought Maggie Riley to London, she had stayed with Madge. He had forgotten how close the two women had become, in spite of their very different personalities. Maggie had told all – or had it extracted from her.

'I want to find that child. It would round things off. The last loose end. But sometimes I wonder if . . .'

'. . . it's best to let sleeping dogs lie?' Madge's head was cocked on one side, her eyes were quizzical. 'We're not talking dogs here, Ben. We're talking babies. She wants to find her son, whatever the consequences. Well, we'll have to see if Sparrow can find you the right person to help.'

* * *

'It sounds expensive, Dolly.' At the other end of the line Dolly was getting exasperated, and Maggie held the phone away from her ear. 'Well, of course I'd like to see Paris. Jim always said we'd go one day. But I'll need to know how much before you can tell them a definite yes.'

When she put down the phone she felt a little shaky. A cruise, even on a river, would cost hundreds. Thousands, even. And all very well to talk about Mrs Webster's will and a fortune coming. Jim had always said believe it when you see it. She had her nest-egg, of course, but that was the money she had put by to pay someone one day to find the baby.

She sat down, feeling her eyes prick. Sixty-four years ago! She had asked if she could be alone with him on that last day, 'Just for a little while.' The sisters had looked at one another and then folded their hands inside the sleeves of their habits, and glided away, although Sister Mary Joseph had said, 'Only for a few moments,' as she went. Maggie had kissed his little face then, wrinkled as though he was thinking as he slept. Then she had slipped the *Milly Molly Mandy* book inside the blanket, and put him back in the crib. 'Are you ready, Margaret?' Sister had called, and she had said 'Yes, Sister,' and walked away because she did not want to see him go.

She was never likely to find him now. He would be a grown man, in any event, a father – a grandfather, even, and in no need of a mother who had given him away. She might as well spend the money on a cruise.

*   *   *

Ben opened a tin of soup when he got back to the flat, and left it ready to heat later. It was growing dark, and outside London was quietening down. He switched on the television and let the news trickle over him. Politics, another death in Afghanistan, some stupid pop star saying something outrageous – all par for the course. He was pouring himself a whisky and soda when the doorbell rang.

'Diana!' He couldn't suppress the surprise and . . . yes . . . displeasure in his voice.

'Look who I've brought to see you!' Diana was looking down, and Ben saw the black head.

'Max!' At the sound of his voice the dog leapt into life, his body twisting in an ecstasy of recognition. Ben bent to stroke the great black head, and with one swift movement Diana was past him and inside the hall. He drew the dog over the threshold, and shut the door resignedly.

'Very nice,' Diana said, when she had installed herself in an easy chair. 'Nice-sized rooms. The furniture's a bit IKEA for my taste, but all in all you've found a good place.'

'Why have you come, Diana?' Ben was not going to enter into a discussion about his habitat, not with her.

'Darling, I thought at least you'd offer me a welcoming drink. A G & T would be nice.'

For a moment he was tempted to tell her he'd see her dead before he offered her a drink, but in the end he went across to the sideboard and poured.

'Ta.' She was looking up at him in a way he couldn't quite fathom.

'I asked you why you'd come.'

'To bring Max, of course. You said you wanted him.'

'I do. I just thought I'd wait. . .'

'Until you've relocated. It could be years before you find the right house. And he misses you, don't you poppet?' Max didn't even prick up his ears at the blandishment. 'Anyway, I don't like to think of you here on your own. You are on your own, I suppose?'

Was that why she had come – in the hope of catching him with some woman? More ammunition for her petition?

'Unlike you, Diana, I don't shack up with the first person who walks by. How is Neil, by the way? Has he settled in with you yet?'

In the old days she'd have flared up at him, but tonight it seemed nothing could ruffle her. 'Neil is still in his own place, Ben. You always did make too much of that. It was just a fling. A blip. If you hadn't taken it to heart in the way you did, none of this need have happened.'

Ben put down his glass. 'I can hardly believe my ears, Diana. You were fucking my chief accountant, my employee, in my bed, in my house – and it was a blip? Do tell me what a full-blown affair would have been like.'

There was silence for a moment and then he spoke again. 'Has he dropped you? Is that why you've come? Better the old dog than no dog at all?'

'The Neil Pykes of this world don't do the dropping, darling. They get dropped. But I didn't come here to discuss Neil.' She stood up. 'I came to bring Max, and to say I hope we can stop being horrid to one another. Thanks for the drink. I'll be in touch.'

When she had gone, Ben stood in the hall, thinking furiously. Why had she come? Surely she didn't want them to try again? If she did . . he shook his head to banish foolish ideas, and went in search of water to give Max.

* * *

When she had showered and got into her pyjamas Barbara curled up on the sofa with the brief. It was all there, just as Terry Bowes and Frank Fisher had described it. The beauty salon in a discreet Mayfair street . . . property was pricey there. She must look into how Julie Carter had managed to acquire it. Even the cost of renting would be astronomical.

Anyway, at the end of that day she was in a salon empty apart from one client just leaving, Lady Jean Darblay. Hugh Darblay's wife, obviously. Britain's man at the UN. She would have got up from the couch, patted her hair into place, paid her bill, and gone down the pile-covered stairs to the entrance. If she had been five minutes later, Terry Bowes would have been pushing past her on those stairs.

Barbara moved on to Terry's statement. He made no mention of passing anyone coming out. Could someone else have slipped in, shot Julie, and left before Terry arrived? But that would have been checked and rechecked, and caught on CCTV.

She read on. There was no mention of a motive, except for 'differences' between the lovers. Terry had seemed so mild-mannered, bewildered even. Was he capable of pumping five rounds into a lover, whatever her offence? The pathologist's evidence was chilling. Five bullets into the body, three in the chest, one in the right cheek and the fatal one in the abdomen.

She turned back to the biography of the accused. Terry had been in the Territorial Army, and was a member of an amateur gun club, a practised shot. So why had he needed five bullets –

six, if you counted the one found in the door – to kill his victim? The pathologist had said the widely dispersed wounds were evidence of a furious assault. To Barbara it seemed more like someone with no expertise firing wildly in the hope of scoring a hit.

Suddenly she wanted to ring Ben, or better still spread the brief out in front of him and ask his help. She glanced at the clock – ten to ten. Too late to disturb him now. She poured herself another drink and went back to work.

Chapter Three

BEN WOKE TO THE GENTLE nuzzling of his arm as it projected from the duvet. 'Max? What is it, boy?' It was 4.45 a. m.

Of course. Last night Max had not had his usual last-thing stroll around the gardens. Because there were no gardens. This was central London. While he pulled on jeans and a sweatshirt Ben wondered again why Diana had landed the dog on him. Not out of kindness, that was for sure.

Outside in the street, the chill struck him and he shivered. Where did you walk a dog a few hundred yards from Selfridges? A side street loomed up and he turned into it, Max snuffling ahead to find a corner to his liking. Was it an offence to allow your dog to urinate in a London street? Thanks to Blair and Brown, it probably was. They'd made laws for everything else.

'You're going to have to go to the country and stay with Adele, old son,' he told the dog as they turned for home. 'But just for a little while.' Tomorrow he would get Madge to look for a suitable house for him . . . except that Madge no longer worked for him and was looking for her own abode in Spain.

'Never mind,' he said, as he settled Max for sleep. 'I'll find somewhere. You can count on that.'

Dawn was already streaking the night sky, turning it into a

patchwork of red and pink and pearl white. 'Eat your heart out Tracey Emin,' he thought. 'You can't compete with nature.'

He had expected sleep to be impossible after so much chill morning air, but he was asleep in a trice.

The telephone woke him. 'My place, 4 o'clock,' Madge said firmly. 'No excuses – you're unemployed.'

* * *

'I'm really glad we're going to work together on this.' The man opposite Barbara – a boy, really – was just out of pupillage, and looked it. 'Have you read up on the case?'

Ian Harper nodded. 'It looks pretty straightforward. I suppose the way ahead is a plea for mitigation?'

'It looks that way,' Barbara said carefully. 'Except I'm not sure I think he did it. I'll be interested to see what you make of him when you meet him. In the mean time, let's look at the depositions.'

The first came from Angela O'Brien, Julie Carter's assistant. She had finished her last client at 5 p. m., looked into Julie's treatment room to wave a silent goodbye, and left the salon. Her colleague, Lena Savage, had left even earlier. Lady Darblay was lying motionless on the couch, and Julie had mouthed, 'See you tomorrow.' There was no one waiting, and no one else in the appointments book, because Julie had wanted to finish early.

'Do we know why?' the boy asked. She must remember his name was Ian, and he was 26 years old, not actually a boy.

'No. Can you find out? So we have an empty salon – no one even manning the phone. That's a bit odd. Check on that, too. It should be in the police report. At 5.30 Julie's client, Lady Darblay, pays her bill and leaves the building. Five minutes later our client appears on camera and enters the building. He says he saw no one – can you question him again on that? And ask

Howard Breen to put his man on to that connecting door . . . both doors.'

They went on dissecting the evidence piece by piece until they were both weary. 'That'll do for today, I think,' Barbara said.

Ian was putting his notes into his briefcase. He looked up at her and smiled. 'I thought it was open-and-shut when I sat down. Now I'm not so sure.'

'It's still open-and-shut,' Barbara said. 'It's our job to disprove that.'

* * *

Maggie shuffled the pages in the brochure and started to read again. Normandy, Provence . . . even Russia. Jim would have liked that, feeling as he did about Lenin, but they all sounded far too foreign and grand for her taste. Dolly had starred one called *The Taste of Normandy*. It would start out in Paris and journey down the river Seine to the coast. That would be opposite Dover, Maggie reasoned, which seemed a bit daft when Dolly lived so far south she was almost there.

The boat would stop at various places: Monet's garden, which she'd never heard of, and the place where Vincent van Gogh had lived and died. That would be cheerful. She'd heard of van Gogh. He'd cut his ear off, and had painted some sunflowers no better than a child in school might have done. They would also take in the D-Day beaches. 'They died like flies there, Maggie,' Dolly had said on the phone. More good cheer.

But there would be evening entertainment, and, according to Dolly, the food would be marvellous. Except it would be French, which might be difficult. 'We'd see Paris,' Dolly had wheedled. 'I love Paris. Eddie showed it to me, and now I want to show it to you.'

Paris! It was a thought. Maggie put the brochure aside and went to take her blood-pressure pill. She would think about it again tomorrow.

* * *

'So what do you think Diana was after?' Adele had swung her legs up on to the sofa and was regarding Ben, wide-eyed.

'I don't know. She said it was to bring Max, because I'd said I wanted him.'

His sister's lips twisted. 'Since when did she care what you wanted?'

They were both remembering the day he had turned up at Adele's house after discovering Diana's lover in bed with her at his own house. They had wound up in hysterical laughter because he had pinched Neil Pyke's shoe. 'Let the bastard hop home,' he had said. It had happened months ago, but it felt like yesterday

'So Max can stay here till I sort something?' Ben asked.

'Of course,' Adele said. 'The kids will love it, and our animals don't mind visitors. However, by the way he's attached to your leg I think you might have difficulty getting away without him.'

Ben bent to fondle the big black head. 'We'll be OK, I'll come over and walk him, and he's a good boy.'

Adele's next remark was a bit too casual. 'Seen anything of Barbara?'

'Yes,' Ben said, trying not to smile at her nosiness. Ever the matchmaker – but on this occasion she was wasting her time. Barbara had become a good mate, no more. 'Yes, we keep in touch now.'

It was true: they did keep in touch. But that was all. So why did he feel embarrassed?

* * *

'Seventeen pounds fifty. That's us square.' Dolly paid off the cleaner and waved her goodbye. It was 1 p.m., time for a snifter. She poured a gin and tonic, and settled on the sofa. Maggie would have the brochure by now. She would ring tonight and find out what she made of it.

She picked up the *Telegraph* but she'd read it from cover to cover over breakfast. No point in rehashing old news. Except that when she sat like this, especially over a drink, the past intruded. She closed her eyes and tried to think of Normandy, of her and Maggie in France. Who'd have thought that back in 1940?

'I don't do nappies, no more.' That's what the Yorkshire woman they were billeted on had said when Mam wanted to go to London and leave them behind with her. 'I don't do nappies no more.' But Maggie had said she would look after Billy's nappies. What was the woman's name? Anyway, she hadn't been kind. Mam had said she took their rations. 'There's not a half of mince in there,' she remembered Mam saying. 'If there is, it's passed through quick.'

And then Mam had gone to London, and had never come back. 'She's gone to Heaven,' they'd all told them, but Maggie hadn't looked convinced.

'I wonder how she died?' Dolly thought now. It would be nice if she could remember her mother's face, but she couldn't. She couldn't remember Billy's either, and he had been a bonny bairn. Perhaps Maggie had photos? Someone must have some. If they went on the cruise, she would ask Maggie.

Dolly was still thinking about photographs when drowsiness overcame her.

* * *

'Ben Webster, Ken Middlemiss.' Having made the introductions, Arnold Sparrow sat back as Madge carried in coffee on a tray.

'Quite the little woman,' Ben whispered as she passed him a cup, and received a glare for his impudence. But it pleased him to see that Madge and Sparrow were subsiding into a state of almost domestic bliss. When he had left the firm, his main concern had been for the woman who had been his PA and his father's before him.

'Right,' Sparrow said when Madge had made her exit. 'I've told Ken it's a tracing job. We worked together on a few of those in our CID days. But you'd better fill him in.'

Ben drew a breath. Where to begin? No need to wash too much dirty linen by saying his family had robbed three orphans of their inheritance. Reparation was being made, and finding Maggie's baby would be the icing on the cake.

He began. 'Margaret Riley . . . she answers to Maggie. . . was put into an institution, a children's home, in 1940. She left there at 14 and went into service with a local family called De Vere Wentworth. In December 1945 she was sent by train to the De Vere Wentworth's London house. She went alone. Troops were demob happy and there was a fair bit of drunkenness on the train. Not long before the train reached London she was raped. It was her first sexual encounter. The man was a soldier – he got off at the next stop, and she continued to London.

'There was a baby. The De Vere Wentworths arranged an adoption, sending her to a home run by nuns and called, I believe, St Clare's. So the likelihood . . .'

Middlemiss interrupted. 'The likelihood is that it was a private adoption, and to a Catholic home?'

Ben nodded. 'I want to find that child. It was a boy. Do you think you can do it?'

* * *

Bruce Forsyth was larking about on the TV. 'He's older than me,' Maggie thought, and felt comforted by the fact that Brucie was dancing like a lad. Perhaps she could go on that cruise – but not if what they said in the brochure about the price was true. The letter she'd received from Miss Vanessa that morning had said she should be enjoying herself. You had to give it to the De Vere Wentworths: they kept faith with their staff.

She felt her eyes drooping, and struggled to come awake. Even when she told them she'd fallen wrong, they'd been kind. 'I blame myself,' her Ladyship had said. 'I blame myself. It was wrong to send you off alone . . . it would never have happened if there hadn't been a war.' So many things might not have happened if there hadn't been a war. She would have had Dad and Mam to take care of her, and Dolly and Billy would not have been taken from her.

She tried not to think of the other baby. 'He'll be very, very happy and grow into a great man,' Sister Mary Joseph had said. But he might be dead like Billy, or in prison, or paralysed somewhere. Fear came and went, and she tried to concentrate on the television. It didn't do to dwell. Ben Webster had raked it all up, asking her questions: 'I can't promise, Maggie, but I'll try.'

But 64 years had gone by. It would be like looking for a needle in a haystack. 'He found you,' hope said. 'And Dolly, and what became of Billy.'

Now she had a sister and a niece. To ask for more might be greedy.

*   *   *

'So she turned up with the dog and dumped him on you?'

Around them the restaurant hummed with conversation. 'Not exactly.' Ben struggled to be fair. 'I had asked for Max. I saw it more as a gesture of conciliation.'

Barbara's eyebrows disappeared beneath her fringe. 'Nothing, but nothing, you have told me about Diana says she does conciliation.'

Ben nodded ruefully. 'True. But why else did she do it? She likes Max, I'll give her that. She wouldn't want rid of him.'

'Maybe she just felt bored and wanted to see how you were living?'

'Why should she bother? Looking back, I don't think she was that interested in me when we were married.' He paused. 'No, that's unfair. At the beginning it was . . . good. We were happy. But later . . .' He fell silent and was grateful that Barbara did not urge him on.

He took a sip of his wine and then leaned forward. 'Tell me more about your case.'

*   *   *

Dolly had put off the night-time ritual as long as she could. Nowadays it seemed to take longer and longer. Take off her wig and put it on its stand. Cream off every bit of make-up, a head-to-toe wash if she hadn't had a bath, and then eye cream round the eyes, night cream to face and neck. 'Pat it in, don't stroke,' the beautician had said.

'I've been doing this for years,' Dolly thought, and suddenly she was back in the 1960s. Christine Keeler was all over the papers. A call-girl, they were calling her, and Dolly had felt a shaft of fellow-feeling for the increasingly haggard face in the papers as the pack closed in. 'That's what I am,' she had thought, and had suddenly been afraid for her looks. There had been tiny crows' feet at the corners of her eyes and she was only 27. What about when she was 30? Or 35? Who would want her then?

She had lain awake all one night, looking down the future and seeing emptiness. That was when the creaming and the primping had begun. By the time Eddie came into her life she was hooked on it. A client at first, he had soon become her salvation. 'You'll never want for anything, Dolly,' he had said, and she never had.

She looked at herself in the mirror now, shorn of wig and mascara and artfully applied concealer. 'You're old, Dolly,' she thought, 'but you're not dead yet.' She would have to put on a good show for Mags when they went on the cruise. 'Lady Muck of Vinegar Hill,' Eddie used to call her when she got dolled up.

'I'll show 'em,' she thought. 'One more time, for our Maggie's sake.' She reached for the jar and began to cream.

Chapter Four

IT WAS NEARLY EIGHT O'CLOCK when Ben woke. He had slept well, but in spite of that he felt an enormous sense of hopelessness. What was what was missing from his life was a reason to get out of bed. He sat up and ran his fingers through his hair. This wouldn't do. He leaned back against the headboard and tried to remember his boyhood. Had he had ambitions? He must have done; they came with facial hair. But all he could remember was other boys at school, eyes shining at the thought of joining one of the Services, or creating great artworks. Smithson Minor had wanted to be an actor. 'What did I want?' he wondered, but could remember only the pain of his parents' death and the growing realisation that Webcon was where his future lay. His grandfather's influence had been subtle but relentless. It was never 'You must,' only 'You will,' in the gentlest of tones.

'I must have had ambitions,' Ben thought, as he swung his legs out of the bed. 'I just have to summon them up again, and choose one.'

* * *

Maggie eased back into her chair. When Dolly got on the phone it was usually a long session. 'I wouldn't like that phone bill,' she thought; but Dolly was not worrying about bills.

'You need to get down here, our Mags.' How easily they had slipped back into the old endearments, Maggie thought. Aloud she said, 'I can't just bob up and down the country, Dolly.'

But Dolly was rattling on about trains, and getting assistance at King's Cross. 'They do you proud, Maggie. Waiting with a trolley. A chair if you need it.'

'I will come,' Maggie said, when she could get a word in edgeways. 'I can't come now, but I will eventually.'

'We'll have to thrash the details out about this cruise . . .' But Maggie was no longer listening. The mention of trains had been enough to trigger memories.

'Demob happy,' a woman had said, when she heard the noise in the corridor. The lights in the carriage had flickered, and the train had come to a halt just as Maggie realised that if she didn't pass water she would disgrace herself. She had tried to push through the massed bodies in the corridor. She could remember the rough feel of uniform cloth, and then hands were clutching at her. A man's voice had said, 'Wait on! We can't . . .' but it had been too late. She had felt the buttons rip from her blouse . . .

'Maggie! Are you listening? I said I fancy the Seine – the Seine River – you know, Paris. What do you say to that?'

* * *

The two men settled in a booth at the back of the pub with beer and huge beef sandwiches between them. 'I'm all ears,' Ben said.

Ken Middlemiss wiped his mouth and frowned. 'I've made progress, but only in so far as I've identified dead ends. St Clare's, the home from which the baby was adopted, no longer exists. It closed in the 1970s. Whereabouts of records unknown. And no one has registered to try and find Margaret Brewis as their birth mother.'

'So what happens now?' Ben tried not to sound hopeless, but it wasn't easy.

'That was the bad news,' the detective said. 'The good news is that this child was adopted in the 1940s, and in the aftermath of a world war. Nowadays, the adoption process is sewn up tight and there's a brilliant paper trail, but there's also a real effort to disperse the children, to get them right away from any future contact with birth parents who've already let them down.'

'I thought they tried to maintain contact nowadays?' Ben's puzzlement was genuine. 'I've heard of cases where the birth parents receive photos, even see the children occasionally.'

'True, in some cases. But a baby taken before – in their opinion – a bond has been formed, there they like a clean break. In 1946 there was a system of sorts. Adoption had to go through the courts, and there was even a period in which a mother could change her mind. On paper, the law made the decisions, but in reality it was left to local authorities or, in Maggie's case, the Church. You said St Clare's was a Catholic home.'

'Yes, run by nuns and a priest called Father Lavery. Maggie says he was kind. Kinder than the sisters, who sound a rum lot, although she doesn't criticise them.'

'And it was in Nottinghamshire.'

'Yes. The De Vere Wentworths, the family where she was in service, had three houses. London, Nottinghamshire – which was the family seat – and another in County Durham, a place called Belgate. Their money came originally from coal, I believe.'

'The Wentworth family had no hand in placing the baby?'

'None that I know of. The priest and the sisters arranged everything.'

'As I said, they made up the rules to suit themselves. But that's to our advantage because it means that the placement was, in all probability, close to home. Almost certainly to a Catholic family, which means there'd have been a baptism ceremony a.s.a.p.'

'So you look up baptism records,' Ben said slowly.

'That's right. Catholic churches were thick on the ground in those days, but it should still be a simple matter of checking for a boy of that age baptised not too far from St Clare's. An adjoining parish, probably. Priest-to-priest transaction. "I've got a good home, you've got a baby – bingo."'

'So you're confident?'

'I'm never confident. Not in this game. But I'm reasonably hopeful.'

* * *

The lad was already at the table when Barbara entered the room, Ian Harper following in her wake with Howard Breen. 'Sit down, Terry,' she said, smiling to put him at his ease. 'We need to check one or two things, nothing complicated.' He put his hands on the table and she saw that his nails were bitten to the quick. 'The prosecution say that you and Julie were always quarrelling, that in fact you had had a quarrel that morning. They're hinting that she threatened to leave you . . . or rather, to throw you out because you were living in her home. Is there any truth in that?'

'No.' The word burst from him. 'We fought sometimes . . . well, not fights, just tiffs . . . nothing nasty. We'd had words that morning because I'd left a wet towel in the bathroom. Julie liked everything nice. But she kissed me before she went – she always kissed me when she went out and when she came in. And then I heard I'd got that job, and I wanted to tell her. It was a big job, well, big for me. I was going to take her out and treat her to celebrate.'

Tears had filled his eyes now, and looking at Ian, Barbara could see that he too was moved. 'OK,' Barbara said. 'Let's move on. Did Julie ever mention making a will?'

'Yes. She said she didn't want everything she'd worked for to go to her aunt because she'd never lifted a finger for her. She used to laugh then and say it wouldn't be the cats' home either. "You'll be all right if I go, Terry," she used to say; and then she'd laugh and say I shouldn't hold my breath because she was going to live for ever.'

Barbara exchanged glances with Ian. If their client said that on the stand, he would put a noose round his own neck.

She nodded. 'I can imagine. But she never actually made the will?'

'No, I don't think so. It was just a big joke to her.'

* * *

As usual Ben felt better as soon as he entered his sister's home. 'Sit down. The kettle's on.'

Max's head was nuzzling at his knee. 'OK, old boy. We'll go for a walk in a moment.' Adele was already bearing down on him with steaming coffee mugs.

'Right,' she said when she had curled up on the opposite settee. 'What's the latest?'

Ben shrugged. With Adele he could be honest. 'There is no latest. I don't think my life has moved on one centimetre since the last time I saw you.'

Adele crossed to his side and put a sisterly arm around his shoulders. 'You're depressed, Ben – and no wonder. Losing a job does that. You were so good at Webcon, and suddenly it wasn't there for you.'

Ben shook his head. 'On the contrary, Del. Bitter though I was at the time, I've come to think the Headey offer was my salvation. We were born into Webcon, you and I. We neither of us chose it. You met Harry, and that was your salvation. Being thrown out of Webcon was mine. I realised that as I walked away.'

'But what will you do now? You're 34, Ben. Even if you've enough money, you can't just . . .' Her voice tailed off, and he finished for her.

'Loaf around? Oh, I think I could. But not just yet. According to Barbara, I have a mission! You know Maggie had a child, a little boy, in 1946? Barbara thinks I should find him. Round off the family, in a way.'

'Good idea. Will Sparrow do it for you?' Adele uncrossed her legs and set her mug on the side table.

'He'll be gone. I think they go to Spain next week. But he's introduced me to a former colleague, Ken Middlemiss. Nice chap, ex-CID like Sparrow. I saw him earlier today.'

'What's he like?'

'Youngish. Took early retirement. Probably gay. Impossibly good-looking. He's keen, and he comes Sparrow-recommended. What more could you ask?'

Adele was pulling a dubious face. '1946 – it seems like a lifetime ago. Well, it is a lifetime. He'll be 63 or 4. He could be . . .'

'. . . dead? Yes he could, or he could be very much alive and on his third marriage. We'll just have to wait and see. Now, how about you? Are the kids OK?'

'They're fine. And before you ask – Harry has a new brainwave. He thinks we should go organic.'

Ben tried to show an interest in the new scheme, but it was

hard to take it seriously. Harry had a new idea every five minutes, and thanks to Adele's money he could try putting them into practice. 'But the two of them are happy. He's what she needs,' Ben told himself. He had thought Diana was right for him, but he had been wrong. And suddenly her voice was in his head: 'I'm your fucking wife and, yes, I have had a gin or two. And before you remark on my language, I need something to make life bearable in this dreary, dreary house!' He had tried to walk away, then, but she had barred his path. 'Go on! For once in your life, say what you think. Don't be such a bloody gentle-man . . . always a bloody gentleman, when what a woman really wants is a man!' Her voice had followed him up the stairs: 'If you had any sense, you'd take Headey's offer and oodles of cash, and then we could get on with our lives.' But Diana's idea of getting on with life had not included him.

'So what do you think?' Adele was looking at him expec-tantly. What was she expecting him to say?

'I think it's marvellous . . . marvellous . . . I mean it's all the rage.' He was talking about organics but the expression on Adele's face told him the subject had changed.

'Sorry,' he said. 'I was thinking about something else.'

'I can see that,' Adele said drily. 'Come on, I'll get some shoes and we'll go walkies. You could do with the fresh air.'

* * *

Dolly had decided to use the Crown Derby dinner service. 'I'm entertaining family,' she had thought that morning, and the idea had really struck her. She had never had a family . . . well, not since the Mayhews had taken her away in the car. They had been her new parents, and for a while that had been good. And at the end of the bad times that had followed, there was Eddie, and those times had been wonderful. But Barbara and Maggie were flesh of her flesh.

She would get Maggie to up sticks and move down here sooner or later, she thought. 'When you put your mind to something. . .' Eddie used to say – which was funny, really, because she never used to have a mind of her own. Except once . . . the day Lassie died. She had demanded a decent burial for her dog, and she had got it. He had made her pay for it afterwards, but she had got her way and that was what mattered.

Now she checked the oven. The chicken was browning nicely, and the veg were peeled, ready to go in the pan. It would be good to have young people in the house she thought, as she went to get ready.

In the dressing-table mirror she caught sight of herself – triple pictures that changed as she moved this way and that. 'You've kept your looks, Dolly,' Eddie used to say, and inside she had glowed. Even Maggie had said it . . . well, said her hair had always been lovely. And then she had had to confess it was a wig. Ah well, something had to go with time. She took her pink Jean Muir from its hanger and slipped it over her head.

There was a nice bottle of bubbly in the fridge, and a trifle from Selfridges food hall, too. If she put out the nibbles, now she could feed Tootsie, and then put her feet up for five minutes before the guests arrived.

※　※　※

It had been hard saying goodbye to Max. 'We'll be together soon old chap,' Ben had said, and Max had settled at Adele's side and let him climb into the car. But his eyes had been sad, and the ears drooped. Tomorrow he would consult an estate agent. There was bound to be a suitable house somewhere. His grandmother's house in The Bishops Avenue was up for sale, but he wouldn't want to live there. Not without her in it.

He had showered and changed before his phone vibrated. Picking it up, he saw there was a text message from Hamish Cameron. 'Free this weekend? Could do with a chat. You're welcome at Cruag Ben any time from Friday noon. Ring me.'

Cruag Ben! He had gone there months ago, before the roof had fallen in on his life. 'Watch your back,' Hamish had warned him then. And he'd said something about looking close to home. He had meant Neil Pyke, of course. 'But I was too thick to see it,' Ben thought now.

It would be fun to drive up to Scotland again. Or do what he did last time – take the train one way, and hire a car for the other. He had driven the hired Audi through Glen Coe and across the infamous Rannoch Moor, and then on through Crianlarich and the Borders to visit Maggie Riley in her little cottage in Belgate. He could drop in on her again if he went up this weekend. See if she had anything useful he could pass on to the detective – he could even bring her back with him, which might delight Dolly.

And Barbara – his conscience pricked him. She had been visiting her client today, a vital meeting, and he had not given her a thought. He would make up for it when he saw her this evening.

*　　*　　*

Ben was getting ready to leave when the doorbell rang. Opening the door, he found Diana on the step, a gold-topped bottle in her hand. 'Again?' he said, unable to keep annoyance from his voice.

'Darling, don't be ungracious.' She was slipping past him, and her perfume was catching at his nostrils, pungent and evocative. 'I thought you might fancy a drink after a day of doing nothing,' she said, her fingers already twisting at the foil capping. 'Get some glasses, darling, I can't do everything.'

'I'm on my way out,' Ben said, but he fetched two glasses just the same.

'Five minutes,' she said soothingly. Her coat had fallen open, and her breasts in the thin sweater were two globes, the cleft between them just showing in the sweater's V neck.

'I want her,' Ben thought and was filled with loathing at his own weakness. He deliberately made his voice harsh as he spoke. 'What do you want, Diana? You didn't come here in case I was thirsty.'

'No.' she said gravely, settling on the sofa and crossing her legs. They were bare in spite of the cold outside. Bare and brown and infinitely desirable, rising from the suede boots. 'No, I didn't come in case you were thirsty. You're a big boy, you can see to your own drinks. I came because I don't like the way things are between us. We used to be such friends.'

'Until you betrayed me, Diana. In my own house my own bed come to that. With Neil Pyke. Just in case you've forgotten.'

'I'm trying to forget. You're the one who seems determined to harbour grudges. I miss you Ben. We were friends once, and we can be again. Can't you accept that?'

She was looking at him and for once her face seemed without guile. Ben would have taken her in his arms then, except for the memory of her face, thrust into his: 'What a woman really wants is a man.' Well, he would give her a man.

'It's really interesting talking over your possible motivations, Diana, but actually I'm meeting someone. Slam the door on your way out.'

He felt triumphant until he caught a glimpse of her face reflected in the hall mirror. It was not affronted or cast down. She was smiling, as though everything was going just the way she wanted it to go.

*　*　*

'That was gorgeous, but I couldn't eat another bite.' Barbara meant what she said. The chicken had been mouth-watering, the vegetables just crisp enough, the summer-fruit trifle melting.

'Let's go in the lounge for a coffee, then.' Dolly was rising from the table, but when Ben made to clear the dishes she stayed him with a lifted hand. 'It can wait till morning. The girl will be in then. Let's get settled by the fire so we can talk.'

Barbara went dutifully into the magnolia sitting-room and sat down on the magnolia sofa. 'How does she do it?' she mouthed at Ben. 'Keep it so spotless, I mean?'

Ben was grinning, but before he could reply Dolly was back, tray in hands. She poured the coffee, and then sat back, her neat little feet together and not quite touching the magnolia carpet. 'We've got to get our Mags down here,' she said firmly as soon as she was settled. 'She's not had much of a life, as far as I can make out. Oh, she was happily married, but they hardly ever left that village . . . Belmont, or whatever it's called. And as far as I can tell, she was a dogsbody before then, somebody's housemaid.'

Ben and Barbara looked at one another, each hoping the other would take the responsibility of deciding whether or not to tell the sad story. In the end it was Ben who spoke. 'She was in service, with a titled family. They . . .'

He hesitated and Barbara willed him to go on.

'They were good to her in their way, though you know how things were then, with servants two a penny. But as far as I know, her marriage was a happy one. Jim was a miner, a staunch trade unionist. They never had children.'

So he wasn't going to tell Barbara thought, and couldn't decide whether or not he had done the right thing.

There was silence for a moment, and then Dolly sighed. 'Poor Maggie,' she said. 'Our poor Mags.'

No one spoke for a while, and then Barbara lifted her glass. 'To Maggie,' she said.

'And a win on the Lottery,' Dolly answered. 'If we're going to give our Maggie a taste of the good life, we'll need all the cash we can get.'

'FIRE AWAY,' BEN SAID AS soon as they had collected their drinks and found a table.

'I got straight on to it after we last met. Nothing definite as yet,' Ken Middlemiss said, wiping froth from his upper lip. 'That's a good pint, by the way. Fuller's is it? No, nothing through the official channels, but I've identified five possibles: boys baptised within a 50-mile radius of St Clare's in the period after the adoption was finalised. I had to guess the actual date, but as she raised no objection to the adoption, it was probably the straight three months after the child was first handed over.'

'So now you eliminate?'

'That's right. Sometimes it's easy – the child is the spitting dab of one of the parents, that sort of thing. Or there's resemblance to a sibling. It's not conclusive, but it allows you to weed out the absolute non-runners . . . ethnicity, that sort of thing. The fact that we're looking for a mature adult makes that more difficult – the adoptive parents may well be deceased. The advantage there is that, once we get face to face with the possibles, there'll be less reason for denial.'

'You mean . . . ?'

'Ask some parents if their child is an adopted one, and

they'll be reluctant to tell an outsider, particularly a private detective. I mean, why is he asking? And sometimes it's the children themselves who don't want to know. But this man has no reason to fear being found. He's mature . . . if he doesn't want to meet his birth mother now, he'll simply say so.'

Long after he had left the detective, Ben was pondering the devastation his grandfather had caused. He had betrayed the Brewis children, there were no two ways about that. He'd left them to God and good neighbours, and the mercy of the council. They could have wound up with a paedophile or an axe-murderer – his grandfather had simply washed his hands of them. His grandmother, too. They had concentrated on the business and on getting rich.

'And Adele and I have benefited.' That was a sobering thought. He had loved his grandparents – loved them still – but their betrayal rankled. 'I've been left to clear it up,' he thought. 'I have to put things right.'

* * *

Dolly made sure she had everything ready: brochure, spectacles, diary, credit cards. It was the only way Maggie would ever agree. Get it booked, then tell her money would be wasted if she didn't co-operate, and to hell with the consequences if she wouldn't budge.

The number was ringing out, and Dolly felt her heart pound. Eddie had been so good about fixing travel, but it was up to her now. Tootsie was regarding her with a beady eye as the number rang. 'You'll be taken care of. When have I ever let you down?' Dolly said out loud. 'It won't be kennels: Barbara says she'll have you, and don't blot your copybook while you're there.'

And then a recorded voice was giving her options. . . bloody options. Press one for a brochure, two for a query, three for a booking – she pressed three, and cleared her throat ready to order.

'This *Taste of Normandy*. I want a cabin for two sharing. The best you've got on the first voyage, 25th of August? . . . That'll be fine. My name is Graham, Mrs Dorothy Graham . . . Yes, I'll be paying the bill.'

* * *

Ben elected to take the A1 in preference to the M1. It was full of speed cameras, but much more interesting than the motorway, and you could stop whenever you wanted to. In fact, he didn't stop until the signs for Durham hove into sight. It was only 11.45 a. m., so he had made good time.

Belgate was as he remembered it, a colliery village strangely unbalanced now that it had lost its focal point, the pit. But the door of No. 37 Laburnum Terrace was still white and spotless. The difference was that this time, as he rang the bell, he knew he would be welcome.

'Come in!' Maggie said, and drew him over the step.

When they were seated, a pot of tea brewing between them, he asked whether she had heard from Dolly. 'Heard from her? She's never off the phone! Made of money, she must be. And this cruise – on and on, but not a word about the actual cost!'

Ben smiled. 'She thinks you can afford it now that you've come into money. And you have, I promise. I know it seems a bit vague until probate is granted, but then there'll be a sizeable amount. My grandmother left the three of you her shares in Webcon. Even in the current climate, that should amount to in excess of a million pounds each. Considerably in excess.'

Maggie's eyes widened, but he could see that the size of the bequest hadn't registered. 'You can afford to take a cruise,' he said gently.

And then he launched into the real reason for his visit. 'I want to talk to you about something else – your son. You know I want to find him if I can, but it may not be easy, and I don't want to raise your hopes.' Her face remained immobile, but her eyes had come alight at his words. 'I need you to tell me everything you can remember.'

She didn't speak, and he reached out to touch her hand. 'It's a long time ago, and perhaps you've tried not to remember? But I need all the help I can get.'

Maggie cleared her throat, and began to speak, haltingly at first and then, as memory took over, with fluency.

'It was 1945 when it happened. I was to go to the Eaton Square house and get ready for Miss Vanessa's party. They said I'd be all right on the train. Trains were packed in wartime, so I wouldn't be alone. It didn't work out that way.' She paused, and licked her lips.

'It was all over in a few minutes . . . ten or 15, I suppose. The men left me in the corridor. When I got to the London house, there was only the butler there, so I never said anything. It was Miss Vanessa who got it out of me. "You look peaky, Maggie." That's what she said –"peaky". I didn't know much about life back then, but I knew what was happening to me. When I dared think about it, that is. Once I'd told Miss Vanessa, they took over and I went to St Clare's. It was a Catholic place although Mam and Dad had been Methodists, so I suppose I was too.

'They never asked me what I wanted to happen. Lady Wentworth said the baby would go to a good home afterwards, and I'd be taken care of. That's how it was. The nuns used to say the babies needed a clean start – the same as they'd said about Dolly and Billy all those years before, whisking them away to "a clean start", whatever that was. When all I wanted to do was keep them and love them.'

'Did you see the people who adopted your son?' Ben asked. Opposite him, Maggie shook her head. 'They let me hold him one last time, and then they took him away. I never saw where they took him or who was there . . . other than the nuns, I mean. But they were pleased with themselves, I do remember that. So I expect he went to Catholics.' For the first time a note of indignation had entered her voice, but when she spoke again it had vanished. 'I went back to the Wentworths. Light work at first till I got my strength back. "I blame myself," Lady Wentworth said. And Miss Vanessa, she was in a right state about it.' Maggie's face lit up. 'She still keeps in touch, you know.'

Ben duly examined the cards and letters kept carefully behind the clock on the mantelpiece. They certainly had kept in touch – or at least Miss Vanessa had. As well she might. A very young girl raped, and all for the sake of a party.

'It's not much,' he said as he left, 'but this new man was recommended by Sparrow, so let's see what we can do. If any other detail occurs to you, let me or Barbara know. I hope we'll see you in London before long. We talk about you often.'

'Remember me to Madge,' Maggie said as he walked down the path. 'Spain! Fancy that. Well, I hope she'll be happy.'

He was half-way down the path when she called after him, and he retraced his steps. 'Don't tell our Dolly about the boy,' she said. 'It would only upset her, and she doesn't need to know. Not yet, anyway.'

In the car he riffled through the various letters and papers she had given him to help in the search. One was a photograph of Maggie herself, aged seven. A happy confident little face looked out at him. Two years later she had lost both her parents, and his grandfather had consigned her to an unknown fate.

'God,' he said aloud. But it wasn't up to God, it was up to him to try and put things at least partially right.

*   *   *

'We can count on the assistant's testimony,' Ian Harper said, trying to sound hopeful. 'She hasn't a bad word to say about him.'

Barbara nodded without enthusiasm. 'The other side will say she's just a girl taken up with romance . . . or that our client has her in his thrall. Unfortunately for us, he's good-looking.'

'That should go down well with women jurors . . .' He almost bit back the words as he realised their implication.

Barbara grinned. 'So that's what you think of us, that we're easily taken in by a pretty face?' He was blushing and she took pity on him. 'I keep wondering if there's anything in the locked door?'

Ian was shaking his head. ''Fraid not. Breen had them look into that carefully. It's always kept locked. In fact when our man questioned them no one could remember it ever being opened.'

'How did the salon dispose of refuse? They must have had bins.'

'No, he checked that. They used a specialist waste-disposal company because most of their stuff was professional waste, bottles, tubes, plastic containers . . . that sort of thing. They had special containers that were picked up by the firm every Friday afternoon. Very discreet Securicor-type operation. They would ring on approach, and someone from the salon would go down, unlock the door, hand over the waste, and lock up again.'

'There's another door to the left of the back door. It leads to the car showroom.'

'Yes, again never used, according to the motor firm. Hasn't been opened since the place was split in two and Julie took over her lease.'

'But both doors were capable of being opened, if you had the necessary keys?'

'In essence, yes – but the people in the showroom say their key is kept under lock and key, so to speak, and hasn't been used since Adam was a boy. And the back-door key was on a hook in the salon. If it had been used to open the door who put it back there? So no joy there.'

'No joy anywhere, as far as I can see. Let's get some coffee and then we'll start again.'

* * *

Maggie sat for a long time after Ben had driven away. He was going to look for, might even find, her son. 'My son' – she had hardly ever used these words, and even now she wasn't sure how she felt about them. Her son. A little old man with a wise expression, and eyes that seemed to look through and past her. 'It's best not to keep him by you,' Sister Mary Joseph had said right at the beginning, 'otherwise it's hard to let go. He'll be very, very happy, and grow into a great man.'

But what if he hadn't? What if she didn't even like him when he appeared? What if he had not existed for years? Ten or twenty?

In the end she made a cup of tea. She would just have to let things happen, because there was nothing she could do about it: all her life it had been that way. She leaned forward to switch on the TV and tried to concentrate on a lot of silly people planning dinner parties.

* * *

Barbara was mulling over the locked salon doors all the way

home, even though they seemed like dead ends. The police would have looked into them, and vetted everyone who worked in the showroom for any sign of a link with the dead woman. The trouble was that there was nothing else to seize upon. It was a relief when her mobile rang as she was garaging the car. 'Ben? Where are you?' she asked, half-laughing. 'I don't hear any bagpipes.'

'That's because I'm still in England – just. Otterburn. How did today go?'

It was a relief to pour out her confusion. 'It's there in black and white, Ben. He clearly seems to have done it. And yet there's this gut feeling I have. . .'

He told her he'd be back in three days. 'We'll go through it then. A fresh eye might help.'

When he rang off Barbara let herself into the flat and made a note: 'Ask Breen's man to check out showroom staff.' Then she fetched a bottle of wine from the fridge and poured a generous glass. 'I like Ben.' she thought. But it was more than liking. She hadn't been short of men in the past ten years . . . from university on, if she was truthful. But none of them had stirred her like this man did.

She sipped her wine. 'He'll probably go back to his wife,' she said aloud. Men usually did.

* * *

Once he was in Scotland and on the M9, the journey became easier. Stirling sped by, Crianlarich, and then Rannoch Moor spread itself ahead of him, sinister in the fading light. The white bridges sped by, and then the road was winding through Glen Coe, and Ballachulish lay before him. He had been looking forward to seeing Hamish again, but suddenly that expectation soured. Whoever was there, even if it was only

Hamish and Penny, would be paired. Diana should have been there at his side. She had always been good company on long journeys, had even shared the driving.

'I want to hate her,' he thought, 'and I do in a way.' But he still wanted her, and that was the sorry truth. 'Damn you, Diana,' he said under his breath. Why had she come the other night and plunged him into turmoil once more?

It was a relief when Cruag Ben came into view, high above the loch, and Hamish Cameron was advancing from the great doorway to bid him welcome.

* * *

Dolly kicked off her shoes and undid the zip on the side of her skirt. That was better. She took up her sherry glass, and sipped appreciatively. In a moment she would give Tootsie his milk and biscuits and start the bedtime routine for them both. For now, though, for twenty minutes or so, she was going to do sweet bugger all. That had been Eddie's favourite saying. 'Sweet bugger all, Dolly. That's what I've done all day and the money's still rolled in.' He had been a good provider – still was, in a way. If the money from the Webster will didn't come in time, she could easily pay Maggie's share of the cruise as well as her own. She might even find her a nice widower on board; get her married off.

'It wouldn't do for me, though.' She almost shuddered at the thought of remarriage. That was when she had descended into hell: when kind Daddy had died and Mummy had married again – to Mr Stainsby. If her real mother had lived, would she have married again? And would that have been a disaster, too? Perhaps it was different with real parents – they didn't let you down.

Except that Mam had gone back to London without them,

and the bombs had got her, and the Yorkshire woman – Mrs Clegg, that was her name – had called it downright selfish of her to run such a risk when she had children. 'How the hell did I remember that?' Dolly said aloud, and put up a red fingertip to wipe a tear from her eye.

Chapter Six

BARBARA ROSE TO HER FEET and adjusted her gown. She was deliberately wasting time, knowing it would put her witness on edge. She shuffled her papers before she spoke. 'You said in your evidence that the man who assaulted you was "big"?' The woman in the witness box gripped the ledge in front of her and swallowed.

'You did say that?' Barbara urged. The woman nodded and Barbara turned to the jury. 'The witness is nodding. She did say her assailant was a big man. Ladies and gentlemen, I want you to look at my client. Would you call him a big man?'

In the dock her client seemed to shrink, doing his best to appear slight. Barbara turned back to the witness. 'Do you still say it was a big man who attacked you?'

'Biggish,' the woman said, licking her lips.

'I've got her rattled,' Barbara thought and pressed on. '"Biggish"? What exactly does that mean? You don't seem to know. I'm going to ask you to look again at your statement.'

She waited as the usher carried the document to its author. 'Now, it begins with a declaration that it's accurate and true, doesn't it?'

The woman's 'Yes' was half-whispered.

'And you signed every page? You're nodding, so you do admit it's your statement? And you did say "big"?'

'He seemed big. I was scared and he just did seem big.'

'He just did seem . . . you're not very sure, are you? You're not at all sure that the slender man in front of you is the big man who felled you to the floor and took your bag?'

The woman was crying now. Time to stop before the jury started to sympathise with her.

Barbara turned again to face them. 'Ladies and gentlemen, I ask you to weigh this witness's evidence. She was subjected to a grievous assault, that is beyond doubt. But not by my client.'

'Well done,' prosecuting council whispered as they gathered up their papers. 'You and I know he did it, but you played a blinder.' Barbara smiled her thanks, although she knew he didn't mean to be complimentary. 'I doubt you'll be as lucky with the salon affair,' he said as he moved away.

She felt like shouting, 'Just watch me!' but discretion prevailed. He was probably right.

* * *

Maggie had suffered from palpitations ever since Ben Webster's visit. 'I'll do my best,' he had said as they parted. Once upon a time she would have welcomed those words, but now she was not so sure.

It was a relief when the phone shrilled. 'Maggie? Now don't get your knickers in a twist but I've booked our cruise. Normandy, on the 25th of August. An en-suite cabin with a French balcony, and every meal included.'

'How much?' Maggie said, feeling behind her for a chair.

'Never you mind. We've got money coming, remember, and I'm not short. We're going to do Paris, our Mags. The Champs-ñlysées, the Sacré-Coeur, even if you're not religious . . .'

There was a pause.

'Isn't that funny? We're sisters, and yet I don't even know if you go to church.'

Long after Dolly had rung off, Maggie sat on in the chair. It was all happening too quickly. For years her life had sailed tranquilly by – now she felt as though she was shooting the rapids. A few months ago she had been a widow with no family, living a safe and ordinary life. And then a man had knocked on her door and suddenly she had a sister and a niece and the prospect of having her child restored to her. She would know nothing about her son if he was found and stood in front of her – not even if he went to church.

And now she was going to Paris. It was all a bit much.

* * *

Ben had declined Hamish's offer of a gun, and elected to be a spectator. It was good to feel the heather crisp underfoot, and see the birds start up into the summer sky at the beaters' approach. He watched as bird after bird thudded to the ground, and felt a little surge of pleasure when one escaped and winged on its way.

At elevenses he supped his hostess's famous bullshots, fiery and salty in equal measure, and then went back to his stance beside the Land Rover. Above him, the grouse were the trickiest of targets, but inevitably most fell, and the dogs ran feverishly back and forth retrieving their treasure. Could he run a grouse moor? A wry smile crossed his face at the thought. He didn't like the slaughter. The camaraderie of a shoot was fine, but not the killing. Besides, what had Hamish said last time? 'Days like this, with friends, are fine. The commercial days are not such fun.' A moor had to pay its way, and according to Hamish the cost of the upkeep was astronomical. Left to nature, the moor would revert to its natural impenetrable form, and that wouldn't be good for the local economy. Land ownership was a responsibility. Those who came with their guns stayed in local hotels and ate out – jobs depended on the shoot.

In the end Ben banished all thoughts of his future and gave himself up to contemplation of the scenery. In the distance were the peaks; before him the moorland, a wonderful mix of grey and mauve and sage green. Perhaps he could be a hermit, living in a cave somewhere, eating berries and leaves?

'Penny for them?' It was Hamish, regarding him quizzically across the bonnet of the Land Rover.

'They're not worth even a penny,' Ben said, and smiled to show the other man that all was well.

* * *

'We've agreed on a cruise,' Dolly said as the junior settled her at the basin and the warm water flowed over her head. The girl had asked if she'd booked a holiday, and she had said, 'Yes. I'm going with my sister.' It had tripped off her tongue, that phrase, which was a wonder.

'Is that water all right?' the girl asked.

'It's lovely,' Dolly replied, 'absolutely lovely.'

In the mirror opposite she could see the other women, all like her with too much time on their hands. That was the attraction of the hairdresser's. For a little while there was no point in fretting or feeling guilty about things done or left undone. You just had to give yourself up to ministering hands. Underneath her the massage chair rolled and pummelled, and beneath her outstretched legs the rest vibrated until her flesh tingled.

She sighed contentedly. In a little while she would be seated beneath the steamer, her head lathered in conditioner, the latest gossip mags in front of her and a tray with tea and bikkies at her side. Not that she had much hair to condition nowadays. Still, she had kept her lovely hair till Eddie died, that was a consolation. After that it was easier to have wigs, but she would never have worn one while Eddie was alive. He had been proud of her appearance, in public and in private. 'Even knowing all about me,' she thought, 'he was still proud.'

* * *

It was a relief to get home early and shed her court clothes. Barbara had turned on the bath taps and was just about to pour in bath oil when the door bell rang. It was 6.30 – who the hell would call at that hour, the moment when every worker reached home and either flopped or hurried to get ready for the evening ahead?

She turned off the taps just in case, but as she crossed the hall, fastening her robe, she prayed it wouldn't be someone who stayed, not even Ben. She needed to clear her mind of today's victory, and turn her thoughts to the bigger trial ahead.

She was still hoping it was someone ringing the wrong bell as she opened the door, but as soon as she saw who it was her heart sank.

'Hello.' Diana Webster was smiling as she held out the posy of freesias. 'I saw these and thought of you.'

Barbara put out a hand but the gesture was automatic. She had met this woman once. At a funeral. Why on earth was she bringing her flowers?

'Can I come in? I won't stay long.'

Diana was half over the step as she spoke, and Barbara struggled to regain her composure. What had Ben said that day at his grandmother's funeral, when she had come upon him with Diana. 'Barbara Tulloch, meet Diana Webster, my soon to be ex-wife.' Diana had scowled then and said something cutting about Barbara's being either a paramour or 'one of the orphans'. She had managed to make 'orphans' sound somehow dirty, something of which to be ashamed. As she remembered the encounter, Barbara's spine stiffened.

'As you're already in, an invitation seems rather superfluous.' Diana had walked ahead of her, and now she sat down on the sofa, one hand nonchalantly over the arm, the other in her lap. 'Don't be like that. I've actually come here to be helpful. Is there any chance of a G & T?'

Barbara poured two drinks with a shaking hand. What the hell did she want? And what sheer neck to walk in like that, as though she had right of possession. She sat down opposite Diana, hoping fervently that her bathrobe was covering her knees. As if she picked upon the thought, Diana said, 'I hope I didn't interrupt your shower. It's just that I felt a word now might prevent misunderstandings later.'

Barbara smiled and raised her eyebrows. 'Misunderstandings?'

'I know you and Ben are friends, and it just occurred to me that you might be confused. You see, my husband has this terribly oversized conscience. He feels you've been wronged, you and those aunts of yours, and desperately want to make amends. I wouldn't like you to get the wrong impression . . . to think that it was anything more than. . .'

She sought for a word and Barbara hastened to supply it. 'Pity? Oh, I recognise pity when I see it, Diana . . . I shall call you Diana as you've come into my home in such a familiar fashion! I also recognise friendship, which is what Ben and I share with one another. You, on the other hand, are his discarded wife. Now, if you'd kindly finish your drink I'd like you to get the hell out of my flat!'

* * *

Ben had dreaded the dinner table, but in the event it was rather pleasant. The last time he had visited Cruag Ben, the other guests had quizzed him about Diana's absence. He had not been aware that she was off somewhere with Pyke. He had told them about her supposed trip to Prague with an old schoolfriend, and had seen mockery in some eyes and pity in others. 'I knew then,' he thought suddenly. 'I knew, and I wouldn't admit it.'

Tonight, though, Diana's name was never mentioned. Around them light sparkled on crystal and silver, talk was of the day's shoot and what lay ahead tomorrow, and he felt himself relax. After dinner, the men sat over their port. As they talked, Ben could see divisions forming, men who obviously worked in the same sphere swapping anecdotes, others drifting away to admire the pictures that lined the walls, or stand by the log fire and exchange what sounded suspiciously like risqué stories.

'It's been good to meet you, Ben. I've known all about you, of course. Whizz-kids tend to be talked about.' This one was Lambert, Tim Lambert, who was in real estate.

Ben smiled in what he hoped was a self-deprecating fashion. 'I don't think I was ever a whizz-kid. You flatter me.'

Tim Lambert was smiling, but it was his companion who spoke. 'The City was expecting you to fall flat on your face when you took the Webcon job, Ben. Elevated to the chairmanship of a biggish company for no other reason than that you were family – that's usually the kiss of death, you know that. But you proved them wrong by earning your place, as Webcon results show. Now we're all waiting to see what you do next.'

'I'm flattered,' Ben said again, but actually he was confused.

* * *

Barbara stayed in the bath for a long time, relaxing into the scented water and brooding about what had just happened.

Diana and Ben were over; Diana had another man in her life. Why would she want, or need, to warn other women away from Ben? 'And why me?'

Inside Barbara, something stirred. I do like him, she thought. And, yes, if we had met in some other way I might have gone after him. But whatever she felt or didn't feel towards him, his only feeling for her was one of concern – a brotherly concern, if you wanted to define it. He was a good man, of that she was sure. He had sought them out and not given up until he found them. He could easily have fobbed off his grandmother, especially when he had so many other things to contend with – the Webcon affair, and Diana's betrayal. What *had* she hoped to gain by coming tonight?

'Do I tell Ben or not?' Barbara said aloud. She put out a hand and turned on the hot tap to warm the cooling water. And if she did tell him, what would he think? She was suddenly overcome with embarrassment, and then with anger. The sheer, bloody effrontery of the woman! She reached for the soap and began lathering for all she was worth.

* * *

Ben was glad when Hamish declined a midnight walk, pleading the cool night air. 'Take the dogs, they'll love it. Lock the door when you get back in.' He had smiled then. 'It wouldn't do to leave doors unlocked for a while in London, but this is Scotland.'

Outside, the night sky was streaked with silver above the blackness of the surrounding forest. The dogs ran ahead of him, sniffing at undergrowth, scenting one or other creature of the night. One day he would bring Max up here.

Looking back, he could see that his friendship with Hamish had grown out of pity. Hamish had known that Diana was betraying him long before he had known himself. He had known about Webcon, as well. 'He is a powerful man,' Ben thought, 'but a kind one, too.'

He walked on, breathing in the night air and trying to let the worries of the day slip away. When he got back he would talk about it to Barbara – if she had time to talk, with the trial coming up. 'She'll make time,' he thought, suddenly feeling happier. 'She's like that.' A sudden feeling of gratitude for his dead grandfather overcame him then. He had thought some hard thoughts about him these past months, but his actions, whatever their motivation, had given Ben a friend. Three friends, for the two old girls were also genuinely nice.

He turned up his collar against the night air and walked on.

Chapter Seven

BOWES WAS NOTICEABLY THINNER, AND the lines around his mouth were turned down now. 'We're working very hard on this,' Barbara said and received a weak smile.

Ian Harper took up the thread. 'Please don't think silence means nothing is happening. Have you had any more thoughts?'

Bowes shook his head. 'I've told everyone over and over . . . I walked in and she was lying there. I tried to pick her up and her head just flopped, and I knew it was too late. That was why I ran . . . to get away from it because it was a nightmare. Worse than a nightmare.'

'God, I can't believe he's lying,' Ian said later, as they walked back to the car. 'But I can't see a way round it. Last night I was concentrating on the possibility of a random attack. If that back door was unlocked, even briefly while someone nipped out for a crafty fag, and a nutter with a gun wandered in from the street . . . that sort of thing. I went over everything, forensics, photographs, but it's a non-runner. There was no sign of disorder in that salon, which means she knew her attacker. If it had been a stranger she'd have tried to get out, things would have been knocked over. But she was felled where she stood – not a paper clip out of place.'

'We just have to keep on.' Barbara clicked her key and the light flared briefly on her car. 'We just go on and on until we do hit on something. It must be there, because there's an innocent man in jail and he's depending on us to get him out.'

But the grim expression on her colleague's face echoed her own feeling that she was whistling in the dark.

* * *

Ben had read through Madge's list of possible houses. '*This is the last favour I'm doing for you,*' her note read, '*so I've half-killed myself doing it. Don't feel obliged to help with any of my burdens. I'm only moving to another country, so no pressure!*'

Ben smiled as he read it. He was going to miss her. She had wiped his nose when he was a toddler, kept sweets in her desk drawer for him as he grew, shepherded him through his first tentative years at Webcon, and moved into his office when he took over as chairman. Now they were both embarking on new lives. He made a mental vow to keep in constant touch with her, and began considering the three-page list she had attached.

He crossed out anything in Twickenham and Richmond, deeming them too far out. Ealing, too, seemed remote, though perhaps worth a look. In the end, there were at least three possibles, although it was obvious that to get any sort of garden for Max he was going to have to take on a bigger house than he had intended. With a sudden overwhelming desire to see Max, he rang Adele and arranged to go over in the afternoon. Then, on an impulse, he dialled Barbara's number. 'Fancy dinner tonight?' he asked.

She hesitated before she said yes, and he wondered why. But only for a moment, before he went back to his house-hunting.

* * *

Maggie walked from Laburnum Terrace to the post office and drew out her pension and her neighbour's. 'How is she?' the clerk behind the counter asked, and Maggie pursed her lips to denote 'poorly'. It was clouding over when she left the post office. If it rained she'd get drenched, but she couldn't get used to the new-fangled taxis – which were really just motor-cars and not proper taxis – driving all over Belgate. People had money to burn nowadays.

She felt a fat raindrop splash on her forehead, and looked around. The Welfare park was on her right. It belonged to the council now that the pits were no more, but to her it would always be the Welfare. She hurried through the gates and scuttled into the old pavilion that now doubled as a shed for old men to reminisce in. It was deserted, which was a pity. She had a fortune in her bag – two pensions. And you never knew who was about, nowadays. All the same she wasn't getting wet if she could help it.

She sat down and clutched her bag with both hands. In the distance she could see the space where the headstock of the pit had been. Impossible to believe that this place was built on coal. The Tories had wiped coal-mining from the face of the earth – or from Britain. There were mines aplenty in other places, like Poland – all of them shipping in mountains of coal to British ports. Coals to Newcastle, all right.

She had liked the life of the pit once she got used to it. Back-shift and fore-shift, tub-loading, and the desirable day-shift. Bait boxes and pit clays and tricks on cavilling day. All gone. Perhaps that was what life was all about, losing things. Things and people. Except that sometimes you got things back.

She cast a look at the sky, less threatening now, and took a last look at the park, then she hitched her bag higher on her arm and turned for home.

* * *

'Good news . . . as I told you on the phone.'

Ben sipped his drink before he spoke. 'I could do with it.'

'Facing a hard day?' Ken Middlemiss's face was sympathetic, and Ben warmed to him.

'In 2010, every day is a hard day. So tell me some good news.'

'There are now three possibles – three boys christened in Catholic churches within a 50-mile radius of St Clare's. I've got someone checking each of them out. As I told you before, we can probably rule out at least one by familial resemblance. After that, in the absence of any other evidence, there'll have to be an approach. Do you want me to handle that?'

'I'm not sure. Let me think about it. Was the stuff I brought back from Maggie any use?' Middlemiss shook his head. 'A lot of letters from the firm she employed years ago. They didn't get anywhere but they certainly knew how to charge. The photographs might come in handy later.'

'As I feared,' Ben said. 'Anyway, let's order, and then we'll talk it through.'

They talked as they ate, but it was mostly pleasantries or moans about their respective spheres of work.

Over dessert, Ben studied the list. All three babies shared the same birthday. Two had been christened Michael, and one Peter. Their occupations were listed: one stonemason, one store manager and one labourer.

'How soon before you narrow it down?'

'A week, no more. So what happens then?'

'I think I'd like to do the approach myself . . . though I'd appreciate company, if you're free. I want to be sure Mrs Riley is not going to be hurt by anything we discover.'

'If it's any consolation, none of them has a criminal record. Not that that's infallible – some of the biggest villains have clean sheets. Every force knows who they are, and can do sweet FA about them. But as far as I can see, all these are upright citizens. Two of them have done quite well, actually.'

'Married?'

'All three are, and two have children. The third is a widower with no offspring. But let me do the final check, and then we can go ahead.'

* * *

Dolly riffled through the garments on the rail, finding one too fluffy, another too bare, another over-ornamented. Eddie had always liked tailored things. 'Clean lines and pastel colours,' he used to say, 'that's what a lady wears. And nothing sparkly before nightfall.' And because he thought she was a lady, she had become one. If someone believed in you, that was really all you needed.

She lifted down a powder-blue trouser suit and carried it to the fitting-room. Once she had her own clothes in order for the cruise she would have to see to Maggie's. This cruise had to be memorable for them both.

She closed her eyes momentarily, imagining herself displaying the glories of Paris to a wide-eyed Maggie. That was how she had been when Eddie first took her there. It had been the end of April, with chestnuts in blossom just like the song. They had still been there on May Day, when Paris had suddenly become awash with lily of the valley, *muguet des bois*. People selling little bunches, and perfect strangers pressing them on the first woman they met with a whispered, '*Jolie madame!*' Eddie had bought her a bottle of the perfume and she had thought it a bit overpowering, but used it just the same.

She suddenly realised she was smiling foolishly at the memory, and began to unzip her skirt.

* * *

'Face facts, Barbara, you have no case,' said Henry Maddox. 'Not even the glimmer of one. No alibi, no rebuttal of anything of theirs, no alternative perpetrator. They have motive, opportunity, and forensics. We are scuppered. You will have to go for mitigation – he did it but he's sorry. It's up to you to persuade Bowes that that's the best course. No, correction! It's the only course. Unless he wants an indeterminate life sentence. This was a nasty crime, Barbara, the cold-blooded shooting of a defenceless woman. If you can't make him out to be remorseful, the jury will eat him alive, not to mention the judge.'

'He says he didn't do it, and I believe him.' Even to her own ears it sounded weak. Hardened criminals with blood on their hands all went down protesting, 'It wasn't me!' Why should Bowes be any different?

Henry Maddox was eyeing her quizzically. 'You're not going soft on him, are you? He's a good-looking lad, but not your style, I would have thought.'

Barbara felt herself blush, with anger rather than embarrassment. Head of Chambers he might be but he wasn't getting away with that. 'Don't be silly, Henry. I have a gut feeling, that's all. But you're right. Mitigation seems to be the only way forward. I'll try him again, but don't hold your breath. He says he's innocent, and he seems to be sticking to it.'

She was back in her own office before she thought of the evening ahead and her own dilemma. Did she tell Ben about Diana's visit or did she not?

* * *

As Ben drove away from Adele's he heard Max barking after him. He must get on with the search for a house. For a moment his worries threatened to engulf him. What did he attend to first? The search for Maggie Riley's child, creating a home for him and for Max, sorting out what he should do with his professional life, or sorting his divorce?

Did he want a divorce: that was the $64,000 question. 'I don't like Diana,' he thought. 'I see her for what she is: shallow, faithless, money-greedy, and quite cruel. So why does the sight of her affect me as it does?' She could be warm at times. Kind – he had never doubted that she would be kind to Max while he was in her care. She was spoiled, imperious, sometimes greedy, but there was another side to her. If he could touch it as he had done in the beginning, perhaps they had a future.

Barbara arrived just after he had sat down and ordered a Campari soda. She opted for the same. 'I know – it's an acquired taste. I'm still trying to acquire it. But they say it has only a third of the alcohol, which is a very good reason for persevering. Anyway, bring me up to speed. You've been to Scotland and called in on Aunt Maggie. It's still strange to say that: "Aunt Maggie". Do you realise I didn't have a single female relative until you came along. Now I have two. And a cousin somewhere? What progress have you made there?'

He brought her up to date with news of the search for the baby, and his stay up north. 'Maggie was in fine fettle as usual, but I think she's a little scared about this cruise.'

'Aunt Dolly is a forceful lady.' Barbara was laughing and he felt his own face crease in return. She was good company, that was certain.

'We must get Maggie to London and discuss the trip with them. Perhaps we can help sort out potential problems.'

She nodded, but her next question took him by surprise. 'Have you seen anything of Diana?'

'Why do you ask? I saw her just before I went to Scotland. She was her usual, charming self! She hasn't done something unusually dreadful while I've been away, has she?'

Barbara shook her head. 'Not that I know of.' But she didn't meet his eye. He would have pressed her, but their starters came at that moment, and then she launched into details of her murder case. He made a mental note to quiz her later on whatever gossip about Diana she had heard, and gave her his undivided attention.

He listened as she off-loaded her worries about the case, and then, as she ran out of words, told her of his own feeling of being adrift. 'I don't know what I'm cut out for, Barbara, that's the problem. I have an academic qualification which I got more by good luck than any real effort, and a few years' experience in the construction industry, which is apparently dying on its feet. Do you think joining the Foreign Legion is a possibility?'

'Perhaps you should give it serious consideration. Now, after the osso bucco, what are you giving me for dessert?'

As she bent her red head over the menu he found his face creasing into an idiotic smile again. She was a character and no mistake . . . rather like her Aunt Dolly.

Chapter Eight

BEN CAME AWAKE WITH A start at the sound of his alarm. He blinked until the clock face swam into focus: 7.45. Time to get up. The dream came flooding back, then, the dream cruelly shattered by the alarm. Diana had been warm in his arms, beside him and yet beneath him, skin on skin, her body soft where his was hard. For a moment he still felt aroused but the thrusts had been in dreams, her groan of pleasure a figment of his imagination. Had he ever satisfied her? Was that why she had turned to Pyke?

To stop uneasy thoughts he threw back the duvet and swung his feet to the floor. The kettle was beginning to seethe when he heard the plop of the post on the mat. Wiping juice from his mouth, he padded through to the hall. Two bills, three circulars, and an official-looking letter in a good-quality envelope. He brewed tea, collected toast from the toaster, and sat down at the table to read. '*Dear Mr Webster,*' it began. '*My client, Mrs Diana Webster, is saddened by the events of the last few months and has asked me to inform you that she would be willing to enter into mediation to see if there is any possibility of reconciliation before formal steps begin to terminate the marriage.*'

His first thought was, 'How bloody dare she?' His second was less of a thought than a feeling, a sudden surge of optimism and well-being. He tried to quell it with toast and marmalade and English breakfast tea, but it seemed to be gaining ground with every mouthful.

* * *

There was a large window in the room, making it seem light and airy at first glance. In fact the window didn't open, and the air was evidence of that. Terry Bowes was already sitting at the table in the centre of the room, and Barbara sat down opposite him. She waited until the instructing solicitor had also sat down and then smiled in what she hoped was an encouraging fashion. 'How are you today?'

There was a long moment before her client replied, 'Scared.'

She nodded sympathetically. 'I understand. But we need to concentrate now because this will be our last chance to talk before the trial.'

Suddenly a female 'screw' appeared with a tray of mugs. 'Thought you might like some tea.' It was hot and pale and probably sweet, but Barbara smiled appreciation. The woman had also smiled at Terry as she handed him his mug. That meant he was a good prisoner. How much easier what she had to say would have been if he had been a shit.

'I . . . that is, we. . .' The solicitor was nodding agreement. 'We need to put something to you. We want you to consider changing your plea.'

Terry was looking at her blankly.

'You've instructed us to put in a plea of "Not guilty". But it's our duty to point out to you the possible advantages of entering a "Guilty" plea. We would present you in the best possible light – it's called mitigation – and that could mean a much lighter sentence than if you continue with a "Not guilty" plea and the jury finds you guilty.'

The solicitor leaned forward. 'It could make a big difference, Terry. Years.'

Bowes's eyes were suddenly bright with tears. 'But I didn't do it. Are you telling me I have to lie?'

Barbara tried to keep her voice even. 'No. We needed to give you that option. If you don't want to take it, then we press ahead with the "not guilty"plea.'

She felt rather than heard the solicitor sigh. It held all the overtones of doom.

* * *

The sun was shining outside, but the wind was brisk and it was unusually cool for summer. Dolly decided to wear a beige trouser-suit and her tan brogue courts. King's Cross was a mucky place, but it wasn't every day you met your sister off a train. 'Your sister': she rolled the phrase round and round, liking it. And she had so nearly shut Maggie out. Barbara too. What had she been afraid of – opening Pandora's box?

As she did her make-up, Dolly thought about how quickly she and Maggie had clicked. Even after all the years apart. They called it bonding nowadays, but to her it was still clicking. But all this closeness could present a problem. As kids they had shared everything . . . their sweets even, although Maggie had always been more generous with her and Billy than she herself had been with either of them. But closeness meant confiding. Telling it like it was . . . or had been. And how could she look into that honest pit-village face and say, 'I turned tricks for a living, our Maggie. And gave a man whatever he wanted, to save a dog.'

She couldn't do it, which meant they could never be as close as sisters should be. Outside the sun was still shining, but the day suddenly seemed to have got colder.

* * *

Trains had changed a lot, Maggie thought, as Durham gave way to Cleveland and then to Yorkshire. The seats seemed more crowded together, and carriages were noisier, but she didn't miss the old compartments. Two rows of people sitting almost knee to knee trying not to catch one another's eye. Or, worse still, being alone in there and the corridor open to any marauder.

Her mouth was suddenly dry and she settled her hat more firmly on her head, telling herself not to be silly. It had been half a century ago, and wartime. Now things were different, more organised, and God knows she had enough to deal with, sorting Dolly and her mad ideas: 'Just get on a train, Mags, and get down here. Or else I'm coming up. Actually, I'd like to come and see where you live . . .' The mere thought of Dolly taking Laburnum Terrace by storm was what had got Maggie on the train. She would settle all the nonsense about the cruise, see a bit of Barbara, and then go home for some peace and quiet. And tonight she was meeting that vicar who took Billy. After all these years.

Outside, the countryside was bursting with promise, but even as she stared out at it she was remembering Mrs Clegg's stuffy little room. Mrs Clegg had told her they were coming for Billy and given her a glare that said, 'Don't dare cry.' She was trying hard not to for fear of upsetting Billy, and Mrs Clegg's voice had softened. 'He's a vicar, Maggie. It's a good Christian home.' She had dressed Billy in his very best suit, white top with a blue collar and blue trousers that buttoned on to the top. He had white socks and his red bar shoes, and she had brushed his hair and put a left-hand parting in it. 'There now,' Mrs. Clegg had said, 'he looks a picture.'

When they came, the woman had a coat with a fur collar and the vicar looked kind, but a bit sad. The woman had held out her arms and Billy went into them. The woman said, 'He's a charmer, isn't he!' but Maggie had felt anger inside her because he was a little traitor. The sad man had taken her hand and said, 'You must be Margaret?' but she just kept looking at Billy because there wasn't much time left. 'We'll take very good care of him,' the man had said then, and looked at his wife. 'Perhaps . . .?'

Hope had sprung up in her. Perhaps they didn't want him after all? But the other man, the man who took children away, was ushering the three of them towards the door. 'Remember me, Billy,' she had pleaded inside her head.

On the path, the vicar had spoken to the woman for what seemed like a long time, and Maggie had hoped they were changing their minds. But the woman had shaken her head a lot, and eventually they had taken Billy into the car. 'There now,' Mrs Clegg had said as she put the curtains back into place. 'It's all for the best. Cling on to that.'

Outside the train it was beginning to rain, the drops running crazily across the windows. It seemed appropriate.

* * *

'Quiches as promised,' Adele said, offloading boxes on to Ben's dining-table. 'And some of Harry's pâté. Two chicken-and-ham pies, and those spicy pinwheels you like. Barbara is bringing all sorts of goodies from Fortnum's, and you, I trust, have sorted the booze.'

Ben pointed to the sideboard. 'And that's only the half of it. Thanks, Del, for cooking. I thought Madge would appreciate effort more than just hiring a caterer.'

'It's the least we can do,' Adele said, decanting food on to plates as she spoke. 'Harry's bringing the ham and chicken, and he'll carve here. Barbara's bringing tempura prawns and all the salads and dips . . . oh, and good bread. You've got condiments, I take it? Do you ever have a meal here . . . you seem to live in restaurants?'

Ben assured her he had salt and pepper. 'I've even got butter, so stop worrying. And very good coffee.'

'Seen much of Barbara?' It was said too nonchalantly.

I can see which way her mind is working, Ben thought, which means I can't tell her about Diana.

* * *

Barbara surrendered her face to the shower's flow, and tried to blot out the memory of how her client had looked. 'I mustn't let him down,' she thought. 'Even if it's hopeless, I have to try.'

She cast her mind ahead to the evening. Had she got everything – prawns, four types of salad, *pain de campagne*, two dips, and accompaniments. It had been good to plan things with Adele. 'I like her,' Barbara thought. 'She's bright and funny, and essentially kind.'

It would be good to see the aunts again, too, and introduce them to her father. His face had lit up when she told him he was invited. 'To meet that little girl again after all this time. My word! I remember walking into the room. She had your father in her arms, obviously her pride and joy. He was all dressed in blue and white, with little red shoes. He came to your Granny quite naturally, putting his little head against her. And smiling – you remember Daddy's smile? Quite devastating, even when he was a grown man.

'I spoke to the little girl, but she didn't answer, just kept staring at her brother. I said, "We'll take very good care of him," but I don't think she heard. I looked at Granny, but she had eyes only for the baby. I felt dreadful, I don't mind telling you, but Granny was adamant. One child was what we had come for, and one child it was to be. It took me a long time to get over it, I can tell you.'

She had wanted to say, 'Granny was such a bitch,' but it wouldn't have done. So she had cuddled him instead and said, 'Well, she's had a lovely life, and you'll see her soon, so it all came right in the end.'

She was putting on eye shadow when she thought of Diana. She wouldn't be there, but she'd be the elephant in the room. 'Should I tell Ben? Does he need to know?'

Diana, she thought, was a hyena circling her prey. Except that hyenas didn't prey on anything. They just moved in to feast on the corpse.

※ ※ ※

It was eight o'clock before they were all assembled in Ben's flat. If there had been a dry eye in the house when the Reverend Edward Tulloch came face to face with Maggie Riley, Ben would have been surprised. It certainly wasn't his.

'My dear,' the old man had said, holding out a hand, 'I've wondered about you all these years, and regretted leaving you behind when we took Billy. It was wrong.'

Ben had felt the room holding its breath but Maggie had risen to the occasion. 'You meant it for the best. And I was all right; I've been happy. You did right by our Billy, that's what matters to me.'

'He grew up to be a fine man. You'd've been proud of him.'
'I am proud of him – and our Barbara.'
Ben looked across to Barbara and saw her grin. The 'our'

had been significant. She moved across and whispered in his ear, 'I think I'm in.'

After that it was a night for fêteing Madge and Sparrow. 'I'll have to get used to calling him Bob,' Ben said. 'And will you be Mrs Sparrow?'

'We'll see. Don't expect an invite, though. I'm hoping I've seen the last of you lot when I fly out.'

'You're such a liar, Madge,' he said. 'You know you're my soulmate. Why try to deny it?'

She sighed heavily. 'For once in your life you might be right. Now dish some more drinks out, stupid boy. Before the evening drags.' She nudged him then. 'Look at the vicar between those two.' Dolly and Maggie had seated themselves either side of Edward Tulloch and were gazing at him adoringly. 'I think he's pulled,' Madge said.

'You and Barbara make a lovely couple,' Adele said smugly when they met later in the kitchen.

'Don't stir it, sister. We're just good friends.'

'I can dream, can't I?'

'Dream as much as you like. Just keep the mouth firmly shut.'

If he told Adele of Diana's offer of mediation, she would go spare. Instead he hurried back to the living-room and told everyone to charge their glasses. 'To the happy couple,' he said. 'And may the door of their hacienda be ever open to their adoring friends.'

'Not on your Nelly,' Madge said firmly. 'Well, not more than once a year.'

Chapter Nine

As light filtered into Dolly's spare room, Maggie decided this was the grandest bedroom she had ever slept in. The Wentworth bedrooms had been grand, but even they had not been furnished like this. As for the servants' bedrooms, they'd been scandalous if the truth were told. But this room – everything off-white, except for the roses on the bedspread and matching curtains. Fancy a Brewis fetching up like this! It seemed sacrilege to put her foot on the off-white rug. She had taken off her shoes as soon as she entered last night, for fear of marks. Come to think of it, the whole place was like that. A bit like a hospital, really except for the ornaments and things.

She could hear the radio in the kitchen as she came down the stairs, and there was the warm smell of frying bacon. 'Sit down,' Dolly said without turning from the cooker. She had a lovely white robe on – you could hardly call it a dressing-gown. But at least she'd put on a pinafore, though even that wasn't designed for standing at the stove.

'You like your white,' Maggie said, hoping she didn't sound critical. White was lovely – just not practical unless you had money to burn. Dolly was cutting a sausage into pieces for the dog sitting expectantly at her feet. 'Even the dog's off-white,'

Maggie thought, but kept it to herself. 'Do you remember breakfast at Mrs Clegg's?'

She half expected Dolly to look blank. She had only been four when they were with Mrs Clegg, after all. But Dolly was putting two loaded plates on to the table, and sliding into the seat opposite. 'I remember some things. I remember Mam crying when a man brought a telegram, and Mrs Clegg . . .'

Maggie interrupted. 'She said, "God almighty, I'll put the kettle on."'

'That's right,' Dolly said wonderingly. 'And I remember, before that, Dad saying he was fit. "Fit as a lop," he'd say, and wriggle the muscles in his arm up and down. And I remember Mam putting something horrible on my thumb when I sucked it.'

'Bitter aloes,' Maggie said. 'She did it to me, too.' They smiled at one another then, joined in memory.

* * *

Ben had fancied poached eggs from the moment he woke up. Now he decanted them on to his toast and carried them and the post over to the window seat. Outside London was busy, but here, a stone's throw from Oxford Street, he felt almost serene. God bless Madge for finding this place when he had left Diana. He had driven to Adele's, the pain of discovering Diana's adultery raw within him, and begged a bed 'for a night or two'. And the next morning Madge had swung into action. 'I've lost my right arm,' he thought.

But she deserved the sun in Spain, and years and years with Sparrow. Why had she not married before? Suddenly Ben realised he had never thought of her as a sexual being. 'We take them for granted, the people who serve us,' he thought. 'I never thought of her as a woman with needs, just as a clever being who made my life easy.'

Thinking of Madge, who had made few if any demands, he was reminded of Diana, who had demanded and got everything. Now she wanted mediation . . . was he going to give it to her? He glanced at the clock: 7.50. Offices didn't open before 9. Another hour and ten minutes when he couldn't do anything, even if he had made a decision. He took up his knife and fork and attacked the poached eggs.

* * *

Ian Harper was waiting at the entrance to the Old Bailey cells, standing with a group of fellow barristers, all wigged and gowned. He fell in behind Barbara as she walked by. There was a murmur from the others waiting.

'Cat. A,' Barbara threw over her shoulder and kept on walking.

She had been to the Category A section before, first as a pupil and then as support. Now the onus was on her. As an alleged murderer, Terry Bowes was classed as dangerous, hence Category A, but a less dangerous individual she had seldom seen. He looked, not to mince words, shit scared, and Ian's expression reflected her own view.

'Cheer up,' she told Terry. 'This waiting bit is hard. Once the hearing starts, you'll feel better. And you must listen to testimony. Anything you think is untrue, or something that strikes you when you hear witnesses – we need to know. One last thing – remember what I said about the plea. Are you still sure you want to plead "Not guilty"?'

Suddenly his face changed, and resolution shone out. 'I'm sure,' he said simply. 'I can't plead guilty, because that would be a lie.'

* * *

Ken Middlemiss was waiting when Ben reached the pub. They sat in a booth and ordered from the day's menu, both choosing lamb chops with minted gravy, mashed potatoes, and green beans. 'Comfort food,' Ben said. 'Very comforting.'

The detective was already opening his file. 'There you are. One Michael Martin, aged 64, living in St Albans.'

'You think this is him . . . definitely?'

'As definite as it can be at this stage – all the stats fit. And there's this . . . you gave me a photo of Margaret Riley aged seven. This is a photo of Michael Martin at the same age. It's only a school group but you can see him there in the front row. Compare them, and I think you'll agree there's a resemblance. It's not enough to go on, on its own – DNA is the only real proof – but it's pretty reassuring, wouldn't you say?'

'How did you get the photo?' Ben asked, curious.

'Newspaper files. Mines of information, they are.'

'What do we know about him?'

'He's a retired shop manager. It was quite a high-class establishment, so we know he's likely to have been reliable, before we make a move. Retired a year ago, when his wife was diagnosed with cancer. She died six months later. He's got one daughter and two grandchildren. They seem a nice bunch. Quite close, by all accounts.'

'So Maggie could have a whole family?'

'If they're up for reunion. Can't be sure of that until we try. What do you want me to do now?'

'Nothing just yet. I want to speak to Maggie first.'

There was silence for a moment, and then Ben leaned forward. 'On the other hand – have you got much else on today?'

It took a little over an hour to reach the outskirts of St Albans. 'Are we making a mistake?' Ben asked as they left the motorway. It had seemed like a good idea earlier. The sought-for baby was now a man of 64 who could well take umbrage if he found two strangers spying on him. 'I didn't intend to make an approach until I'd spoken to Maggie,' Ben had said to the detective, 'but I've reconsidered. If . . . to put it bluntly . . . he's a shit, she need never know we found him. If he's OK, then we can put the facts before her.'

There was silence for a moment as they both thought deeply.

'OK. We'll just take a look,' Middlemiss said at last.

'We won't commit ourselves or Maggie to anything. I just want to see if he has a nice face.'

'Eminently scientific.' The detective's tone was dry. 'Peter Sutcliffe had a nice face, so they say.'

'You know what I mean.'

'I do.'

They drove on in silence until they reached the address on Middlemiss's file. 'What if he doesn't leave his house?' the detective asked.

'We turn round and go home.' He couldn't make contact until he had Maggie's permission, but you could gauge quite a lot from observation.

After 20 minutes their prayers were answered. A man emerged from the house and moved towards the gate. He didn't go outside the garden, just stood there watching. At last a figure appeared, a schoolgirl, satchel on her back, and let out a whoop. 'Hi, Grandad! Wait till you see what I did today.'

The man was smiling, bending to kiss the child, relieve her of her satchel, and usher her into the house.

* * *

'Maggie!' Dolly sounded exasperated. They had picked out two nice dresses with bolero jackets, and a pair of white flat-heeled shoes perfect for shipboard days, and Maggie was looking like a rabbit confronted by a stoat.

'It's all very well for you, Dolly, but I haven't got that kind of money . . . well, not to spare anyway. And I can't flash a card around like you for the simple reason that I haven't got one.'

Dolly let out a theatrical sigh. 'For the umpteenth time, our Mags – we've come into money. We haven't seen it yet but it's there. In the mean time, I've got more than enough. I'll buy the bloody things for you, come to that – we're sisters, after all.'

Maggie's chin came up. 'I can pay my way, Dolly, thank you all the same. Jim and I never believed in debt.'

'Nor did my Eddie, but I tell you, Mags, I couldn't have got by without a bit of tick . . . until I met him, that is.'

Maggie leaned forward. 'How did you meet him? Jim turned up on my doorstep one day, cadging votes for Labour. I sent him off with a flea in his ear, but he still came back.'

She was waiting, and Dolly sought desperately for a lie. How could she tell her sister that Eddie had first engaged her services as a prostitute? Escort, they had called it, but there had been no doubt about what was expected.

'I met him in a dance hall, Maggie. He walked me home and after that, we just clicked, and he popped the question, and we never looked back. I hoped for a baby, but it never came. "If we have none to make us laugh, we'll have none to make us cry,"' Eddie said. He never wasted time regretting things. He was good like that. Now get in that cubicle and try those on, or I'll find a few more things – and you won't like that.'

* * *

Prosecuting counsel was still outlining his case. 'It was not unknown for the accused to call in at the salon. He had worked there as a jobbing builder, which led to the unfortunate relationship that ended in Julie Carter's brutal killing. You will hear from the pathologist that there were five bullet wounds, one of which tore out the carotid artery and caused death. One further bullet was found in the plaster of the wall. Six bullets, ladies and gentlemen. Whoever fired that gun did so with deadly intent.'

Barbara made a note. Six bullets, one of which had missed its target altogether. Terry Bowes had been in the Territorial Army and was a practised shot. Why six bullets, when he could presumably have killed with one?

She looked at the jury. Seven women, five men. Would the women sympathise with the man in the dock or with the victim? Their only qualification for sitting in judgement was that they had lived in Britain for five years, hadn't been convicted of a criminal offence, and appeared to be sane. Which they couldn't be, to be sitting there in the first place. Really sane people found a good excuse to get out of it and get on with their lives. She tuned back to the sombre tones of the prosecution.

'You will hear from the officer in charge of the case that the accused was the only person in the vicinity of the crime. Testimony which will be backed by CCTV evidence shows only Terry Bowes entering the building, and then exiting moments later in a state of disarray.'

Barbara made a note: '*Not carrying a gun.*' Well, not visibly. Not much of a rebuttal, but better than nothing at all.

* * *

It was two weeks since Ben had visited his grandmother's grave, and his first task was to remove the dead flowers from the stone vase. The earth had settled but it was still uneven. Her name had been added to the stone however. Beneath his grandfather's name the newly chiselled words stood out: '*And his beloved wife, Gwendoline Winifred Webster, who died secure in faith.*' That had been Adele's idea. 'She believed in God, Ben,' Adele had said, smiling through her tears. 'That was why she had you chasing after the orphans. She didn't want to meet her Maker with a dirty trick on her record.'

Ben was smiling at the memory as he put fresh carnations into the vase, filled now by last night's rain. He had a matching bunch for his parents' grave. *'They were lovely and pleasant in their lives, and in death they were not divided.'* They had died together in a car smash, and he and Adele had found refuge with their grandparents. Now all four of the people who had guided him through life were gone. 'I'm head of the family,' he thought, and was suddenly afraid.

He carried the dead flowers and discarded wrapping paper to the bin, and turned back for one last look at the graves. Together those people had built up a mighty business from little or nothing, and in wartime, at that. 'I have their genes,' he thought, and was somehow cheered.

* * *

It was a relief to get home and step out of her heels as she hit the hall. Sinking on to the sofa, Barbara felt her tension ease. It had been a tough day, but, on the whole, not as bad as she had expected. She had entered their plea and then had tried to concentrate on every word that issued from the prosecuting counsel's lips. Most had been damning, especially when he had emphasised the impossibility of anyone but Terry's having access to the salon.

The impeccable credentials of the prosecution's chief witness, Lady Darblay, had been emphasised. Ironically, her husband was on every front page that day, receiving an accolade from the United Nations for his services to world peace. That was bad luck, having to cross-examine the wife of an international philanthropist, a near-saint. 'If I have to come down too hard on her I'll be pilloried,' Barbara thought. 'But I need to shake her certainty that there was no one else in the building, and if I don't go for the jugular with prosecution witnesses we haven't got a case.'

Somehow, some way, someone else must have been present at the murder scene. She was still mulling over the possibilities when she heard her phone. It was Ben.

'How did it go?'

She murmured vaguely about it having not been too bad, well, not as bad as it might have been, and then accepted his invitation to dinner tomorrow evening. 'I need some of your mega-clear thinking,' he said.

She felt a frisson of pleasure at the compliment, which lasted until she was safely tucked up in bed.

* * *

It was luxury kneeling on the thick carpet, and Maggie stayed kneeling for a long time, asking blessings for everyone she could think of who needed a boost, but especially for Dolly. There had been times tonight when she had looked tired. She was still pretty, though. What was it the WVS woman had said – adoption would be no problem for Dolly and Billy because they were 'lovely children'. She had leaned against the door and heard the next words. 'Only problem is the eldest . . . she's a plain little thing, and her age is against her. Not much chance there, I'm afraid.' And she had been right. For Billy and Dolly it was adoptive parents, for her it was a children's institution.

'But I've been happy,' she told herself. She didn't have an all-white bungalow, but she had a nice little house and she'd had Jim. That had been the main thing.

The thought that she had a child, too, somewhere out there, intruded. Dolly had never had that. 'I want to tell her about him,' Maggie thought, 'but I never can.' Some things were better left unsaid. Dolly had had a cushy life, that much was obvious. But she had never known the joy of looking at the child you had created. 'And I had that. Even if only for a few days.'

The thought of Ben's quest surfaced – she might have to come clean then. Except that it would never succeed. She climbed into the spotless bed, and put out a hand to the bedside lamp.

* * *

It was a relief to get out into the night air, Max gambolling ahead of him, snuffling at the roots of trees and running back to him every now and then. Dinner tonight had been a family affair, but even as he joked with Adele and Harry, the decisions he must make weighed on his mind. He had thought about Diana all day, thought he smelled her perfume, felt the pressure of her thigh against his. Damn sensuality, it prevented rational thought. Diana was a bitch. Not only a bitch, a money-grabbing one at that. 'But I want her,' he thought ruefully.

Tomorrow he would confide in Barbara about the offer of mediation. Barbara had a cool head – she would lay out the pros and cons for him.

Tonight Max was less interested in snuffling around than in running back to check that Ben was indeed there. 'Not long now, old boy,' he said, 'and then we will be together full time.' Quite what he would do with Max during the day, and where he would walk him in central London, he wasn't sure, but he would manage. Once he got into the house . . . But without Madge to do it for him, how would he furnish and fill it?

'Barbara will help me,' he comforted himself. On an impulse he reached for his phone to text her, but common sense prevailed. She was probably out enjoying herself somewhere, or getting an early night. To the west there were still pinkish streaks behind the cloud pattern, and the moon was a faint silver disc in the night sky. He breathed in the cool air and then, whistling to the dog, turned for home.

Chapter Ten

T HE FACES OF THE JURY were rapt now. It was still early and they were drinking in every word the detective in charge of the case was saying about the finding of the body.

'We were responding to a 999 call made, as we later discovered, by the defendant. He told us he had found the body of his fiancée, Julie Carter, in her salon. The operator taking the call asked him if he was there in the salon, and he said no, he was in the street. The next street. He gave no explanation as to why he had left the crime scene.'

The voice of prosecuting counsel was silky-soft. 'No explanation at all as to why he hadn't summoned medical help immediately?'

'None whatsoever.' The detective's voice was firm.

'Am I right in thinking there was a phone in the salon which he could have used?'

'There were four phones, m'lud. One in the treatment room, another on the receptionist's desk, a third in the small office used by the deceased, and a mobile later identified as belonging to the deceased, which was lying in plain sight near the body.'

Again the deliberately understated question. 'The defendant had his own mobile, I believe, which he later used to make the emergency call?'

Barbara groaned inwardly as the detective replied. It looked bad. Even allowing for shock, why hadn't Terry dialled 999 as soon as he saw his fiancée on the floor?

* * *

'Ring me as soon as you get home, so I know you're safe. And start your packing . . .'

Maggie felt a lump in her throat. This was her sister getting agitated over their parting, after all these years. 'I'll sit up all night filling me case, Dolly, so stop worrying.'

'Next time I see you it'll be our cruise. Two more weeks. The time'll fly.'

Maggie kept smiling but inwardly she was wishing time would fly right now and the train would pull out of the station. It would be a relief to get home, but she would miss Dolly. It was strange the way the years had fallen away . . . especially when their lives had followed such different paths. 'I've made out my life was rosy,' Maggie thought. 'Not as rosy as our Dolly's but a pretty smooth run.'

Sooner or later, she might have to tell Dolly about the baby. But how did you tell a secret like that . . . even to your sister?

* * *

Edgerton Gardens was leafy, slightly faded, but charming just the same. One of a row of four-storey town houses set back from the road by pocket-sized front gardens, with sweeping paths to the door. Four storeys for one man and his dog. It didn't make sense. All the same, he might as well take a look.

A grey-haired woman in a Barbour jacket was hovering on the path. 'Mr Webster? Oh, good. I wasn't sure you'd come.'

The house had been her brother's, was now the property of her son who was working in New York, and they wanted rid. The asking price was £2.5 million but the agent had reckoned Ben would get it for two.

'So you see, there'd be no hold-up. The sale could go through immediately . . . you could be in in a matter of days,' the woman was saying hopefully. Why squash her optimism by pointing out surveys, solicitors, conveyancing?

'Sounds ideal,' he said and followed her into the hall. They were in the master bedroom when he remembered his dream. He had woken from it with a pounding heart and sweat upon his brow and reached out for her. Except that she wasn't there. The body that had responded to his every touch, rocked to every thrust, felt warm and wet to his probing fingers, was gone. There was only the empty bed. Remembering, he felt himself blush, and hastened to ask about plugs and internet access points. Damn Diana. Even in a strange house she still held sway. It was Diana who accompanied him through a trawl of bathrooms three, cupboards too many to count, loos five, and a mini-wine cellar. She was even there in the garden.

'I like this,' he said to the woman, trying to drive the shadowy interloper away. But she was there, even in the charming, large, oddly shaped tree with a celluloid umbrella, a child's plaything, planted between its roots.

* * *

'You said in your evidence a moment ago that the defendant at first refused to talk?'

'Yes,' said the detective. 'He appeared to be too over-wrought to speak.'

'And yet he had managed to make a 999 call?'

'That is correct.'

'You thought he was attempting to fool you?'

'That was my . . .' Before the witness could finish, Barbara was on her feet.

'Objection, m'lud. The witness is being asked to conjecture.'

The judge was looking over his spectacles. 'Granted. Confine yourself to matters of fact, Counsel.'

'Of course, my lord.' Prosecuting counsel was all deference, but the damage had been done. He had established that an experienced detective thought Terry Bowes a liar . . . or at least someone capable of pretence.

* * *

'Ben!' The man advancing on him was his brother-in-law, Neville Carteret, the man who had cast the vote that gave Webcon to predators and had lost Ben his job. Yet here he was, bold as brass, hand outstretched.

Instinctively Ben recoiled, but the other man was upon him, one hand closing on his arm, the other seizing his hand. 'No hard feelings, old chap? A fellow has to do what has to be done, you understand that, don't you? And it's such a pity about you and Diana. My sister can be a pain occasionally, but her heart's in the right place.'

It was too tempting to resist. 'What heart, Neville? If you're speaking about my soon to be ex-wife, she doesn't have a heart. In the right place or not.'

The memory of Carteret's face carried Ben all through his Campari soda, and on to his *croque monsieur*.

* * *

By the time the train reached Doncaster, Maggie had made up her mind. She would write to Dolly tonight.

'The plain truth is, Dolly, that there's a child out there . . . a boy . . . and he's mine,' she'd write. 'He'd be 64 now, if he's alive. There was no father, well, no one I knew. I was raped on a train. October 1945, it happened. I never saw the man's face. He was a soldier. Some soldiers, like the old joke. I was a virgin but that didn't help. Do you know what I thought of when it was happening? I thought of Dad coming home on Friday nights. I could smell beer, you see. Do you remember Friday nights? Well, you wouldn't, being little. But he always had chocolate in his pocket. For my best girl, he'd say, and that was me. And there I was on the floor of a train corridor and someone pounding away at me. "A husband passes a seed, and the seed grows into a baby" – that's what they told me at Northfield.'

She was woken from her musing by the guard announcing that they were approaching York. She couldn't tell Dolly any of that, not when Dolly's life had run on oiled wheels. Still, everyone was hiding something. It was the way of the world.

* * *

'And you subsequently searched the area between the salon and Honiton Street without finding a gun?'

'An area of 1¼ square miles was searched at great length, but no weapon was recovered.'

'How do you think the gun was disposed of?'

'Impossible to say. It could have been passed to an accomplice, or thrown into a passing truck. We searched all empty premises in the vicinity, and the post boxes with the assistance of the Royal Mail.'

'The defendant claims he never had a gun.'

'That is correct.'

'Do you believe him?' Barbara let it go. There was no point in a protest.

'A gun was used in the murder. The defendant was the only person who had accessed the property.'

He didn't need to say that Terry Bowes had fired the fatal shot. The expression on his face said it for him, and the jury were drinking it in.

* * *

The bungalow felt strangely empty now that Maggie had gone. Dolly put down some full-cream milk for Tootsie, and switched on the television. Cookery on one side, and on the other some man ranting and raving about his wife while a lip-licking presenter goaded him on. The way people raked over their problems on telly was a scandal. 'We could all do that,' Dolly thought, 'except some of us have some decency.'

She herself could say a lot, if she had a mind. Tell them what it was like to put on a dead girl's gown – slipper satin slit to the knee – and stand up in front of men and trick them into buying coloured water at the price of champagne. She had smelled Rebecca's sweat on the dress when it was slipped over her head – Rebecca, who had lost her family in Ravensbruck and died of septicaemia after a botched abortion. She had once spoken harshly to Dolly: 'You've got a lot going for you, kid, with a face and a body like that. Don't waste it on *drek* like this lot.' The *drek* had done for Rebecca in the end.

Would Maggie even know what *drek* meant, the Yiddish word for shite? Not that she would ever tell Maggie about the bar or the agency or the endless, endless procession of men. Not upright Maggie who had never put a foot wrong in her entire life.

* * *

It was a relief to escape from the court, and make her way back to the flat. She would wear her Catherine Walker suit with the mandarin collar and her pearl choker, Barbara thought. No, not the choker: mustn't look tarted up for Ben. It was only a bite of supper, after all.

She was seated at the dressing-table applying mascara, eyes wide, mouth agape, when it struck her. 'I am behaving like a teenager . . . mooning over a man who sees me as a friend, and nothing more.' She couldn't even be sure of the friendship. Ben felt guilty about his grandfather's ruthless robbery of the birthright of three children – that might be all it was. Guilt, and possibly friendship . . . that was what Ben felt for her, and the sooner she accepted that the better.

* * *

'So it didn't go well?' Ben was sympathetic.

Barbara shrugged, 'It went as I expected. It's a fact that Terry ran from the salon and along two streets before he took out his mobile. They haven't found the gun . . . the gun he says he never even saw, let alone fired. And he was apparently the only person at the scene. I know all that, so it was no surprise. But the prosecution are so smug. They know they have me boxed in, and they're loving it.'

'Tough,' Ben said. 'But you don't believe he did it?'

'With my head I totally accept his guilt. My heart says "No way." Still, enough shop. Tell me about your search. Any luck?'

'Yes, in fact. It looks as though we might have found him. We actually went up to St Albans – that's where he is, if he's the one – and I saw him. He looks . . . OK. And he's a grandpa!'

'Good grief. He's my cousin and he's a grandpa . . . I can feel the grey hairs.'

'Don't worry, you're wearing well!'

'Beast!'

'Only joking. He looked OK, but there's a lot of ground to cover before we can say it's a success. It's in abeyance until I've had a chance to talk to your aunt.'

He told her then about Diana's request for mediation. 'What should I do?'

She didn't answer for a while, and then she smiled at him. 'I think you know. You should take the mediation, and hope it works.'

'You make it sound simple.'

'I'm a genius.' She was grinning, but for some reason her eyes were sad. Perhaps she had some problem of her own, and all he could do was bang on about his affairs. On an impulse Ben put out his hand and covered hers where it lay on the table. 'You're a good friend, Barbara. I can't believe how close we've become in such a short time. God bless Sparrow for finding you. And you know I'm there for you, don't you?'

'You're getting sentimental,' Barbara said, withdrawing her hand. 'Now pour me some of that excellent Chablis, and let's talk about something lighter for the rest of the evening.'

Chapter Eleven

BEN'S FIRST CALL WAS TO the estate agent. 'I want to go back to Edgerton Gardens. Yes. I know it's larger than I said I wanted, but there's something about the place I liked. Anyway, I want another look.' As he was replacing the receiver, he heard the post plop on to the mat, and went into the hall to collect it. Circulars, bills, a bank statement, and an envelope addressed in Diana's unmistakable hand.

'*Dear Ben,*' she wrote. '*I'm so glad you've agreed to mediation. It would be foolish to throw away what we had without exploring every possibility.*' He pursed his lips at her words. What had she said at his grandmother's funeral? Her tone had been cold as ice, her words clipped: 'I've filed for divorce, you'll get the papers any day.' And instead she was now backtracking. She wanted him again. Well, well, well! He ought to feel exultation at her vanquishment. Instead he felt excited, like a 17-year-old embarking on his first affair.

To calm himself, Ben went on with opening the mail. Two bills, and then, right at the bottom, a letter in a hand he knew. Tom Finch. That was a blast from the past. The letter was short and, if not sweet, at least intriguing. '*Dear Webby, I hear you're at a loose end. I have something which might interest you and, anyway, a meet-up over a beer to discuss old times would be good. Give me a buzz. I'll be at the London address from Friday on.'*

*　*　*

The next witness was Lady Darblay. Jean Darblay, as she was called on her witness statement. 'She's serene,' Barbara thought. 'Worse still, she's composed.' No chance of rattling her under cross-examination. She wore a beige suit which shrieked money – the understated elegance of real money. Jean Muir, probably. Her hair hung either side of her face in a glossy bob ending at pearl-studded ears. Barbara settled back in her seat and waited for testimony to begin.

The witness answered the prosecution's questions smoothly enough. She had gone to the salon for a back massage and some reflexology. It was her third visit, and she had been very satisfied with the quality of the treatment. 'I would have remained a client,' she added. 'But of course . . .'

Prosecuting counsel nodded. 'So you paid the bill for this satisfactory treatment, said goodbye to the therapist, and left?'

'That is correct.'

'What time was this?'

'It was 5.30. I remember I said I hoped I hadn't kept her late, as her colleagues all seemed to have gone.'

'Did she react to that?'

'She laughed, a little ruefully, and said it was her own business and she couldn't expect the perks her staff received. I remember I commiserated with her, and then I left.'

'The exit from the salon is down a staircase to the street, is it not?'

'Yes, that's true. Quite a narrow stair.'

'Were you alone on the stair?'

'Quite alone. There was no one in the hall or the passage at the side of the stairs. I remember looking down and thinking it was rather bleak compared with the comparative luxury upstairs.'

'So you're satisfied that there was no one else on the premises?'

'Quite sure. Other staff had looked in to say goodbye and each of them said they had left their room tidy. And I had used the WC myself.' Barbara found she was smiling at the archaic phrase. How long since she'd heard a lavatory described in that way? It was both quaint and charming.

Prosecuting counsel was looking distinctly smug. 'Bastard,' Barbara thought.

'So Julie Carter was alive and well when you left the salon?'

'She was. She called after me . . . goodbye, I think, or come again. Something like that.'

There was a pause then. Was he finished? No. The questioning went on. 'What opinion did you form of Julie Carter's mood?'

Barbara was on her feet. 'Objection, m'lud. Counsel is asking for an opinion.'

The judge peered down at counsel for the prosecution.

'The question is relevant to what we will claim was the motive for the crime, m'lud. As the last person to see the dead woman alive, this witness's opinion is surely valid.'

The judicial glare intensified but the judicial voice was clear. 'Objection overruled.'

Inside Barbara alarm bells rang. One of the few avenues she had to explore was absence of motive, so what was all this about?

'I'll repeat my question. What did you make of the victim's mood that afternoon?'

'I thought she was rather tense. Pre-occupied. It didn't interfere with her therapy, but I felt she was unhappy. Or not as happy as she had seemed on previous occasions. Once or twice she sighed. I've always felt beauty therapy must be rather boring for the therapist, but Julie was always enthusiastic, so the sighs were unusual.'

* * *

They would depart St Pancras station at 9.25 and arrive at the Gare du Nord an hour and a half later. Once aboard the ship, they would have a stateroom with a French balcony. Dolly closed her eyes, seeing sunlight shining in, water rippling below, and swans. There were always swans on waterways.

She opened her eyes eventually, and went back to the literature. They would call in at Conflans, which apparently had charming lanes and the imposing tower of a medieval church. Dolly sighed. And hopefully a few coffee shops and bistros. Once you had seen one medieval church, you'd seen them all. Vernon sounded more inviting: Monet's garden. For a moment she thought he was the one who cut off his ear but no – with Monet it was waterlilies. She read on with mounting pleasure.

* * *

'Did you have any reason to think that Julie Carter might have made enemies?'

'No. She was extremely pleasant – a simple soul, I think I would say. And she was a very competent masseuse. As I said, I would undoubtedly have returned if . . .'

'. . . it had not been for the tragic turn of events? Precisely. Tell me, Lady Darblay, when you came out into the street did you see anyone lurking about?'

A small smile flitted across the witness's face, 'Not lurking.

People were passing by. I think there was a girl with a baby in a pushchair standing in the doorway opposite. But no one lurking.' She gave the word an almost comic ring.

'And you hailed a cab?'

'Yes. I started walking towards Connaught Street, then I turned back. I thought I'd stand a better chance on the opposite corner but just then a cab came towards me and I hailed it.'

'This must have taken a little while?'

'A moment or two, yes. I think I hesitated, looked up and down, that sort of thing.'

'And you saw no one else enter the salon?'

'No one.'

* * *

Diana's call had come at 11.15. 'Can we meet for lunch? My treat. Just to talk through the mediation thing.' She sounded young and scared, and Ben tried to remind himself of Diana defiant when he had thrown Neil Pyke in her face. 'Diana, go to hell,' he had said, 'and take Pyke with you.' And now they were seated in the Wolseley restaurant, contemplating one another over the glittering glass and silverware.

'Thank you for coming,' she began. Ben hardened his heart at the sound of her little-girl voice. She had other octaves, and he had felt the lash of them all. 'I sometimes wonder how we got here,' she said now.

He crumbled his bread roll. 'Well, your adultery with my employee springs to mind.'

'You've a right to be angry, Ben, but Neil wasn't the start of it. I feel quite ashamed at the way I have treated him. Used him really. I felt you and I were drifting apart. You were wrapped up in Webcon, and concerned about your grandmother. I was alone in the house, just me and Max. I felt abandoned.'

He took a sup of his Campari. 'I'm waiting.'

She was nonplussed. 'What do you mean?'

'For the violins. There ought to be violins. Or clowns. You were shagging another man, Diana – tell it how it was. I used to come home to an empty house. A note on the fridge and a Marks & Spencer meal in the microwave. You'd come home later, swearing you'd been at a girlfriend's, with the odour of another man still upon you. Give me some credit.'

'You're right, and I'm sorry. I did neglect you, but that doesn't mean we can't make things work if we try.'

Ben looked at his watch. 'I hope they hurry up with the steak. I've got a house to view at three o'clock.'

* * *

'You'll love it, our Mags. Monet's garden, all those waterlilies . . . and then the beaches, the D-Day beaches. That's right down by the coast. And there's a trip to van Gogh's place. The artist who cut his ear off. Or you can go to a wine place . . . I think that's on the same day. Anyway, have you checked your passport?'

Maggie half-listened as Dolly rattled on. The last time she had used her passport was 1981, the year before Jim died, when they had gone to Amsterdam. Thank heavens she had renewed it when it ran out – quite why, she didn't know, because she would never have gone abroad on her own. But she had been proud when she got it, complete with an official stamp and her picture in there bold as brass. It was a mercy it was up to date because Dolly would kill her if this trip fell through.

She kept on murmuring 'Fancy that,' and 'Well, I never,' as Dolly rhapsodised about Normandy in particular and France in general, but all the while she was thinking that her life had changed so dramatically in such a short time that any moment the Red Queen would walk through the looking-glass and the White Rabbit appear at her door.

* * *

Barbara let her clothes fall to the floor, and padded naked through to the bathroom. It was always a relief to get out of court clothes. Today had been tough. She would get her chance to cross-examine Lady Darblay tomorrow, but at present she didn't see a way in. The only thing she had was Terry's assertion that he had found Julie dead, but the prosecution had been at pains to impress the jury with the empty salon and the absence of anyone else lurking in the vicinity. And they had CCTV to back them up. Terry had come through the door and ascended the stairs and seen no one.

She had checked all that with him when she visited him in the cells at the day's close. After a moment she had spoken again. 'Terry, you heard Lady Darblay say that Julie seemed unhappy?'

He was shaking his head. 'She wasn't. She was over the moon about me getting that job; she told me so on the phone that morning. "It's great, Terry," she said – because if I made a go of it, it meant she could ease up a bit. That was what she wanted to do when we got married. There'd be kids then, she said, and . . .'

The end of the sentence disappeared, and Barbara put out a hand to console him. He had cried, then, and she had tried to tell him to keep up his spirits. But her words were hollow and they both knew it. Tonight's *Evening Standard* had contained a picture of Lady Darblay being presented to the Queen at some function. The press were loving her ritzy connections. 'She basks in her husband's saintly aura,' Barbara thought now, as she sank further into the scented water. 'If she says Julie was upset, the jury will believe her.' Perhaps she could suggest that to someone as imperturbable as Lady Darblay even the most trifling of mood swings could seem magnified. It wasn't much, but better than nothing.

She thought of Ben as she dried herself and applied moisture cream liberally to her body. Perhaps he too was at a loose end. She pulled on a robe and went in search of the phone, but all she got was his answerphone: '*Leave a message and your number and I'll get back to you as soon as possible.*' She didn't leave a message. He might think she was desperate for company, and that would never do. She poured herself a whisky and ginger, and curled up on the sofa with the newspaper.

Chapter Twelve

THE WITNESS WAS A PRETTY girl of 27. Lena Savage. She gave her evidence in a low voice, obviously over-awed by the court surroundings.

'Julie was so happy. "This is it, Lena," she kept saying. "He's the one."'

Counsel nodded sympathetically. 'So I believe. But on the day in question you left the salon early?'

'Yes. I was going for a fitting. I'm . . . I was getting married this month. We've put it back. I couldn't . . .' She was on the verge of tears.

'Julie Carter was a good employer, then? She understood about things like wedding dresses?'

'Yes.' The answer was fervent. 'She was lovely. Good to everyone. So how could he do this? She loved him . . .'

Barbara was rising to her feet to intervene when the opposing counsel beat her to it.

'Quite so. That completes my examination of the witness, m'lud.'

Barbara kept her voice gentle. No point in spooking the girl further. 'I'm sure we all understand how devastated you are by what has happened. But can I take you back to that day? You left at 4.15?'

'Yes. My client went at 4, then I tidied my treatment room and I went to say goodbye to Julie. She was showing a client into her room, and she smiled and said, 'Watch they don't stick pins in you.' She was teasing me about putting on weight and getting into my dress. It's vintage 1980s . . . I'm having it taken in.' She looked suddenly agitated. 'It's been cleaned and everything.'

'I'm sure it has,' Barbara hoped she didn't sound sarcastic. 'But to come back to that afternoon. In your opinion, Julie was in a good mood. Happy, even?'

'Yes. Like always. She was a happy person.'

'So you had no reason to think that anything had upset her?'

'No. Like I said, she was happy.'

'Thank you. No more questions for this witness, m'lud.'

Prosecuting counsel was on his feet. 'Rebuttal, m'lud. Miss Savage, is it true that Julie was a kind person?'

'Very kind.' The tone was fervent.

'So it's perfectly possible that, in order not to diminish your enjoyment of your day, she might have hidden any upset from you?'

'I suppose so.' This time the tone was less sure.

'Thank you. That's all, m'lud.'

As her opponent sat down, Barbara was making a note. Julie's close friend and associate had seen no sign of stress in the dead woman. And yet Lady Darblay yesterday had said she was tense. Had something happened after Lena Savage left the salon, or had the girl been simply too wrapped up in her vintage dress to notice?'

* * *

'So as you'll see, we're going to be cosseted.' Dolly's handwriting was large and childlike. Maggie let the letter fall into her lap, remembering she had taught Dolly how to write her name, 60 . . . no, 69 years ago. More than half a century. Where had the time gone? Dolly's tongue had stuck out of the side of her mouth and her stubby little fingers had gripped the pencil so hard the lead kept snapping. 'D . . . O . . . L . . . L . . .' She had formed the big fat letters and then looked up at her sister, eyes shining. 'I can write my name, our Maggie. Aren't I a good girl?'

And then they had taken her away. 'I want our Maggie,' she had shouted, and tried to wriggle free, but the man had said, 'Now, now!' and lifted her up, legs kicking, to carry her down the path towards the car.

'Please, Maggie, please,' she had screamed – and then, just before he closed the car door, 'I want my Mammy.'

'It's for the best,' they had told Maggie, and perhaps it had been. Dolly had gone up in the world, and owned a palace of a house. 'And I've been happy,' Maggie told herself stoutly. She might not have a house of her own, but her rent was up to date, and now she was going on a cruise.

* * *

'Webby! Good to see you again.' Tom Finch hadn't changed much, except for a faint greying at the temples which was rather distinguished. 'I've been meaning to look you up for ages, but you know how it is . . . I fly in to London full of good intentions, and then, suddenly, I'm back on the plane again.'

'Where are you based?'

'Geneva. Let's order, and then I'll fill you in.' Over smoked salmon Ben learned of Tom's two marriages. 'This one's for keeps – can't afford the alimony. Seriously, she's lovely. You'll like her. And she's a huge help to me, a very social animal. And very shrewd.

'Actually,' he went on, 'she goaded me into contacting you. The fact is I'm expanding fast . . . too fast. I need someone I can trust, someone who knows how to manage a wide-flung work-force, can read balance sheet . . . that sort of thing.'

Ben held up a hand. 'Before we go any further, what exactly do you do?'

'Property development. In Europe mostly, but a little in the Americas. There are several companies, but the parent company is Pantheon.'

'I've heard of Pantheon,' Ben said slowly. 'I just didn't realise you were behind it.'

'I am it, old chap. Hence the call. We're growing fast. I need a trusty lieutenant, and I think you might be the ideal person.'

*   *   *

Counsel was getting into his stride, tugging on his gown with one hand and shuffling papers with another. 'Get on with it,' Barbara said under her breath, and, as if he heard, he obeyed.

'Officer, you conducted an exhaustive search of the sur-rounding streets for the weapon, I believe.'

'We did, m'lud. No weapon was found.'

'Do you have an opinion as to what happened to the weapon?'

'I think the defendant passed it to an accomplice, or disposed of it in a passing vehicle.'

'Let me turn then to the bullets. You obtained six, I believe?'

'That is correct. Five were retrieved by the pathologist. The sixth was found in the plaster of the wall.'

'And these bullets were from a 7.65 mm Webley Automatic?'

'That is correct. It's a type commonly sold on the black market.'

Barbara came alert. For some reason the man was sweating – and yet he was a seasoned officer, a firearms expert giving straightforward evidence. Why should he be uneasy?

When it was her turn to cross-examine, she by-passed the whereabouts of the gun and went straight to the bullets.

'Bullets have an identity, don't they? You can tell things from the rifling?'

'That is correct.' Sweat was beading his upper lip and, more significant still, his eyes were flicking across to prosecuting counsel. She asked one or two stilted questions, and let him go. Something was up, but for the moment she would bide her time.

* * *

Ben pulled up in Edgerton Gardens, and sat contemplating the house. Could he be happy there? He needed a four-storey town house like he needed a hole in the head, but it seemed to be drawing him towards it. He had felt at ease there, almost high. Suddenly he remembered how Diana had intruded into his thoughts on his first visit, and his cheeks burned at the memory. All the same, he might as well take another look . . . at the garden, at least. If he could get it for £2 million, he might bite.

He cut down the side of the house to the garden. 'I like this,' he had said to the woman showing him round, but it was really the oddly shaped tree that had attracted him. It still did, but this time he looked more carefully at the rest of the lay-out. Lawns and flower-beds, big but not too big. A place for children. Except that he was never likely to have children now.

And would he need a house at all, if he might be moving to Europe? What had been said over lunch was whirling around in his head. What did he know about property development? Well, quite a lot actually, compared with most people. But what would become of Max? And would his working abroad appeal to Diana, supposing he were foolish enough to try again? Vague ideas of pet passports flashed through his mind before he started up the engine, and turned for home.

*   *   *

'You don't need a bath, Maggie, if you've got a shower. It's en suite . . . it'll be lovely.' At the other end of the line Maggie was getting herself worked up about the absence of a bath.

'It maybe en suite, or whatever you call it, but I've never had a shower in my life. Water pouring on your head . . . I'm not starting that at my time of life. It'll have to be all-over washes.'

'It doesn't pour on your head, Maggie, you can divert the jet.'

'Well, you divert the jet, Dolly; I'll use a flannel. Still, the sliding windows'll be nice. When you said a French balcony I thought it would be like a little veranda, with seats on – but if you can slide the windows back, that'll do. And entertainment every night . . . will it be in French?'

'It might be, Maggie, but if I'm any judge the passengers will be mostly Americans. They don't do French, so I guess it'll likely be English. Now, before we get on to our Barbara, is anything else worrying you?'

They talked of Billy, then, and how he would have felt about having his daughter spread all over the papers. 'Defence counsel, that's what they call her,' Maggie said.

'He'd've been proud of that. So would our Mam and Dad.' Dolly felt suddenly weepy. 'I never forgot them, Maggie. Well, perhaps for a bit, when I was still little. But I remember Mam putting rags in my hair. "You've got lovely hair, our Dolly," she said. Yes, I remember that.'

'She used to say you had a pretty mouth: "Our Dolly's got a

cupid's bow." You've kept your looks, I must say.'

'If our Dad hadn't died in the war, it would all have been different, wouldn't it? We'd've grown up together, watched our Billy grow into a man. He might even be alive today.'

'It's no good talking like that, Dolly. Life happens – especially to kids.'

* * *

Barbara caught the prosecuting counsel in the corridor outside the robing room. Without his wig and gown he was less imposing.

'David, I won't beat about the bush. Is there anything on the bullets that you haven't disclosed?'

His eyes flickered momentarily, but he recovered his composure. 'Nothing relevant. I passed on all the relevant stuff.'

'If you don't mind, I'll decide what is and is not relevant to my case. What did you hold back? I reserve my right to take this to the judge if I need to.'

'No need for that. It's nothing. Bullets with a similar rifling were retrieved from a crime scene in the Lake District last year. They have absolutely no connection with this case. Believe me, we tried very hard to place your client in Kendal that day, but his alibi was cast-iron. There is no connection, none.'

'How can you say that for certain? When did this happen?'

'A year, 18 months ago, I forget exactly. The gun is obviously one of those weapons that are hawked around. It would have been got rid of in the Lakes, and shipped to the other end of the country for resale. Your client would have bought it in some East End pub. There is nothing whatsoever linking that crime scene to your client or the victim. We checked very thoroughly.'

'Then why didn't you release it to me, if it was so unimportant? Why conceal it?'

'Because I knew exactly what you would do with it – what you will do with it now: use it as a red herring to hold up the case. I hope you'll be sensible and see the futility of doing so, but I doubt it. You'll have the file in the morning.'

'I meant what I said, David. I may take this further, if it's in my client's best interest to do so.'

'Your privilege, Barbara. And now, if you'll excuse me . . .' He swept off. But he was rattled, Barbara thought. Good!

* * *

Ben had rung Barbara on a whim when he left Farringdon Street, and as he expected he got her answerphone. He left a message: *'Do you fancy dinner tonight, if you're not bushed?'* She had rung him an hour later. Now he settled back and watched Corrigans of Mayfair seethe around him. If there was a recession it wasn't reflected here.

When Barbara walked towards him he saw heads turn to watch her, men and women alike. She was striking, the red hair made sure of that, and she carried herself proudly. He felt a little frisson of satisfaction that the table she was joining was his. He rose and greeted her with a kiss. 'Sit down. We've both had quite a day.'

'How was yours?' she said as she settled back with the dry sherry she had requested.

'Interesting. I'll tell you all about it later. Tell me first how the case went.'

He listened as she outlined the day's events. 'D'you think anything will come of these other bullets?'

'Not really. I think my opposite number was being truthful. He's got an open-and-shut case, and he didn't want me creating a diversion, even if it was a cul-de-sac.'

'I know rogue guns do change hands. Would Terry have

been able to lay hands on one?'

'Easily. Before he met Julie, he frequented pubs – he worked in construction. A word in someone's ear – it would have been simple. He's a good shot, thanks to the TA which he joined four years ago. Which makes me wonder about the pattern of bullets. He could have done it with one shot, so why use six?'

'Can you make something of that?'

'I can try to make something of everything, that's my job. The trouble is that I have no substantial witnesses, and they've got Lady Darblay, to mention but one. The unimpeachable witness for the prosecution.'

'Unimpeachable?"

'Akin to a saint. She's married to Lord Darblay, the diplomat, and is a loving wife, devoted mother.'

'She has children?'

'One, a boy. Ten or eleven, and the apple of her eye, by all accounts. She said the salon was deserted and Julie Carter was on edge, and the jury drank in every word. I could see it in their faces. The only time Lady Darblay seems ever to have blotted her copybook was over the boy. She's very protective of him, doesn't like publicity, that sort of thing. Paparazzi were after her husband, when he won the UN peace award, and the boy got in the way of the cameras, and they snapped him. She flew right off the handle. It made the papers briefly.'

Over their starter, they talked about Maggie's baby. 'I like Sparrow's man, Ken Middlemiss. Knows his stuff. In theory, you can go through official tracing channels: the government set up the scheme a few years ago to help adopted people trace their natural parents, and you can signify your willingness to be found there. But that could take forever and, of course, there's no guarantee our man is looking for his birth mother – or even knows he's adopted. Nowadays children must be told, but back in 1946 a lot of adoptive parents preferred not to tell.'

'So what did Middlemiss do?'

'What we did to trace you and the aunts – parish records, birth and baptism registers. He's convinced he's found the right man, but we have to be mega-sure.'

'You do realise he's my cousin?'

'You've already pointed that out. And he has children, so you'll be Aunty Barbara.'

'Heaven forbid. I like having the aunts, though, and wish I saw them more often.'

'When you're free of this case and they're back from their cruise, we'll have a get-together.'

'The cruise! Do you really think Maggie will do it?'

'I'd back Dolly against the world. She may look fragile but what she wants she gets. She wags her foot when she's cross . . . she did it with me the first time we met, when she didn't want to admit who she was. If she says Maggie's going, go Maggie will.'

Over coffee, Barbara regarded Ben quizzically. 'What are you not telling me?' He pulled a 'Who? Me?' face, but it cut no ice. 'Come on, spit it out.'

'I was offered a job today. Mostly in Europe . . .'

Chapter Thirteen

Barbara opened the file and began to read what was inside: details of a crime committed in Kendal, in Cumbria, almost two years earlier. The victim had been a 63-year-old pensioner named Beryl Rutherford. She had lived alone in a rented house, and had been retired for three years from her job as a midwife. There were no signs of a break-in; no strangers had been seen in the vicinity; no one had heard any disturbance. She had been found, shot to death, by her sister-in-law, who had called at the house after getting no answer to phone calls over several days. Cumbria police had carried out exhaustive enquiries that revealed precisely nothing.

According to the sister-in-law, nothing had been taken from the house, and from the description of the scene there had been nothing of great value to take. The bullets were the only clue; and they had yielded nothing, either. No weapon had been found. When she closed the file, Barbara was forced to conclude that the prosecutor spoken the truth when he said that, once they had checked Terry Bowes's whereabouts, they had found no connection between this murder and her case.

Terry was seated in the interview room when Barbara went down. 'I'll be brief, Terry. I need an answer and it has to be a truthful one. There's no one else here, so you must be truthful with me.'

He was nodding and looking apprehensive.

'Do you know . . . did you know . . . a woman called Beryl Rutherford?'

'No. I don't know anyone called Beryl. If she says I did she's lying.'

'She was a nurse, Terry. Does that ring a bell?' Again a shake of the head.

'She lived in Kendal. Have you ever been there?'

'No. I don't even know where it is? What is this, who is she? The police went on and on about Kendal. I told them I'd never been there, never heard of it . . . but they didn't listen. Until it turned out I was with the TA at the time.'

'You were away with the TA? Where?'

'We were camping on Salisbury Plain –' suddenly he was grinning. 'They had to believe me then.' The grin widened.

'Why? Why did they have to believe you?'

'I was in the police station at the time . . . the cells. Me and Trev Matthews. Drunk and disorderly.'

Barbara tried not to smile but couldn't resist a quip. 'That's what I call an alibi. And you're sure you never knew Beryl Rutherford?' He shook his head vehemently.

'That's OK then. Don't worry about it.'

Walking back up to the court, Barbara felt the same conviction that the man was telling the truth. But what could she make of the second set of bullets?

In her office, she picked up the phone and dialled. Through to her opponent, she laid down her terms. 'I want the file submitted in evidence. I may or may not refer to it, but I want to be sure I can.'

She could feel the shrug at the other end of the line, hear it in his voice. 'Fine by me. But that gun may turn up again if

Bowes passed it on. More wild-goose chases. I have him bang to rights, Barbara. The sooner we get a result the better for everyone. If he changes his plea, I won't go for the jugular. It's up to you and your client, but I know which way I'd play it, if it were me.'

'Well, fortunately for him, it's not you, David. It's me.'

* * *

Ben had suddenly made up his mind to go again to St Albans, but now, as he was nearing his destination, the thought of what he was doing filled him with trepidation. How did you walk up to a man and say, 'I think I know your birth mother?'

Perhaps he should have written first, or used a trained intermediary, as Ken Middlemiss had suggested. The trouble was, he wanted to see for himself. To make sure that nothing could hurt Maggie Riley, not even her son. His family had damaged her life already; the least he could do was rule out further trauma, as far as that was possible. If nothing else he could verify that the man was indeed the person they were looking for. The trouble was, if he started asking questions, the man was entitled to say, 'Mind your own business.' Confidence deserted him as he raised his hand to knock on the man's door. Perhaps he wouldn't be in, and he could retreat to the car. But the person who opened the door was the man they had seen on that first trip.

'Michael Martin?' Ben said. 'I wonder if I might come in?'

The door didn't open wider – if anything it closed an inch.

'I'm not selling anything,' Ben said desperately. 'It's just . . . could I ask you one question? Were you adopted?'

For a moment there was silence, and then the door opened an inch or two wider. 'You'd better come in,' the man said.

* * *

Collecting her pension always made Maggie feel good. There was something about crisp notes in her hand that made her feel secure. Jim's pension from the union was paid straight into her bank account and, nice as it was, it never really seemed real. Cash was different. When Jim died, her pension had been not much more than £20. Now it was nearly £100, and this morning she had received a letter from London solicitors telling her she was in line for what they were calling 'a considerable sum' in shares in a business she had never heard of until a few months ago. 'It's moving too fast,' she thought, and turned into the Welfare park that had once been the property of the National Coal Board, and once would have been full of miners relishing a day off above ground. Now it belonged to the council, and was almost deserted, except for pale young women with pushchairs and a wee-un or two hanging on their coat-tails.

Sometimes it was hard to accept that some women had children so easily, and others didn't. When she first came to Belgate, girls who fell wrong were consigned to a place in Sunderland, and their babies were removed for adoption, unless a supportive family claimed the baby and took it home.

'If I'd had a family, it might have been different with my baby,' Maggie thought. But she had only had an employer. In a way it was Hitler's fault: he had killed her father, and then her mother – he had even been responsible for those soldiers being on the train! She stood up suddenly. There was no point in going over and over it: it was a long time ago. More than 60 years. Time for her son to grow into a man, an old man.

'They'll never find him,' she told herself. 'And if they did, what would he want with a stranger like me?"

* * *

The man sitting opposite Ben looked stunned. 'I can't take it in,' he said at last. 'Over the years I wondered – especially when our own baby came along. "How could my mother have dumped me?" I thought . . . well, I knew what I was feeling about my child, so it didn't make sense. And then, in the last few years, I've thought, "Well, she must be dead by now." And you say she's alive.'

'She didn't want to give you up. She was very young, almost still a child, and they gave her no choice.'

'I'm sorry,' the man said, but it was obvious he was still bewildered.

'Her parents had been killed in the war, so your mother grew up in a children's home. She was in service, just a young parlourmaid, and . . .' He hesitated, wondering how much to tell. 'She has never stopped hoping that one day she'd find you.'

If Ben had hoped for an enthusiastic response, he didn't get it. Michael Martin was shaking his head. 'I'm sorry,' he said at last. 'Once upon a time I might have said yes . . . but not now. Tell her I bear her no ill will, but I can't face an upheaval at my time of life. I have my daughter to consider, and that's what matters to me.'

* * *

The witness had a ferrety face and a composure that exuded self-satisfaction. 'Stop being prejudiced,' Barbara told herself but she had found the witness's statement equally off-putting, full of spite and innuendo. The prosecutor obviously didn't share her distaste.

'You've lived in Earl's Court for a long time, Miss Honeysett?'

'Twenty-seven years.' The voice was firm and full of confidence.

'You're active in good works in the neighbourhood, I believe?'

Barbara groaned inwardly. There would be violins next. He was painting his witness as an urban saint.

'I try to do my best.'

'So when Julie Carter moved in to the next flat you made her welcome?'

'No more than I usually do with newcomers. I took in a pie and some scones on the first day, to tide her over. She was in a bit of a state, so I gave her a hand. No more than any neighbour would do.'

Counsel was almost licking his lips. 'You and Julie went on to have a good relationship, I believe?'

'We did . . . always popping in and out. You know what it's like.'

'She was a good neighbour, then?'

'Very good . . . until he moved in.'

'By "he" you mean the defendant?'

'Yes, him. Terry Bowes, or whatever he calls himself.'

Barbara was rising to her feet to intervene when opposing counsel beat her to it.

'You mean he was sometimes called Terence Bowes?'

There was only a momentary hesitation before the woman caught on. 'Yes. That's what I mean.'

'Things changed then?'

'Yes. She was a different girl, too busy to pass the time of day with anyone.'

'And it wasn't always a happy relationship, was it?'

'No, definitely not. I sometimes thought they would come crashing through the wall . . . screaming and shouting. Him most of the time, shouting her down, not letting her get a word in.'

She was painting a picture of a discordant, even violent, relationship and she was doing it very well. But when she got up to cross-examine Barbara kept her voice smooth. No point in bullying a witness – juries never liked it.

'I'm sure you meant to be a good neighbour, Miss Honeysett.' Barbara hoped she didn't sound sarcastic. 'But isn't the truth that you tried to take over Julie Carter's life, and it wasn't until Terry Bowes came on the scene that Julie had the strength to put an end to your interference? And isn't that why you're so keen to paint him in a bad light?' From a quick glance she could see that the jury were taking notice. Good!

But Miss Honeysett wasn't going to go quietly. 'I'm only telling the truth.'

'As you see it, Miss Honeysett. As you see it. And you see the defendant as the man who got in your way.'

* * *

Dolly sat with a G & T, trying to concentrate on the television screen. She'd always liked *Corrie*, lived for it sometimes, when life was rough and escape to Salford, or wherever it was supposed to be, was a welcome relief. But tonight it wasn't working its magic. She lifted the lemon slice from her glass with pink-tipped fingers and sucked on it. The tartness stung her tongue, and after a moment she dropped it back into the glass. Her nails looked lovely. She'd had them done today, in Shanghai Shimmer. Where did they get these names from? She'd bought some more clothes also – at the rate she was going she'd need a ship to herself to accommodate her wardrobe. Still, nothing wrong with retail therapy. She tried to relax, swirling the liquid round in the glass before she sipped again. In little more than a week, she would be being pampered, entertained, cosseted . . . and so would Maggie. She stuck her foot out and surveyed her new shoes. Glacé kid in taupe. She was wearing them to break them in. It didn't do to take brand-new shoes on holiday.

Why was she so uptight tonight? 'I'm resentful,' she thought. 'I feel hard done by.' Which was silly, really, when she had so much. 'But not what I should've had' – that was it. She hadn't had the hand God had dealt her. She should have grown up with a mam and a dad and a brother and a sister. She'd have married eventually, a nice boy next door – no abortions, no men paying to use her, just the life of a housewife, with a week in Bognor once a year. But there would've been no Eddie – and she wouldn't have missed him for the world. He'd given her everything. She looked around. She had a lovely home, perfect to the last detail. And now she had a sister and a niece. It hadn't turned out as badly as it might have done.

She reached for the remote and turned up the volume. Rita was having a row with Norris, and that was not to be missed.

* * *

'It's lovely to have you here . . . no need to have brought all this food.'

Barbara went on unwrapping. 'I had to get it from M & S. Sorry . . . but I tried to get your favourites.'

'You're my favourite. Come here and give your Grandpa a hug. You look tired. I want to hear all about your case.'

They sat with plates on their knee, glasses on side-tables, and shared their news. 'I heard from young Ben yesterday . . . or was it today? My mind plays tricks,' her grandfather said. 'He sounds confident of finding Margaret's baby. I do hope so. I've felt such guilt all these years. I wanted so much to take her along with your Daddy.'

'Don't beat yourself up about it, Grandpa. We both know Granny wouldn't have let you.'

'She meant well. She always meant well. But sometimes . . . she was a little extreme.'

Barbara let it go. No point in tormenting him now. 'Eat your prawns,' she said. 'There's three more courses to come. And leave Maggie to me and Ben. Aunt Maggie, I mean. Aunt Maggie and Aunt Dolly . . . you can't beat it, can you?'

'They said Dolly was pretty, all those years ago. The woman who was looking after the children said the one that had gone was a pretty little thing. She's still pretty, and she must be . . . well, 70.'

'She's very well preserved. Look at her hands, and compare them with Aunt Maggie's. Their lives are a world apart. But I'm growing fond of them both.'

'And Ben?'

'I like Ben. Rather a lot actually.'

'But he has a wife?'

'Yes, Grandpa, he has a wife. They're semi-detached at the moment but she's still a presence. Don't worry – you brought me up well. I wouldn't do anything foolish, even if I got the chance. Now, let me give you some of this quiche, and then I'll tell you about what's happening in court.'

'Will you win? That's what I want to know.'

'Probably not – which is a pity because I feel it in my gut that my client is innocent. It's just that the evidence is stacked against him.'

'Well, do your best, my dear. That's all you can do. Give me some more of that crunchy green thing as well, and set out the facts. You never know, I might just come up with an inspired observation.'

* * *

On the way home from St Albans disappointment had lain heavy upon Ben. Had he done the wrong thing in going there? Would someone else have done better? But there had been a finality in the man's tone that suggested he had made up his mind.

Now, in Corrigan's, Ben tried to put the day's events behind him and relax. He'd liked his dinner companion ever since their schooldays and he'd looked forward to having dinner with him, but his pleasure was diminished by the sight of Neville Carteret sitting three tables away. Diana's brother, and the man who had cast the fatal vote against him. 'I put him on the bloody board and he shafted me,' Ben thought. He tried to concentrate on his guest, but whenever he looked up Carteret's eyes were on him. Once he even raised his glass in a mock salute.

They ate Corrigan's famous crab cocktail and mouth-watering skate, followed by a raspberry mousse, all washed down with Chablis. As they ate, Ben mentioned his meeting with Tom Finch. 'What do you know about him . . . since school, that is?'

The other man was enthusiastic about their old school-friend. 'He's built up a huge business, Ben. An empire . . . and he's done it without losing sight of himself. You could do worse.'

Ben felt pleasantly mellow when they got up to leave. He nodded to Carteret and followed his friend to the entrance. They parted in the street, and went their separate ways, promising to meet again before long. A few moments later Ben was in a cab and speeding home towards Margaret Street.

He had paid off the cabbie and was turning away when Diana stepped out of a shadowed doorway. 'Hallo Ben. If the mountain won't come to Muhammad . . .' So Carteret had phoned her from the restaurant. 'I see the jungle drums are ahead of me, Diana.' He tried to sound aloof but felt he only succeeded in sounding like a boy.

'Come on, Ben.' She was moving forward, and he could smell her perfume, see the shape of her body under the belted trench coat. He wanted to take her to bed and fuck her for all he was worth, but what he was actually going to do was get rid of her as soon as he decently could.

Chapter Fourteen

BARBARA SPREAD THE PAPER OUT and put her plate of poached eggs on top. She ate without taking her eyes from the newsprint, lifting the fork to her mouth automatically. There was a big picture of Jean Darblay, showing her to great advantage. Not that there had ever been an unflattering photo of her. 'She is truly beautiful,' Barbara thought. The clothes and make-up were the best that money could buy, but she would look equally stunning in a Primark shift with a freshly scrubbed face. It was bone-structure that counted. She finished her eggs and pushed away the plate.

Miss Honeysett's evidence was given prominence in the newspaper report, and there was a blurred photo of Julie, looking incredibly like Marilyn Monroe. Where had they got photo that from? People came out of the woodwork at a time like this, all with something to sell. As the law demanded at this stage, the story made an attempt to appear impartial, but the reporter had obviously decided Terry was as guilty as hell, and it showed. She could only hope the jury thought differently.

'What am I going to do?' Barbara thought as she closed the paper. Well, getting to court on time would be a start. She carried her dishes to the kitchen bench and got on with dressing.

Tonight she was going to Adele's to meet the aunts before they went off on their cruise. She was coming home to change, but she'd have fifteen minutes at the most – less if she showered. She laid out her black and white checkerboard dress and some patent pumps all ready for her return, and then gathered up briefcase and handbag, and hurried down to her car.

*   *   *

'So I've decided I want it. If you can start the ball rolling . . .' At the other end of the line the estate agent was trying to disguise his jubilation. Property sales were thin on the ground at the moment, and a £2 million sale was never to be sniffed at. Putting down the phone, Ben rocked back in his chair and gazed skywards. Had he done the right thing? Did he really want the house in Edgerton Gardens or was it just the magic tree? It would be a bolt-hole to come back to if the job in Europe went pear-shaped – although he still hadn't made any decision about that.

Perhaps he was trying to rush a move because he feared being drawn back to the other house, the house he had bought for Diana, and where they had lived together quite happily . . . but he couldn't even be sure of that. He had thought she was happy, but then he had thought she was faithful, and that had been the biggest mistake of all.

He had held to his intention and got rid of her last night as soon as he could, but he had been sorely tempted to let her stay. The sooner he made up his mind about Finch's offer the better. He would have less time to brood then.

He reached for the phone and dialled his sister's number. 'All OK for tonight? Yes, Barbara's coming; I'm picking her up at 6.45. The aunts too. We should be with you about 7.30. And by the way, you won't be lumbered with Max much longer. I bought a house today.'

'He's not lumber, he's adorable, and I'm not sure the kids will let him go. But you've bought a house. A whole house?'

'A very whole house. Four storeys. A bit ridiculous for a man on his own but I've done it anyway. You'll love it. There's this marvellous tree in the garden – straight out of Disney, knot-holes and all.'

'So you've decided that you're not going to try again? You and Diana, I mean.'

'Yes.' He tried to sound calm and determined but this was his sister he was talking to.

'Oh Ben, I have to admit I'm relieved . . . but it's your decision. I mustn't butt in.'

'Don't worry Adele. I'm not going there again, although I think it's open if I want it.'

'I know how much she meant to you but I have to say it – she's such a bitch!'

By common consent they changed the subject, moving on to the evening ahead and making sure it would go well. 'I'm glad you're bringing Barbara,' Adele said in parting. 'Now there's a thoroughly nice young woman!'

* * *

'So the defendant was often short of money?'

'You could say that.'

'I am saying it. I believe that at one time he owed you in excess of £9,000?'

'Something like that.' The witness seemed to wish he were anywhere else but the witness box.

'He paid you back however, didn't he?'

'Yes.'

'In the summer of 2009? Not long after he had . . . how shall

I put it . . . allied himself to Julie Carter.'

'About that time.'

'I put it to you, Mr Smeaton, that the reason he could repay the sum he borrowed from you, plus your exorbitant interest, was that Miss Carter was bailing him out.'

'He said he'd got a big job, and that was where the cash came from.'

'He had indeed got a big job. A very big job. He was going to marry Miss Carter and live comfortably off the profits of her business?'

The witness was shaking his head as if in incomprehension.

'Well, Mr Smeaton, you must have an opinion?'

Barbara was on her feet. 'Objection, m'lud. The witness cannot know my client's intentions, nor indeed his circumstances.'

The smirk on the prosecutor's face was a yard wide. 'No further questions, m'lud.'

So that was his game. He was going to say that Julie had been the golden goose. That was the reason for getting Lady Darblay to say she had been tense. They were going to say that she was getting fed-up with bankrolling him, and about to pull out of the marriage – that was why he lost his rag and killed her.

As she sat down again, she looked at the jury. They were all intent. 'They're buying it,' Barbara thought.

* * *

Maggie looked out at the familiar passing countryside. Durham, Cleveland, now North Yorkshire. Green fields splattered with sheep and cows. Why did anyone want to go on foreign holidays when England was so beautiful? Why was she going to a place full of names she couldn't pronounce, let alone spell? The brochure was in her suitcase, but it might as well be in Double Dutch.

She had woken at four in the morning, worried that her alarm wouldn't go off and she would miss the train; then she had got to thinking about the money. If it was as much as Barbara had said, it would change everything. She'd be like the man in Belgate who had won the Lottery. Everyone had shirked speaking to him for fear of his thinking they were sucking up. 'I could lose my friends,' Maggie thought. Or be like that woman with the good voice, the one who'd wiped the smiles off the judges on that talent show. She'd come into money overnight by becoming a star, and hardly ever got back to her own house now, by all accounts.

It was a relief when she saw Dolly on the platform at King's Cross, a porter in tow. 'Let him take the bags, Maggie. He's getting paid. And get a move on. We're due at the hairdresser's in half an hour.'

'I've had my hair done,' Maggie said feebly. 'I had a perm last Monday.'

But it was useless to argue with Dolly. It always had been even when she was a little bairn.

* * *

The jury were looking weary now, and there were still two or more hours to go. Barbara straightened her shoulders. Mustn't lose concentration. Prosecuting council was into his stride.

'I want you to tell me exactly what the defendant said to you. Use the exact words if you can.'

'He said he'd fallen on his feet.'

'He was speaking about meeting Julie Carter?'

'Yeah, that was what he meant. He said she was beautiful and loving; a good . . . well, he said she was sexy, you know . . .'

'Yes, we know. But she was something else, wasn't she?'

'He said she was rich. "I've fallen on my feet, Lee", that was what he said.'

'Prior to this he'd been hard up, hadn't he?'

'Always on the cadge. People would see him coming.'

'And all this . . . cadging . . . ended with his meeting Julie Carter?'

'Yes. After that he seemed to have money to burn.'

'No further questions, m'lud.'

Barbara stood up and faced the witness. 'Did you tell anyone about this conversation at the time?'

The man shrugged. 'I might have.'

'We don't do "might have" in this court, Mr Templeman. We like absolutes. Did you or didn't you tell anyone what the defendant had said?'

'No . . . well, I didn't think anything to it.'

'Exactly. It was the chuntering of a young man who has had a drink and wants to unwind. Isn't life rosy, he says, my girlfriend'll do anything for me – that sort of thing. He knows she may not really do what he wants, but for the moment he can say anything and make it sound right.'

When they left court she followed her client down to the holding cells. 'Did you tell that man Julie was rich? Did you boast about falling on your feet?'

He was shaking his head. 'I might have done. I can't remember. But not the way he said it . . . not like that.'

'You'd better remember by the time I put you on the stand. Your testimony is the only thing we have going for us, so don't get all high and mighty and say, "This is not for me." We're fighting for your life here, and don't you forget it.'

* * *

They sat opposite each other at identical basins 'How much does it cost?' Maggie hissed across the space between.

'For God's sake, forget about the money. I've told you, there'll be plenty when the time comes. Have you got your chair on?'

Maggie nodded. Something like a moving hand was working its way up and down her spine, and the rest on which her legs reposed was quivering, for all the world like a whirling dervish.

'Nice, isn't it?' Dolly mouthed, and Maggie nodded unenthusiastically. The only reason for staying put was that she was frightened of what Dolly had planned for her next.

* * *

They gathered round the table in Adele's diner-cum-kitchen. The shadows under Barbara's eyes seemed to lessen as she talked with her aunts. 'They get on,' Ben thought and gave thanks. What if he had reunited them and they had loathed one another on sight? They were disparate creatures: Barbara sophisticated, professional, a little cold on the surface but warm at heart; Dolly a delightful eccentric with enough money to satisfy her whims; and last but not least, Maggie, a simple woman whom he would back against the other two if it came to it.

They all wanted to know about his new house. 'We'll have a party,' he told them. 'As soon as it's mine – Barbara's case will be over; you'll be back from France – we'll have a housewarming. That's a promise.'

'We'll come round and scrub,' Barbara offered. 'I do a mean line in scraping wallpaper.'

Maggie's face lit up. 'I love papering. If you get your first roll right you can't go wrong.'

'There you are, Ben,' Dolly said. 'I'd take her up on that offer.' Tonight Dolly looked like a girl. In the lamplit room, the years seemed to have fallen off her. 'She's a stunner,' Ben thought and smiled to himself.

After the meal, when he and Adele were alone in the kitchen, she looked at him quizzically. 'You've bonded with them, haven't you? Especially Barbara.'

'What are you talking about?'

'She fancies you. Never took her eyes off you over supper.'

'We're friends, Del. You can't make more of it than that. Or you shouldn't.'

'Well, your niece is champing at the bit to be a bridesmaid . . . Still, better get rid of one entanglement before you take on another.'

He didn't want to be reminded of Diana. He had been happy tonight. Why spoil it?

'You decided not to say anything about Maggie's baby?'

'Let the aunts have their cruise,' Ben said. 'Time enough for bad news when they come back.'

* * *

Maggie and Dolly parted on the landing with a hug and kiss.

'It was nice tonight wasn't it?'

'Yes, Dolly, a really nice night.'

'Our Barbara looked lovely. Do you see her dad in her?'

'A little bit. Except for the hair.'

'She likes that Ben . . . did you see her watching him? Do you think anything'll come of it?'

'You never know. Now, get to bed, Dolly, we've got an early start.'

'Do you remember when you used to read to us? *Milly Molly Mandy*? And our Billy would suck his thumb and struggle to keep his eyes open. He was a lovely bairn.'

'He was, and so were you, Dolly. A little picture.'

'We're getting old though, Mags.'

'I know. Now, go to sleep, there's a good girl.'

Chapter Fifteen

THE STRAIN WAS TELLING ON her client, Barbara thought. Terry looked somehow diminished in the dock, bedraggled, compared to when the trial had begun. The face was still handsome, the body that of an Adonis, but the spark had gone out of him. Even the close-cropped blond curls looked faded. He wasn't the sharpest knife in the box, but even he must feel the weight of evidence bearing down on him. Was she being stupidly idealistic because this was the first time she alone was in charge of a man's fate? Not that she was in charge – his fate lay in the hands of the jury.

She looked at them now. They all looked alert, so that was a bonus, but one or two of the women had tight lips – not a good sign. Two of the men looked like Jack-the-Lads, so that should count in her client's favour. She turned her attention back to her opponent.

'And you knew of his previous gambling addiction, an addiction which accounted for the morass of debt in which he found himself?'

The witness was supposed to be a friend of Terry's, but she was doing a pretty comprehensive job of damning him. 'Yes he'd run up big debts. It was a well-known fact.'

Barbara made a note: '*A woman scorned?*'

Prosecuting counsel was relishing the testimony. 'The accused's lifestyle changed after he met Julie Carter, didn't it?'

The girl was nodding vigorously. 'She was always buying him things, things you flash around. And he had money, what seemed to be a lot of money . . .'

'Supplied by Miss Carter?'

'Where else could he have got it from?'

'Precisely. So if this tap – this enviable supply of money was suddenly to be turned off, that would be a source of some distress to the defendant, wouldn't it? His rosy lifestyle would be gone in a puff of smoke, and he would be destitute once more.'

Barbara rose to her feet. 'Objection, m'lud. The witness is being asked to give an opinion.' But he was murmuring, 'No further questions,' and resuming his seat. His job was done.

Barbara hitched up her gown and began to cross-examine. 'You seem to take a remarkable interest in my client's affairs, Miss Jollitte.'

The girl looked disconcerted but only for a second. 'You can't help noticing things when they're under your nose.'

'I'm sure that's true. But do you take such a minute interest in all your friends, or could it be that Terry Bowes is just a little special to you?'

'He's no different to anyone else. He's not even a friend, come to that.'

'Oh, but I put it to you that he was once much more than a friend. That you and he had . . . what shall I call it . . . a fling, prior to his meeting Julie Carter?'

'That's a lie. I wouldn't touch him with a barge pole.'

'I didn't have a barge pole in mind. But I do say that you and he had a sexual relationship for four months prior to his going to Miss Carter's salon to do some work for her, and that after meeting her his interest in you diminished. In fact, he told you it was over. You didn't like that, did you, Miss Jolliffe?'

'It wasn't like that.' She was sullen now.

'Are you saying you never slept with him? Remember, you're on oath, and the punishment for perjury is not a slight one.'

'We might have, once or twice. But it wasn't a . . . what you said.'

'I put it to you Miss Jolliffe, that your involvement with the accused was much more than once or twice, that when he met another, more attractive woman he dumped you, and that your testimony in this court this morning is nothing more than the outpourings of a woman scorned.'

* * *

Ben had perused the dossier Tom Finch had given him, looked through recent trade journals, and Googled Pantheon, and what he had found was impressive. In a less than favourable climate, the company was forging ahead. He put the papers aside and walked to the window. Could he survive away from London? Of course he could. You could survive anywhere if you were enjoying your work.

And he didn't foresee any problems in being a Number Two after being Number One for so long. 'I won't be on your back, Webby,' Finch had said. 'Rather the reverse. I'm moving around so much that you'll be sending plaintive requests for a meet. That's what happens at the moment, and with you at the hub I'll be even more free to get about.' Perhaps it was fate that had brought an old schoolfriend into his life at this stage.

He moved to the phone, and dialled the number Tom Finch had given him. 'Tom? You're where – Mumbai? You do get around! I'll keep it brief, then. Let's meet when you're next in London. I'm interested in your offer. We may have a deal.'

He had scarcely put down the receiver when the phone rang again. 'Peter? What can I do for you?'

'Have you checked the Webcon share price today, Ben?'

'Not yet . . .' Something unpleasant was coming, he could tell that from the other man's tone.

'It's down a point . . . and that's the third day in a row. I don't like it, Ben. Business may be slow, but it's like that for everyone at the moment. I would say we were steadier than most.'

'So something has spooked the City?'

'Obviously. I'm keeping my eye on it, but I felt you ought to know.'

*　*　*

They had shuffled through crowds at St Pancras, looking in vain for the guide they had been told to expect. 'We're lost,' Maggie said despairingly, but Dolly was having none of it. 'Look up there . . . it says "Paris Gare du Nord Platform 4." Just follow me!'

She used the trolley containing their luggage like a battering ram to charge through the crowds, until at last they found themselves in a waiting area. 'There's a chair, you sit down,' Dolly commanded. She then fixed a beady eye on a weedy youth lost in his IPod and didn't take it off him until he got to his feet and let her take his place. Twenty minutes later they were aboard Eurostar, and sinking into luxury.

'The carriage is nearly empty,' Maggie said wonderingly.

'That's because we're in First Class. I thought we might as well splash out seeing as we've come into money.'

'We haven't got it yet. I read in the papers that no one wanted to buy it. Webcon, I mean.'

Dolly wondered if she should try to explain the intricacies of takeovers to her sister but decided against it. 'Sit back and enjoy it, Maggie. We'll get a meal and a drink in a minute. Might as well have our money's worth – we've paid the best part of two hundred quid for the privilege.'

The upgrade to First Class had actually cost £178, and it was worth every penny to see the look on her sister's face.

* * *

The man was looking across at Ben and Diana. 'As you've probably been told, I specialise in mediation. I'm told by your respective solicitors that you've agreed to this attempt to iron out any problems arising from your separation. However, Mrs Webster has expressed a wish to see if there is any prospect of a reconciliation, which would, of course, obviate the need for other discussions.'

Diana was smiling sweetly, the smile of a much put-upon spouse anxious, above all, to preserve a union solemnised in church and sacrosanct. In spite of himself, Ben smiled.

'You're not averse to that idea, Mr Webster?'

'It's not a question of being averse . . . or in favour, come to that. I feel a little as though we've wandered into *Alice in Wonderland* territory here. I didn't break up the marriage, my wife did. Her words, as I recall were, "There's no point in discussing a reconciliation." She said I never pulled my weight in our marriage, I gave her no emotional support, I begrudged her having fun . . . I could go on, but we'd be here all day. And now she wants to try again. I'll say one thing for my wife, she's a glutton for punishment.'

Diana didn't speak, but her eyes were on him and the expression in them was one of triumph.

'Fine words,' Ben thought, 'but she knows I want her, and she's right.'

* * *

Barbara had discarded her court clothes and was heading for the car park, hoping to get back and find that Tootsie hadn't wrecked the flat, when she saw DCI Frank Fisher ahead of her. She hesitated for only a moment before she caught up with him. 'If you aren't dashing off, I'd appreciate a word?'

He hesitated for a moment and then he smiled. 'OK. I don't know if it's protocol now that the case has started – but what the hell! The Carlton Arms?'

They settled in the snug of the small, murky pub in the shadow of the Old Bailey.

'What's the problem?' he asked when she put down the drinks.

'You know the problem. I haven't got a case.'

'Not much of one. Well done with Jolliffe, though. You were spot on there. I was surprised counsel put her up.'

'Tell me honestly, what do you think of him? Terry Bowes, I mean. You said before that you had doubts as to whether he did it.'

He took a drink of his beer and licked his lips. 'Well, the evidence says he did it. But he's not your typical murderer. He's about as calculating as Little Bo Beep. So my head says he's guilty, but my heart seeks excuses. I thought you'd go for a plea of mitigation . . . daft young lad, older woman holding the purse strings, you know the score.'

'He wouldn't have it – I've tried. He's either innocent or I've failed to make him understand what changing his plea could mean.'

'Pity. The judge'll clobber him. He takes no prisoners, that one.'

'Don't rub it in. What d'you make of the bullets with the

same markings as the ones in this case? The prosecution deliberately withheld that information to begin with. They must've thought it had some weight.'

'Unless you could unearth something more, I don't see it carrying much weight. Everyone knows there's a market in dodgy guns. They're passed from hand to hand after use . . . anything to get rid of them. There are men who specialise in recycling firearms. But we tried very hard to tie Bowes into the northern crime and we failed. You could challenge the prosecution on that: create a doubt in the jury's mind as to whether it was the person who used the gun in Kendal who also killed Julie Carter.'

'Thanks for that,' Barbara said. 'But you wouldn't have given me that tip if you hadn't had your own doubts about his guilt?'

'That's for you to guess and me to know. Maybe I just want to offer a drowning woman a straw. Want another?'

* * *

It was pleasant to be sunk into one of Adele's comfy sofas, Max's head heavy on his knee. Ben had told her about Tom Finch, and her face had fallen at the idea of his moving away.

'Still, if it's what you want . . . but you'll be lonely so far away on your own. All the same, a job's a job, even when you have money. God knows I appreciate my Webcon dividends. Harry is talking about starting a vineyard now. I've told him English wine tastes like gnat's pee, but you know what he's like when he gets an idea.'

'I thought he was writing a novel? In between introducing organics, that is.'

'He still is, but he also imagines himself producing vintage Cabernet. I love him, though. It just means we rely on my

Webcon money, so God bless Dad and Grandfather . . . and you for keeping it going. It will keep going, won't it?'

He reassured her, and then she turned the talk to Barbara. 'Her case is all over the papers. Have you seen much of her?'

'We're in regular contact, but you can take that nonchalant note out of your voice. There's no romance – on either side.'

'You never did have the sense you were born with, but I hoped for better from her. Anyway, I've got to see to the coq au vin. Help yourself to plonk. Harry should have got the kids to bed by now. He'll be down directly.'

She was leaving the room when Ben remembered the letter. 'I heard from Madge this morning. They've settled in. She sends her love to everyone and an invitation to visit.'

'Spain? I suppose I'll go out one day. Now, put your feet up and relax, and give that sloppy dog your undivided attention. He misses you like crazy, daft mutt that he is.'

Ben fondled the great head. 'Do you miss me boy? Does no one scratch behind your ears? We'll be together soon in a house with a big garden, and a huge tree you can pee against to your heart's content.'

* * *

'Do I look all right?' Maggie sounded uncertain.

'You look lovely, Mags. Really nice. That navy suits you, and the white at the neck. But try these earrings.' The pearl drops softened her sister's expression, and Dolly stood back, satisfied. 'Just right!'

Maggie regarded herself in the mirror and was reassured. 'You look a picture, our Dolly, and no mistake. Do you remember Mrs Clegg? I heard her say that I was behind the door when looks were given out.'

'Nasty bitch. She only took us in for the money.

'I know. She wasn't that bad, though. It can't have been easy for people having East End kids foisted on them. We spoke another language.'

'You always make excuses for people, Maggie. I don't. She was a bitch and she took our meat coupons. You told me that the last time you were in London.'

'Well, I'm not thinking about the last war tonight, Dolly. We're going up there to face a lot of strangers, and that's frightening enough.'

'They're Yanks, most of them, Maggie, and we're British. Walk in there like we owned the joint. If you don't do that with Yanks they take over. And stop being frightened. You went on and on beforehand about being in the Channel tunnel – what if it all caved in? – and when it came to it we were through and you'd never even noticed.'

Maggie could hear the buzz from the restaurant as they walked along the companionway between the cabins. Why had she ever agreed to this? And why wasn't it Jim there beside her? He had been afraid of no one: 'We're all born equal, Maggie.'

Remembering him saying that, she lifted her chin and followed her sister into the glittering throng.

* * *

When she emerged from the shower, Barbara dried herself, applied deodorant, and then wrapped herself in her oldest dressing-gown. She needed comfort right now. And a drink. She allowed herself a generous Cointreau, and settled down to review her options. Tomorrow the prosecution would complete their cross-examination; after that it was up to her.

On the opposite sofa, Tootsie regarded her solemnly. 'Cheer up,' she said. 'Your Mum'll be home soon.' He gave her a look which she thought was one of contempt, and put his head on his paws.

She put her bare feet on the coffee table and considered her case. She had two witnesses to testify that Terry Bowes and Julie Carter had been in love, blissfully happy, and planning marriage; and the witnesses for the prosecution had been decidedly shifty in their testimony about the state of the relationship. The trouble was that the idea of Terry as a gold-digger seeing his pot of gold vanish was so bloody plausible. The age difference between them wouldn't help either. Julie had been 37 and Terry was 27, a discrepancy of ten years. That would have been nothing, if they had been similarly wealthy. But Julie had held all the money and all the power . . . what would Terry have done if she had, in fact, threatened to snatch it away?

* * *

In the west the sky was striped turquoise and pink, the occasional cloud tipped with gold. In the east was the dark outline of a distant hill, the sky behind it luminous and pale. 'Blue remembered hills . . .' Ben recalled the Housman poem he had learned at school. Nature is beautiful, he thought, feeling suddenly diminished. Man was so small, so petty, running in his pitiful race to get ahead. And all the while nature went on producing miracles. He felt his eyes prick. Bloody sentiment – absolutely useless, and yet getting at you whenever you thought of anything except the daily grind. 'I feel small', he thought, 'because I am small.'

Above him the sky was changing as the sun was sinking. To the west the moon was already ghostly pale, and somehow chilling. He heard a rustle, and then Max was there, thrusting his nose into Ben's outstretched hand. 'I'm in a hell of a mess, old boy,' he said. 'I really am.'

Chapter Sixteen

THEY SAT UP LATE THAT night, marvelling over the captain's welcome dinner, and then took turns to use the bathroom and get ready for bed. They were both a little awkward in the confined space. When Maggie had stayed at Dolly's, she had had her own room, and a bathroom to herself, too. Here they were on top of one another, sidling past to reach cases and drawers. Outside Paris was brilliantly lit, the Eiffel Tower a glittering cascade of light when they had sat on the upper deck for a while after dinner. But here in the cabin it felt almost claustrophobic, when each had grown used to her own space.

It was Dolly who grasped the nettle. 'It's weird, isn't it, being in here together? You've been on your own for years, and so have I. D'you remember when we used to share a bed, with our Billy peeing in between us?' They laughed then, remembering.

'You've got a good memory, Dolly, considering you were only four. A lot of time has passed. I thought you might've forgotten.'

'I thought I had – but you coming, and that detective and Ben stirring it up . . . it's come back, some of it. I think I blocked it out at the beginning. The mind does that, draws a veil.'

They climbed into bed, then, after a good-night hug, neither of them expecting to sleep. But sleep overtook them as soon as their heads hit the pillow.

They awoke to a bright morning, feeling easier about sharing the cabin. 'Get a move on,' Dolly said. 'I'm going to show you Paris, our Maggie, and you're going to love it. The Moulin Rouge, the Sacré-Coeur . . . oh, and the bridges. We'll go on a boat.'

'We are on a boat,' Maggie said.

'I mean take a trip on a sightseeing one. And then there's the shops – you'll love the shops.'

'I'm not spending a penny, Dolly. Not a penny. You'll have me bankrupt.'

              *   *   *

Ben's conversation with Peter Hammond had been on his mind since he woke, and now a look at the *Financial Times* showed yet another fall in Webcon's share price. Something was up. He dialled Hammond's number.

'There's no news, Ben. Well, nothing definite, but Headey's have gone ominously quiet.'

It was a hell of a long time since the Webcon board had voted to accept the offer from Headey's, a rival construction firm, and in doing so had precipitated his own resignation. And now they'd gone quiet. Were Headey's having second thoughts, and was that knocking City confidence in the shares? 'That sounds bad,' he said cautiously.

Hammond's tone was upbeat. 'Or good, Ben. I won't grieve if it all falls through. I told you that we've had Headey's crawling over everything here for some time, and I haven't been impressed with them. I hear a whisper that they may be backing off. I think they've bitten off more than they can chew.'

'If they do pull out what happens?'

Hammond sighed. 'We return to the status quo. The legal bods may call for compensation from Headey's, but my guess is that everything would just return to the way it was before the Board's decision.'

As Ben put the phone back in its place, he felt shaken, not reassured. What would happen to the shares if the offer did fall through? And to the staff? Would prospective clients get suspicious and drop away? Worst of all, would anyone expect him to take back the reins? 'I don't want to,' he thought.

He had fought to stave off the takeover because it seemed the right thing to do. In the end it had been his brother-in-law, Diana's brother Neville Carteret, who had cast the fatal vote, whispering, 'Sorry, old boy,' as he did so. But as Ben had walked from the boardroom that day, feeling defeated, he had also felt relief, as though he had suddenly been set free. Still, that had been then. Should he now tell Adele the Headey offer might be faltering? His grandmother had left her shares in Webcon to the three Brewis descendants, that is, to Barbara and her aunts. If Webcon suffered, so would their legacy. Better keep quiet for the moment. But there was one thing he could do.

He dialled his stockbroker. 'Donald . . .' He was making rapid calculations about his cash reserves. 'I want you to buy up every Webcon share you can get your hands on.'

*   *   *

'I hope I've demonstrated . . . or rather that the evidence has demonstrated . . . that this was a young man on the make. That Julie Carter was a chicken ready for plucking, and the man you see in the dock was the fox. Not a particularly cunning fox, I grant you, but one that was capable of ending a life. A man who killed as easily as a fox kills . . . because he could.'

Barbara tried to calculate the effect her opponent's words

were having on the jury. They were all paying attention to his winding up, but was he going over the top? Terry Bowes looked an unlikely Reynard . . . perhaps Mr Oh-So-Clever had not been as clever as he thought?

* * *

They had seen the Sacré-Coeur' from a distance as they toiled up the narrow street, but as they ascended towards it on the funicular railway, the sight was almost overpowering. 'It is a big church,' Maggie said, her tone respectful.

'Look down there,' Dolly said. 'It's the best view of Paris you'll ever get.'

As they entered the scented darkness of the basilica, Dolly heard her sister's breath come out in a soft rush at the sight of Christ, arms outstretched, in the dome above their heads. 'He looks as though he's coming down to you, doesn't he?' Dolly whispered, remembering her own shock when Eddie had first brought her there.

They settled in a pew at the back, drinking in their surroundings.

'They beheaded St Denis under here,' Maggie said.

Dolly nodded. 'Been swotting, Mags?' – but she said it indulgently. She was proud of her big sister.

* * *

The judge was shuffling his papers. When he looked up, he looked directly at Barbara. 'It's ten to three. I assume Counsel would not wish to begin cross-examination for the defence at this comparatively late hour?'

'Thank you, m'lud. I'm sure you're right.'

'In that case, I think this is an appropriate moment to

adjourn and reconvene tomorrow.'

'All rise.'

Terry was standing up and turning to go down from the dock. Barbara nodded at him, and gathered up her papers. She would have to try and instil some confidence into him but it wouldn't be easy. 'You're my only real witness,' she would say again to him. 'You have to believe that truth will out.' But she had been around the legal system long enough to know that that wasn't always true.

She nodded curtly to her opponent and went off to lie to her client.

She was almost at the door when Howard Breen caught up with her. His face was flushed, and he looked less than his usual immaculate self. 'There's been a development. Remember you asked me to put our man on to the motor-showroom staff again? Well, it's paid off. The senior salesman is a man called Jed Hughes. Married, and a bit of a drunk by all accounts. When they were first interviewed he claimed to have had no contact with Julie Carter. It now turns out that he and Julie had an affair – an affair that ended when his wife found out. Just before Julie met Terry.'

* * *

Ben had been back at the Margaret Street flat for an hour when his phone rang. He pushed aside the sheaf of Pantheon figures that he was studying, and sat back as Diana's voice floated from the receiver.

'I thought you were horrid the other day, Ben. When I'm trying so hard to work things out, you throw bitterness in my face.'

'Your own words, Diana, that's what I threw at you. Things you said and, presumably, meant at the time.'

'I was confused. I know I said things I didn't mean. So did you, but I haven't carried them around for months, brooding on them. It's in the past, as far as I'm concerned.'

'How convenient, I wish I could do that.'

'Do what?'

'Consign things to oblivion.'

'You left me, remember; I didn't ask you to go. You ran off to your sister and left me alone in the house. If I hadn't had Max . . . and now you've taken him too.'

He couldn't help laughing. 'My dear Diana, you are what Liverpudlians call a piece of work. You really believe that I left you . . . no question of my being driven out by the sight of another man making free of my wife?'

'You make it sound sordid. I was silly and he confused me . . .'

'He filled your head with tales of how he'd run Webcon when Headey took it over, and you fell for it. He was a second-rater with a good patter, and it took you in. Now, for God knows what reason, you think you'll return to the old comfort zone. I think not.'

'It isn't like that. I loved you, Ben, I still do. Please, please, let's meet. We need to talk. Remember how good it used to be? We're good together, you know that. Mediation is a waste of time we need to work this out for ourselves. Neil is . . . eminently forgettable. And I've said I'm sorry.'

She sounded suddenly lost and Ben felt his resolve weaken. But his grandfather had had a phrase he used before making big decisions: 'Retreat and consider.'

'I can't talk about this now, Diana. But I'll be in touch.' He put down the phone without waiting for her to say goodbye.

* * *

The day in Paris had passed by in a blissful whirl of visits to places whose names Maggie had only heard of – the Moulin Rouge, Montparnasse, the Trocadéro. Best of all had been the Sacré-Coeur, where she had sat at the back, watching people come and go, smelling the incensed air, and seeing the shimmer of candles at the feet of statues. She had walked and walked, and now it was a relief to sink into a chair and look forward to dinner.

Their table soon filled. 'Yanks,' Dolly mouthed, and made a face. But looking round, Maggie thought they looked pleasant, all of them. 'I'm Mamie,' the woman opposite said. 'And you're . . .?'

'Margaret Riley. Well, Maggie really. Pleased to meet you.'

The woman, tiny and bright-eyed, was friendly and not at all pushy. She was from Milwaukee, she volunteered, and seemed interested to know Maggie came from County Durham, although she pronounced it Durr-ham. The courses came and went, looking mouth-watering on the plate and seeming to vanish on the tongue.

They were on something called butterfish, which Maggie had never heard of, when she sensed someone at her elbow. It was a woman who she had seen goggling at Dolly yesterday, and from the sound of her voice she was British – Yorkshire, or maybe Lancashire: it was hard to tell. It was Dolly she was speaking to, hastily because she had just nipped over from the next table. 'I know who you are,' she was hissing. 'But I won't tell . . . I know you want to stay private. They won't hear it from me. I've followed your career since the *Carry On* films. And *EastEnders* – you'll be a miss there!'

Dolly was smiling and nodding as though she understood, and she kept smiling till the woman had slipped back to her seat.

'What was all that?' Maggie whispered, as the wine waiter refilled her glass.

'She thinks I'm Barbara Windsor.' Dolly was looking quite

smug, but Maggie was scandalised.

'Barbara Windsor! Didn't you put her right?'

'No, let her dream. I'm quite flattered, really. She's a smart little thing is Babs. Now stop gawping, Maggie, and choose your pudding. It's just a bit of fun.'

* * *

After he put the phone down on Diana, Ben sat for a long while. Sooner or later he would have to deal with it, but not now – he couldn't think about it now. He picked up the phone and dialled Barbara's number almost on impulse.

A few hours later they sat facing one another across a table in Little Italy.

'You sounded stressed when you phoned,' Barbara said. 'Bad day?'

'Bad doesn't even measure it.' He was tempted to tell her about Diana, but instead he said, 'The Webcon share price has come under pressure. The City isn't liking the uncertainty about the Headey deal.'

Her brow creased. 'I didn't realise there was any uncertainty. How will this affect the aunts?'

Diana's first question would have been, 'How will it affect me?' Ben thought, putting down his knife and fork and aligning them neatly. 'Broadly speaking, it shouldn't make any difference. If there's a new bid, which is quite likely, they'll get a decent price for their shares. I must chase up how probate is going, actually. If there is no offer, Webcon will continue as it is, and the aunts will get dividends . . . or they can sell their shares, whichever they prefer.'

'But how will Webcon fare without a chairman?' She was looking at him directly.

'It has a chairman.'

'A cipher, you've told me that.'

Ben shook his head, but before he could speak she went on. 'I bet they'll ask you back. If they have any sense, they will. I've looked at the data. You took that company to new heights in an increasingly hostile climate.'

'Are you saying it's my duty to go back?'

'No. Just that they'd be lucky to have you.'

'It's difficult. There are times when I wish I was on the Seine with the aunts. I hope they're enjoying it.' They were into safe waters now, talking about the cruise, and holidays in general. He sat back and let the pleasure of Barbara's company wash over him.

*   *   *

'I don't know how you dare, our Dolly!' They were back in the cabin, and getting ready for sleep. 'I was wishing the ground would open and swallow me up.'

'Deck, Maggie, not ground. Not in the middle of a river. You were sitting on the deck.'

'Never mind splitting hairs, madam. You know what I'm getting at. You pretending to be something you're not.'

'Yes, and I'm loving every minute of it. Eddie used to say I was born for the stage.'

'The dock's where you'll be going if you're not careful. That American woman was looking at you really funny. She knows something's up. And her husband looks like an ex-policeman to me. He could be ringing Scotland Yard, for all we know.'

'Ooh, you mean I could be taken off in Paris in handcuffs? Just make sure the paparazzi are there, if that happens.'

Dolly had to duck, then, as the cushion from Maggie's bed came whizzing across the space between them.

Chapter Seventeen

THE SHARE PRICE WAS UP a point – so far, so good. Ben dialled Barbara's number and waited. When she came on she sounded breathless. 'I hope I didn't get you out of the shower?'

'No, I've been up for hours. Reading, revising . . . I still can't see a loophole.'

'You haven't presented your evidence yet.'

'True. But it's thin, Ben, paper-thin. Still, did you ring for anything special?'

'Just to wish you luck today.'

'Thank you. That's really nice . . . I need it, Ben. So does poor Terry Bowes.'

She sounded more cheerful when he rang off, and Ben was glad. He sat for a moment, contemplating the phone, then he reached out with new purpose and dialled.

'Diana, I've been thinking over what you said. You're right – we should meet . . .'

*   *   *

Outside the cabin window, Paris had slipped away. 'It's a huge city,' Maggie had said wonderingly. 'All those bridges!' Now they were in the industrial suburbs and heading towards open country.

'It's Conflans next,' Dolly said, 'Conflans-Sainte-Honorine, to give it its proper name. It says in here that it has a rural tranquillity.' She was quoting from the brochure.

'Haah! Swans!' Maggie was standing at the open window gazing out on the river. Sure enough a cob and a pen were leading their brood downriver.

'You'll see plenty of them before we're finished. Now, do you want to go ashore in Conflans? We could look at the shops, have a coffee somewhere. Or we can go up to the sun-deck and have long tall drinks in a deck chair.'

'Drinks? It's only two o'clock.'

Dolly shook her head. 'You're on your holidays, our Maggie. You can drink when you like.'

'Well, I hope you're not going to tell any more lies, Dolly.'

'I didn't lie, Mags. She said I was Barbara Windsor – I just didn't say I wasn't. That's not lying.'

'It's precious close. You could get arrested for it . . . impersonating a celebrity.'

'I can't help it if I have an aura of glamour. Now, get a move on. I didn't come all this way to sit indoors.'

* * *

Barbara tried to make eye-contact with each jury member as she spoke. 'And I hope to show, to prove to you, members of the jury, that my client is not the shameless, money-grabbing monster the prosecution has tried to make out, but a good and kind young man who has lost the love of his life and is devastated by what has happened.'

She looked up at the dock willing her client to look less hang-dog and more like the hero she was describing.

'Furthermore, I will demonstrate that Julie Carter was not

the foolish victim of a gold-digger, but a clever business woman, capable not only of building her own successful business but of helping my client to find his feet also. Above all, I will show how happy they were together, what plans they had for their joint future. And then I will pose one question: why on earth would any man want to murder the one person who could . . . who had . . . transformed his life?'

* * *

They lunched at the Ivy, at Diana's request. 'You brought me here the first time you dated me. Remember?'

Ben did remember. He had thought her the most desirable woman he had ever seen and had marvelled at the fact that she was there with him. Men passing the table stared at her, and he had glowed. That had been years ago, but she was still the most attractive woman in the room, and she knew it. In vain, Ben tried to hang on to the memory of her face the last time he had brought her here. They had met then to discuss their separation, and she had kept him waiting for 15 minutes. He had chosen scallops and green beans, and she had sneered at him: 'Always so predictable, Ben. And please, not a Chardonnay.'

Today she was being less direct. In fact, she was being positively emollient. 'She's playing me,' Ben thought, and knew with a sense of despair that he was ripe for playing.

* * *

Her first witness was up, and she was nervous. 'That makes two of us,' Barbara thought.

'You had known Miss Carter for several years, Miss O'Brien?'

The girl was nodding and trying to smile, but it was obvious that she was on the verge of tears. Julie smiled warmly. 'Can you tell us how long?'

'I went there for work experience. I was 15, then, so it was 2002. She was lovely to me, showing me things. She was like that, very kind with everybody.'

'She helped you get into college, I believe?'

'Yes. I went to the North London College and did my course. Julie let me work at weekends, so I got some practical experience, which meant I did well at college.'

'And when you'd completed your course and got your qualification, she gave you a job?'

'Yes, she took me straight from college, and I've been . . . I was . . .' The tears came now. Good! The jury would be impressed.

'Take your time. We understand this is painful for you. So you were close to Miss Carter?'

'Yes. We were friends as well as employer and employee.'

'She confided in you?'

'Yes, she did.'

'Did she confide in you about her relationship with the accused?'

'She said he was the best thing that had ever happened to her. She said even though he was younger than her, she could rely on him. She wanted to help him get on. She was always helping people, but with Terry . . .' She hesitated then, and Barbara prompted her.

'With the accused . . .?'

'Yes, with him it was special.'

'Do you think she was special to him?'

'Yes.' Her voice was firmer now. 'Yes, he loved her. He'd've done anything for her.'

*   *   *

Ben had timed his arrival to coincide with Adele's return from the school run. The children were pleased to see him, and the welcome he received from Max when they entered the house was overwhelming. 'Not much longer now, old chap,' he said, fondling the square head.

'I'll be sorry to see him go when you take him.' Adele had flung off jacket and shoes, and was padding around the kitchen making tea. 'How long before you complete?'

'Who knows? Another month, probably. And then there'll be furniture to get, carpets, all that stuff.'

'You'll miss Madge. She did it all for you with the flat. But I'll help, and so will Barbara.'

'Yes, I'm sure she will help, if I ask. Her own place is nice – minimal but comfortable. She could well be helpful . . . particularly as my sister has such lousy taste!'

'Pig. Just for that I won't give you one of my caramel shortbreads, homemade this morning.'

'It cooks! Wonders never cease.'

'Cut the cheek and tell me what's been happening. Have you heard any more from Diana?'

For a moment Ben was tempted to lie, but she deserved better. 'I had lunch with her today, actually.'

'To discuss the divorce?'

Again the temptation to lie and avoid a row. 'Not exactly. We just talked in general.'

'You surely wouldn't take her back, would you?'

His silence was more eloquent than words, and Adele shook her head in despair. 'How can you, Ben, after what she did? With Pyke, of all people.'

'They're not together now,' he said defensively.

'I'm sure they're not.' Adele's voice was tart. 'As soon as she saw that he wasn't going to be Headey's top honcho, Pyke was toast as far as Diana was concerned.'

'It wasn't like that.' Even to his own ears, he sounded weak.

'I think it just fizzled out.'

His sister didn't answer, but her silence was eloquent.

Ben told her then about Headey's and the dip in the share price. 'But it's rallied again, so don't worry.' He didn't mention his own intervention.

'I don't, but I'd worry less if you were back at the helm. Would you consider it?'

'Not now. I've tasted freedom, in a weird way, and I quite like it. But there are other people to consider. If Webcon were to go down . . . there's a workforce there, Del, and I know them. Men like English, who was prepared to drive me after I'd resigned even though it could have cost him his job. And Hammond, and others, all dependent on Webcon to keep them afloat.'

'And me,' Adele said. 'I need my dividends.'

She was attempting to lighten the mood and he smiled at her. 'And of course my big sister, whose capacity to swallow money is legendary. How could I forget her?'

* * *

Counsel was tugging at his gown and shuffling his papers. She had tried to prepare the girl for his cross-examination, and she seemed ready for it, but he was deliberately wasting time in an attempt to rattle her. At last he spoke.

'You're very young, aren't you, Miss O'Brien?'

'I'm 23.'

'My goodness! But I wasn't referring to actual years. You're a delightful young woman and I bet you like romance . . .'

Barbara shot to her feet. 'Objection, m'lud. Irrelevant!'

The judge looked coldly, first at Barbara then at her opponent. 'Get to the point, if you will. If there is a point.'

'There is, m'lud, I assure you. Miss O'Brien, you were very

fond of your employer, weren't you?'

'Yes, I was.'

'So you were delighted when romance came into her life?'

'Yes. She'd been hurt in the past, and now she was happy again.'

'I put it to you that you don't want to contemplate the possibility that this "romance". . .' He was emphasising the word, trying to trivialise it, and Barbara's heart sank.

'. . . might end. You didn't want to think that this Prince Charming might have feet of clay.'

The girl looked across at Barbara, puzzlement on her face, but there was nothing Barbara could do. Not yet. The eyes turned away, disappointed.

'I don't know what you mean, but if you mean he did it you're wrong.'

Counsel merely smiled. 'No further questions.'

Barbara rose to her feet. 'Rebuttal, m'lud.' There was a judicial nod and she turned back to the witness.

'Miss O'Brien, on that last day did you see any sign at all that Julie Carter was unhappy.'

'No.' The voice was firm and strong now. 'Just the opposite. She was humming under her breath when I left. "See you tomorrow," she said, and she was smiling.'

Tears came now, but they only added to the effect. 'One up to me,' Barbara thought.

*   *   *

Conversation at dinner that night centred on Conflans. One man, who sounded like John Wayne, threw out facts and figures about the town in between courses. He told the table that it was called Conflans-Sainte-Honorine because the bones of that lady-saint had been buried there since 876.

'Get away!' Dolly said in wondering tones, and batted her eyelashes.

'She's up to something,' Maggie thought, and felt herself break out in a sweat. Still, giving a man the glad eye was less dangerous than impersonating a famous star. She had scanned the tables as they entered the restaurant, terrified the woman might be there, but mercifully she hadn't seen her. Perhaps, and hopefully, she had left the boat, even gone overboard – anything as long as Dolly didn't dig herself in deeper.

The American man was still wittering on about Conflans, which had seemed full of boats and barges to her – that, and restaurants on every corner. It was true what they said: the French loved their food.

Maggie was half-way through her crème brulée when the woman loomed up at their table. She kept on walking past, but not before she had given a huge wink to Dolly and received a finger to the lips in return.

'Never mind hush,' Maggie thought to herself. When they got back to the cabin she would put her foot down. No more dangerous nonsense, or she was getting off at the next stop.

* * *

In the taxi taking her home from chambers, Barbara dialled Ben's number. It was late, for she had spent three hours going over witness statements ready for tomorrow. But if he was free they could find a late-night restaurant somewhere, and she could unload the angst of the day. All she got, though, was his answerphone. She hesitated for a moment and then rang off. If she left a message, he'd feel obliged to answer her. Better to leave him free. She would soak in the bath instead, and open a tin of soup. And then, wrapped in her snuggler, she would watch the most mindless thing she could find on the television, and chill right out. She would have Tootsie for company, which was not as good as a hunky male but better than nothing.

She was trying to decide between cream of mushroom and broccoli and stilton when the phone rang. It was Howard Breen. 'I've just heard from our man. He says this affair between Julie and the salesman could have legs. The salesman has access to the key to the inter-connecting door, and he's known to have a hot temper. Anyway, we're still digging, but if we're going to get the salesman in the box we have to move now.'

'Call him,' Barbara said decisively. 'We'll declare him as hostile if necessary, but do the paperwork. And tell your man to keep digging.'

* * *

In a way it was inevitable – Ben had known that from the moment he had agreed to go to the house. All the time he was pouring drinks, talking about what had been on the six o'clock news, he knew what was going to happen. Diana wasn't being overtly sensual – if anything, she was more demure than he had ever seen before. In the end, though, she made the first move, coming to kneel before him and lift her face to be kissed.

He wanted to say, 'How dare you?' but instead he said, 'Are you OK?' in a voice so slurred it hardly seemed his own. What a bloody silly thing to say!

But Diana was nodding and rising to her feet to lead him towards the stairs that led to the room they had shared together. He tried to blot out a mental picture of her leading Neil Pyke in this same way. That was all over now – if it had not been, he could never have been here, like this, wanting . . . no, needing her. And then they were naked, skin on skin, her body soft and yet firm beneath him, her legs gripping him, her mouth seeking his as though desperate for air. And it was like it had been at the beginning . . . an ecstasy that must never, ever be allowed to end.

He slept then, for a while, and when he woke he could tell from her breathing that she was awake too. He reached for her, and her skin was as soft beneath his fingers, her mouth as desirable as it ever had been. She was laughing softly, and he lifted his head. 'What's amusing you?'

'Nothing. I'm just happy.'

He let his lips travel down her throat to her breast, and felt a tremor within her. 'Really happy?'

'Very. That's good. That's good, darling.'

'She wants me,' he thought, and was suddenly in need again, sliding into her with the old familiarity. 'I love you, Diana.' He said it again and again, more fiercely with each thrust. He nails were digging into his back, urging him on until the climax. 'Yes,' she said then. 'Yes!'

It was much later, when she was lying asleep beside him, that he realised what she had not said – 'I love you too.'

Chapter Eighteen

HE WAS STILL AWAKE AS light filtered into the familiar bedroom. Beside him, Diana lay sleeping, just as she had done on that fateful morning when the phone had rung and he had been summoned to his grandmother's side. What a fool he had been! He had managed the business of finding the children his family had wronged, and he had made a true friend in Barbara; but he had not kept hold of Webcon, which now hung in the balance as people with little or no concern for its future, except as a business proposition, jostled for place.

But his greatest mistake had been in his handling of his marriage. He looked at Diana, innocent in sleep, and as beautiful as ever. Last night they had made love insatiably, except that it hadn't been love. It had been lust on his part and calculation on hers.

'She wants me back,' Ben thought, 'but only because my substitute hasn't come up to her expectations. I can see it clearly now.' But when the next siren call came, would he give in as easily as he had last night?

He left Diana sleeping and made his exit from the house. He wanted to get home, back to Margaret Street, and work out what was to be done – but even in the safety of his own flat he felt wretched.

Diana rang him at 10.15. He didn't answer, just listened to the message she left. *'Darling, it was sweet of you to let me sleep, but naughty too. I wanted to cook you a ginormous breakfast.'*

In spite of himself, Ben smiled at her cheek. 'She thinks she's done it,' he told himself. 'That's how easy she thinks I am.'

But his revulsion at her complacency was tinged with foreboding. Could he handle this? She kept prattling on about how glad she was that they'd *'sorted things out. I was a fool, darling, and you know that I know it. At least I hope you do. We'll talk when you get home tonight . . .'*

She was still enthusing, but cold fear had closed his ears. Diana thought he was going to walk in tonight as though nothing had happened. No doubt she'd be preparing a meal, something she knew he liked. There'd be wine cooling, and of course there'd be appropriate music.

'. . . what time will you be back, darling? Don't worry – any time will do. I just need a rough idea.'

He was remembering other nights, when he had come home full of love and trust. The night he had come home to the smell of coq au vin, a special effort. Special because she was going to tell him she was off to Prague. She had broached the subject over smoked salmon with avocado, dropped in the fact that the trip was the next week as they ate the chicken with green beans and duchesse potatoes. Or had it been over the summer pudding 'made with my own fair hands'?

What she had not made clear, over any course, was that the 'girl chum' who was accompanying her to Prague was in fact Neil Pyke. That he had found out later.

*   *   *

'Hurry up, Dolly. We'll miss the bus.' Maggie was already at the cabin door, her bag in her arm.

'Plenty of time,' Dolly said, tweaking her neckline into place. 'It's not council transport, Maggie. It's laid on for us. It'll wait.'

Maggie shifted her handbag on her arm and bit her lip. It had always been the same with Dolly, a law unto herself. She wouldn't change now. Last night she had argued with Dolly until she was blue in the face, and got precisely nowhere. 'What am I doing wrong?' Dolly had countered. 'I haven't said I'm Barbara Windsor.'

'You haven't told her you're not, and don't tell me you don't need to put her right because we both know different.'

'I don't know much about this van Gogh,' Dolly said now. 'Except about his ear.'

'He didn't cut it off,' Maggie said, preening inwardly. She had spent all last night reading up on today's excursion, and for once she knew more than her sister. 'He only cut a bit of it off, the bottom bit, the lobe. His dad was a vicar, like our Billy's. Twice van Gogh fell in love, but it never worked out and he couldn't keep a proper job. We think we've had our troubles, Dolly . . . well, I do . . . but nothing like him. Went mad and killed himself in the end.'

Dolly's eyebrows shot skyward. 'Sounds like it's going to be a cheerful outing. Still, there's a bottle of wine in this packed lunch, and I dare say there'll be a handy pub in Auvers-sur-Oise. We'll just have to make the best of it!'

* * *

'You've known the defendant for five years?'

The witness was ex-military, and obviously liked to think he was in command of situations. 'That is correct.'

'You are a Warrant Officer in the Territorial Army, and you

were previously a regular soldier?'

'Seventeen years' service, ma'am.'

'Please address your answers to his lordship.'

'Sorry, ma'am, m'lud.' A bead of perspiration had appeared on his brow. He had taken in the solicitor's pre-trial advice but the atmosphere of the court had got to him.

She ploughed on. 'You have been with the TA for seven years now and you're a firearms expert?'

'Correct, m . . . m'lud.'

'And in that role you trained the defendant in the use of firearms?'

'Yes, m'lud.'

'Was he a good student?'

'One of the best I've had through my hands. A born marksman.'

'Quite.' Inwardly Barbara relaxed. She had wanted that point driven home. 'The usher is placing in front of you some photographs of the body of Julie Carter. Marked 46 and 47, m'lud. You've seen these photographs already, but please look at them again. In your opinion, is the pattern of those bullet holes likely to have been made by a trained shot, an expert marksman?'

'No it is not, m'lud.'

'Let's be clear about what you are saying. Terry Bowes would not have sprayed bullets in that haphazard fashion because he would have been able to kill quite cleanly with one shot?'

'Definitely.'

'Thank you. No further questions.'

Prosecuting counsel was rising to his feet ready for rebuttal. 'You have a proud record, Mr Winston.'

The man was visibly inflating. 'Some people have said that.'

'So I'm sure you're very good at your job. You train men to

do things the right way?'

'Certainly. That's my job.'

'You teach them to concentrate, fix their eye on the target, select the area they want to hit, and only then pull the trigger?'

'Correct. Calmness is all important.'

'Calmness is all important. Indeed it is, Mr Winston, indeed it is. But what happens if that person, that man you have trained so carefully, gets a red mist before his eyes. Feels such all-consuming rage that all he can do is squeeze that trigger . . . bang, bang, bang! What would happen to his training then?'

The witness was looking confused, his eyes flicking from Barbara to the judge and back. She stood up. 'Objection, m'lud.'

She knew it would be overruled, and it was, but opposing counsel was already sinking into his seat with the look of a man who had just scored a hit.

*   *   *

Ben tried to concentrate on reading up on Finch's companies, but thoughts of Diana kept intruding. It was obvious that she considered their reunion a foregone conclusion, but he knew now, with a dreadful certainty, that it was over. She wanted him back simply because her lover had not lived up to her expectations. He was contemplating making coffee when the doorbell rang. He opened the door expecting a postman or a canvasser, but it was Neil Pyke who stood there.

For a moment Ben contemplated refusing him entry, but that would only be postponing things. 'Come in,' he said shortly.

The man was as handsome as ever, but the cockiness had left him. 'Thank you for seeing me,' he said.

Ben merely nodded in reply. Nor did he ask the other man to sit down. There was a moment's hesitation, and then Pyke infiltrated his long frame into a chair.

'What can I do for you?'

'I want . . . I was wondering . . . look, we both know I'm good at what I do. I want to rejoin Webcon, and it's to their advantage to take me back. I've had legal advice that says you should never have ousted me.'

'You were fucking my wife behind my back and . . . even worse . . . giving vital information to my competitors – and I was wrong to throw you out? I'm willing to challenge that in any sane court in this country.'

'It wasn't like that . . . and it wasn't just me.'

'Oh, there I'm sure you're speaking the absolute truth. I'm quite sure you had a willing accomplice in my wife. Did she rat on me to Headey's too? Repeat bits of pillow talk? Not that we talked much about business – she was more interested in spending my money, as I recall. And now I suspect she's dumped you. She has a tendency to jump ship when something better sails into view. She thought I was going to lose Webcon, and that you would step into my shoes, hence the transfer of her affections.'

'I didn't come here to rake over the past.'

'I'm sure you didn't. It doesn't make for comfortable discussion, does it? But I like a good rake, myself, especially when I hold all the cards. You want to know if I'd put a block on your return to Webcon? I wouldn't, even if I had the power. But I'm pretty sure that they have your number now. Headey's, too. You, my friend, are history. Now buzz off.'

It wasn't elegant, Ben thought, but it was probably the most satisfying thing he had ever done.

*　　*　　*

The room was small and entirely bare except for a van Gogh

print on a wall, and an appeal for money to buy the original and hang it where it belonged: in his workplace.

'There's no window,' Maggie whispered.

'Poor bugger. No wonder he shot himself,' was Dolly's reply. Outside on the landing the guide was holding forth to the rest of the group. 'It's the cemetery next,' Dolly whispered. 'Do you fancy pleading tired legs and popping in somewhere for a drink?'

For once Maggie was up for breaking the rules. 'If I see his grave, Dolly, it'll just about finish me off. And to think he painted sunflowers in a miserable place like this.'

Safe in a roadside inn, she cheered up. 'At least he had his brother, Dolly. He stuck by him right to the end.'

'Not according to the guide. She said he shot himself because Theo turned the money tap off.'

'Only because he had another bairn coming, and he couldn't afford it any more. And they're buried side by side, it says in the bookler, so they didn't fall out.'

'If you've shot yourself dead, there's not much scope for a family feud, Maggie. Still, I take your point. There's nothing like family. Which is why I'm here running after you.'

* * *

Barbara didn't have much hope of her next witness, Edward Cousins, but something had to be better than nothing.

'Mr Cousins, do you remember the morning Julie Carter died?'

'I do.' He suddenly remembered his coaching and looked up at the bench. 'M'lud.'

'It's quite a long time ago. Why does it stand out?'

'Because the police came asking questions . . . that was just a week . . . no, five days after. So at that time I could remember everything.'

'You could remember – that's good. Tell us about that evening.'

'I was at work as usual.'

'Work is the garage you co-own on the Edgware Road?'

'That's right. Like I said, I was there. Terry . . . the defendant . . . he was a regular customer. He came in most days. Anyway, he came in that evening about quarter past five.'

'About quarter past five. Can you be more precise?'

'It was exactly quarter past five – I checked his receipt in the till. He paid at 5.24, and he'd been there eight or nine minutes. I had a mug of coffee, and he asked for one. He was lippy like that, but no harm in him. He often came in cadging a coffee or a fag . . . a cigarette.'

'Let's stick to that particular afternoon. How would you describe his mood that day?'

'Good. He was in a good mood. Cracking jokes. He said he was getting married. "I'd ask you and the wife," he said, "except it'll be a posh do!" I said, "Cheeky bugger!" . . . excuse the language, but that's what I said. But it was all good-humoured, you know. No malice.'

'So he was in a good mood. A happy man?'

'Very happy.'

'And he went directly from you to Julie Carter's salon?'

'That's what the police said. They had all the times and things like that.'

Barbara thanked him, and resumed her seat as opposing counsel rose.

'You say the defendant came in almost every day?'

'He did. He was a good customer.'

'So you had many such friendly encounters?'

'I suppose so,' the witness said reluctantly.

He's seen the way this is going, Barbara thought. He's cuter than he looks!

'Many such friendly encounters . . . so how can you be sure you are remembering that particular day? What more natural than that your memory should play tricks when you are asked, days later, to dredge up one particular memory?'

Barbara's voice was a shrill. 'Rebuttal, m'lud!'

Counsel resumed his seat, and she fixed her eye on the witness.

'Are you sure you're remembering the correct day? The correct one, and no other day?'

'Very sure. He made some remark about my mug being chipped and said he'd get me a new one for my birthday. I said he needn't bother: my birthday was yesterday, and if I'd wanted a mug I'd've asked for one. My birthday is on the 14th. He came in on the 15th.'

'Yes!' Barbara said, but only under her breath.

¤ ¤ ¤

Ben tried to concentrate on the economic facts in front of him. Slowly but surely the indicators were creeping up. It was too early to talk of a recovery from the credit crunch yet, but it was better than the decline that, at times, had threatened to turn into a downward spiral. The sooner there was another election and a single hand on the tiller the better. Labour was blaming world banking for the crisis but that was only half the problem. Britain had been living beyond its means – that was the sad truth everyone was unwilling to face.

For a little while he drifted off into a pleasant fantasy of firm government, a stabilisation of land values, sensible lending rates, and an end to boom and bust. He was woken by another phone call, which the answering machine picked up. Diana's voice filled the room.

'Where are you, darling? See if you can get here early. I am making the most brilliant meal, and I just want you home. Last night was amazing, but tonight will be even better.'

It was only delaying the evil day to hide behind the answer-phone. He couldn't escape her forever. She was expecting him back, just like the old days. But it wasn't the old days, and no amount of sex could disguise the fact.

* * *

Henry Maddox leaned back in his chair. 'I told you your only chance was a guilty plea.'

'I can't ask him to lie, Henry.'

'Don't be naive, Barbara. We both know the man's as guilty as hell. It was your job to ask him to be truthful, in his own interests. Unless you can get him to come clean, we know the outcome. They'll throw the book at him.'

'If he's guilty!'

Maddox threw his hands in the air. 'I can do stubborn, Barbara, Intransigence is beyond me. You obviously have the knack. Get on with it, then, but on your own head, et cetera.'

It was a relief to get back to her room. She was going to lose, and it would hurt like hell, but what would it do to Terry? That was what mattered.

She took out her mobile to check for messages. There was one from Ben, and her heart soared.

* * *

Diana opened the door before Ben could fish for a key. 'He's come! The elusive Pimpernel. Come in. I've an icy G & T waiting.'

She was turning towards the kitchen when she saw his arms

empty at his side. 'No bags? Oh well, I suppose most of your stuff's still here.'

'I'm not coming back, Diana,' Ben said determinedly. It was out, and relief swept over him. Her eyes were darkening – there was going to be a row. 'We need to talk. Let's sit down . . .'

'Sit down? You shit! No wonder you were out of here so early this morning. I might have known. You lied to me, you bastard!'

'I never lied to you, Diana, but you're right: I was less than honest. I wanted things to come right, and I fooled myself. Last night . . .'

'Last night!' She moved towards him until he could feel her breath on his face. 'Don't dare mention it! You conned me, you bastard, you fooled me into letting you back into my bed! I must have been mad.'

'I'm sorry you feel that way. I want to be fair . . .'

'Fair? Fair? Get out, you shit.'

Her fists were beating his chest now, driving him back towards the door. He tried to capture her hands, to stop the onslaught and talk sense, but she evaded his grasp.

'Let's have that drink,' he began. Suddenly she sprang away from him and dashed into the kitchen, returning with a cut-glass tumbler in her hand. 'You want a drink? You're welcome to it.'

The glass caught the bridge of his nose, and pain shot through him. It was useless. He turned for the door, feeling the slightly sticky liquid trickle over him. He was half-way down the steps, and trying to remove a slice of lemon from his lapel, when her voice rang out again. 'Anyway, you always were a lousy fuck!'

Chapter Nineteen

THE WEBCON SHARE PRICE HAD gone up another point, and
there was a postcard from Paris among his post. '*Having a
wonderful time. Ship nice, food superb, Paris dazzling. Every
good wish, Dorothy and Margaret.*' Ben smiled as he read it,
trying not to wrinkle his nose as he did so. There was a faint
bruise where Diana's glass had struck him, but that was a small
price to pay for the sense of relief he felt. For a while he had
been crazy, but he was free of craziness now.

He pushed his coffee aside, and got ready to face the day.

* * *

Barbara faced the police firearms expert with as much of an air
of confidence as she could muster.

'You examined the bullets taken from the body of Julie
Carter?'

'That's correct, m'lud.' He exuded the confidence of long
experience in the witness box.

'You also examined the bullets taken from the body of a 63-
year-old pensioner named Beryl Rutherford. She lived in
Kendal, in Cumbria, and was shot dead last year.'

She looked up at the police expert. No signs of unease as yet. 'There were no signs of a break-in,' she went on, 'no strangers were seen in the vicinity, no one heard any disturbance. The bullets were the only clue. You identified them as having been discharged by the same weapon as that which later killed Julie Carter.'

'Partially correct. I did not initially examine the bullets taken from the body of Beryl Rutherford. The bullets from that crime were reported on by the forensic laboratory attached to the Cumbria force. I accepted their findings, although I did have the opportunity to examine the actual bullets at a later stage.'

'So you did examine them,' Barbara said firmly. 'The riflings on the two sets of bullets were identical, were they not?'

'That is correct, m'lud.'

'For the benefit of the jury, can you spell out what that means?'

'It means that the same gun was used in both crimes.'

'Thank you. Have you any explanation as to how a gun used in Cumbria could also be used in a similar crime in London?'

'With respect, that is not my province.'

'We know that, Detective-sergeant, but give us the benefit of your long experience.'

Counsel was on his feet, 'Objection, m'lud!'

Again the cold glare directed at both counsel. 'Is this leading somewhere, Miss Tulloch?'

'It is, m'lud. I wish to establish that there must be a link between the two crimes.'

'Go ahead, but I hope we are going to come to some conclusion eventually.'

'Sergeant?'

'It's obvious the same gun was used in both crimes, but it does not follow that the same finger was on the trigger. There is a wide black market in illegal guns, and guns used in a crime are shifted very quickly, usually to London for resale there.'

'But you couldn't swear to that in this case, could you?'

'No, m'lud, I couldn't swear . . . but I know what I think.'

He had bested her and they both knew it. The prosecution counsel rose to cross-examine.

'In your long experience, how many crimes have you been associated with where the gun in question had been recently purchased?'

'I would estimate 20 to 30, m'lud.'

'And how many of these guns had been used previously by other criminals?'

'Impossible to give exact figures, I'm afraid.'

'How many of those cases of which you have personal knowledge did not involve the same person pulling the trigger.'

'Again, it's impossible to be exact, but I'd say the vast majority, m'lud.'

Barbara's heart sank. No point in taking it further. The prosecution had fleshed out the idea of guns passing from hand to hand, and it was too late for her to change it.

* * *

Dolly and Maggie had grumbled at the need for an early start until the guide explained: 'If you don't get there early, the place gets so full you can't move, and I want you to see everything.'

Now, beside the lake, with the waterlilies still closed until the sun rose higher in the sky, the trees leaning towards the water, and the bridges leading from one enchanted pathway to another, they looked at one another in agreement. 'It was worth getting up,' Dolly said, and Maggie nodded. The guide was ahead of them now, holding her umbrella aloft to make sure none of her charges lost sight of her.

'I've seen the paintings Monet did of this,' Dolly said at last.

'But they don't do it justice.'

Maggie had put out a hand to the fronds of a willow weeping towards the water. 'He was a lot happier than van Gogh,' she said. 'Apparently there's a lovely house up there, and he had a lovely family and everything.'

'You've been swotting again,' Dolly said, but she said it indulgently. 'You always were the little bookworm.'

'I haven't read for years,' Molly said wonderingly. 'You just get out of the habit with the telly on. I might start up again now. Anyroad, he was a founder of the Impressionist movement because he did a painting called *Impression, Sunrise*.'

Dolly was rolling her eyes. 'Get away, I never knew that.'

'If you're going to be scoffy I'll shut up.'

'No, carry on. We'll both be on *Mastermind*, at this rate.'

'Well, Monet's father tried to make him work in the family greengrocery business, but he was determined to paint. He went to art school but then his mam died. It took a few years for him to get famous, but he did and then he married his model and they had a baby. Only she had the baby first.'

'Go on,' Dolly said. 'I'm all ears.'

'All mouth more like. Anyway, he came to England but they wouldn't put his pictures in the Royal Academy, so he went to Holland. He came back to France, and they had another baby, but then Camille died, and he painted her on her deathbed.'

'That's a bit gruesome, Maggie . . . although I suppose artists are different.'

'Well, he was a genius, Dolly. You can't expect them to be normal. He got married again, and then he looked out of a train window and fell in love with this place – not that it looked like this. He married a widow, and they came here, and he made this garden with his own hands.'

'And they lived happily ever after?'

'More or less . . . although the guide said the second wife

wasn't keen on his children.'

They were both silent for a moment. 'He lived to 86,' Maggie said at last. 'That's a good age for those days, so she must have looked after him.'

* * *

Hamish Cameron wiped his lips. 'That risotto was good. I called on spec, hoping that you'd be free for lunch, because I heard something interesting today. Headey's are retrenching. A man I know acts for them, and he told me. If they're regretting their bid for Webcon, we . . . that's my company, with one or two others . . . might make an offer for Headey's shares. It would be a fair offer, and I think they'd take it. They'd be fools if they didn't.'

Ben felt, first, elation that Headey's would be out of Webcon, and then uncertainty. Why was Hamish telling him? Deals were usually kept close to the chest until they were done deals.

'We want you back on board, Ben. In fact our offer to Headey's and Webcon would be based on your being back at the helm.'

Ben laid down his knife and fork, and sat back in his seat. A few months ago he might have welcomed Hamish's offer but he had come to terms with losing Webcon. True, he had not yet decided on what he wanted to do instead, but the thought of going back into that building, feeling the weight of responsibility settle on him once more, was far from appealing.

He smiled at his companion. 'I'm surprised at your suggestion. I lost the confidence of my Board, remember? Why would you want me back?'

'Why do you think we want you back? We're none of us philanthropists, I can assure you. You were good, Ben. It was the

Board who were weak.'

Ben promised to think over Hamish's proposition, and they stood up to leave the restaurant. It was then that he saw Diana, sitting two tables away with Flicky Everett. They were in animated conversation, but as if she sensed his eye on her, she turned and smiled, then rose to her feet. She moved towards them, taking in each man in turn, her smile dazzling. Inside Ben fear grew. After the other night she would want revenge. What would she do?

What she said came as a surprise. 'I've been a very good wife, and not interrupted your business, gentlemen. Isn't that splendid of me?' Hamish rose to the occasion, and greeted her formally, before managing to extricate them and get them out to the waiting car. On the pavement, he turned to Ben.

'You didn't know Diana was there, did you? Tell me to butt out if you will – you'd be entitled, God knows. But I like you, and I can't believe that meeting was accidental. Diana is a clever lady. Anyway, not my place, but I mean well. I know what a lot you have on your plate at the moment. Take your time, but please, be assured of our good will towards you if you come on board.'

It was flattering Ben thought, as Cameron's car moved off. They really did want him. And Hamish was a good friend. All the same, his flesh crept with embarrassment that a friend felt the need to warn him about the woman who was still officially the most significant person in his life. And even scarier was the knowledge that Diana had only played the good wife because she still felt she could lure him back.

* * *

Barbara was returning to court after the lunch break when she encountered her opponent. He feigned sympathy. 'Pity you didn't get anywhere with the gun issue . . . I did warn you.'

'It's not over yet, David,' she said as sweetly as she could manage.

But he was right. She had not managed to plant the possibility of a linked crime, and that was a pity. The postcard she had received at breakfast flashed into her mind: Paris at sunset. Somewhere on the Seine, her aunts were relaxing in summer sunshine, and she fervently wished she could be there now. But she was in the confines of the Old Bailey.

She hitched up her gown and went in to do battle. If she could get through this afternoon, she had one more day, two at the most before her opponent's closing statement. And in those two days all she could do was put her client in the witness box and hope for the best.

* * *

The voice at the other end was Tom Finch's. 'Webby, I'm back in the UK. Can you meet me tomorrow? I'll get my PA to fix it?'

Ben agreed to a meeting and walked to the window. He couldn't muck about with a man like Finch. Tomorrow he would have to give him a straight yes or no. He must tell Adele of his decision about Diana, too. Remembering yesterday, in the restaurant, he felt his cheeks burn.

* * *

'All you have to do, Terry, when the time comes is tell the truth. Keep your eyes on me, unless the judge addresses you, which is unlikely. If counsel for the prosecution opts to cross-examine, you have to pay attention to him, but I'll be watching him too. If he tries any funny business, I'll jump in. I can't say exactly when you'll be called – probably the day after tomorrow.'

'Will it last all day?'

'It will last all day – it may even go into a second day. But don't dwell on that. Just listen hard, and then answer truthfully. We have a good case, we just have to get it across. What are you going to wear, when the time comes?'

'They put a blue shirt out and my grey jacket.'

'Make sure it's clean and pressed, and wear a matching tie. What you're wearing will do for today, but I'd smarten up for tomorrow. Do you have another tie?'

He was nodding. 'I'm scared, Miss Tulloch.'

'Good,' she said briskly. 'Nothing could be worse than you going in there feeling cocky. Juries don't like it. I want them to see the real you . . . not a bully, and not an impulsive idiot who'd fly off the handle. You're a nice, ordinary young man who finds himself in an impossible situation. A situation he doesn't deserve to be in.'

'I want them to see I'm not guilty.'

'They will.' She said it with a confidence she was far from feeling. 'You'll be a free man, and able to get on with your life.'

He was shaking his head. 'That's not the point – my life's finished, whatever happens. But they've got to see it wasn't me, because if they think it was me no one will look for the bastard who really killed her.' There was silence for a moment and then he said, 'Who did do it?'

'I wish I knew, Terry. I wish I knew.'

* * *

Almost everyone on their table at dinner had been on the visit to Monet's garden. 'They say there was only a handful went on the other excursion, Bizzy Castle, or whatever it was called.'

The speaker was Mamie, the little American woman they had met on the first night.

'Mind, I was glad to get out at the finish.' Dolly was rolling her eyes to denote terror. 'Have you ever seen so many people? And half of them Japs.'

'They'll have come to see the Japanese prints,' Maggie offered. 'Monet collected Japanese woodcuts; they're all there at the house. That lovely house, all pink and green and the roses climbing everywhere. He moved in there in 1883.'

'Do you know my sister, Margaret?' Dolly asked the table. 'She swallowed the encyclopaedia, but we've got her some tablets for it.'

'Go on,' a man sitting across from Maggie said. His face was the colour of leather but his eyes were kind.

'Well, he did,' Maggie said. 'He was famous for collecting them.' The man was still smiling. 'He should have stuck to his own paintings, they're much better. Me, I love the weeping willows hanging like curtains. . .'

Maggie was into her stride now. 'You know why he painted those? It was for the soldiers who died in the war. His son was in the war, and he wanted to pay tribute to them.'

'You don't say.' The man was looking kindly at her, and Maggie felt herself blush.

'You've clicked there,' Dolly whispered when the man went off to choose his dessert. As Maggie was searching for a suitable put-down, her worst fears materialised.

'It's just me,' the woman said. 'And I haven't breathed a word to anyone. But I wonder, before we split up, could I have your autograph?' Dolly was nodding and smiling, and Maggie felt sweat break out on her brow.

'You never will?' she asked Dolly, when the woman went off, jubilant.

'I might and I might not. Now let your meat stop your mouth. You've never stopped talking since we left that garden.'

* * *

Ben felt himself relaxing as Adele's family life flowed around him. Max's head was on his knee, he had a good Merlot in his hand, and the prospect of a walk with Max after dinner.

'Right,' Adele said. 'The lasagne's browning, and I've turned off the veg. Bring me up to date.'

He filled her in on what Hamish had asked him.

'What will you do?'

'I honestly don't know. I like Hamish, but as you know I felt a certain relief when I walked away from Webcon. This would be a permanent commitment – or as permanent as any executive job ever is nowadays.'

He hesitated to tell her about Diana, but eventually the need to unburden himself overcame him,

'Poor you,' she said, as he finished. 'It must have been awful.'

'That about sums it up.'

'Well,' she said, sighing. 'Far be it from me to tell you what to do but I know what I'd like to see.'

'What's that?'

'You finally walking away from someone who has never, ever placed you first in her life. And taking up with someone who would do just that.'

*   *   *

Barbara curled up on the sofa after her shower, a drink at her side, and the dossier on the salesman in front of her. Howard Breen's man had done his work. Jed Hughes was dissected on the pages, and his liaison with Julie well documented. They had been lovers for 11 months, perhaps more, but 11 months was all that could be proved.

And Julie had not been alone in Jed's affection. In addition to his wife there had been at least two other women, one of them a single mother who had earned a precarious living cleaning cars at the showroom. 'What a rat!' Barbara thought.

The important thing, though, was that he had lied in his statement to the police when he said he had not had any connection with Julie Carter. 'I can get him on that,' Barbara thought, and felt a little surge of optimism run through her.

Chapter Twenty

BARBARA FORCED SCRAMBLED EGGS DOWN, and mechanically ate half a grapefruit. She had never felt less like food in her life, but there was a gruelling day ahead of her and she might have to skip lunch. Better to take some nourishment now. At her feet Tootsie was sitting expectant. 'You've eaten, Mr Greedy. Mrs Briggs will give you something when she comes in, so be a good boy until then. Your foster-mother's got a big day ahead of her.'

She plastered on her make-up. This time it really was 'war paint'. 'I have to go out there and conquer,' she told herself. But however brave her thoughts, they couldn't dispel the queasy feeling in her stomach. 'I haven't a single thread of real evidence to support my case,' she admitted, and no amount of blusher and concealer was going to alter that.

But she had Jed Hughes, and the ambiguity about the Kendal crime. That would have to do.

* * *

'Ben?'

It was not yet eight o'clock. Ben rubbed a hand across his

forehead and transferred the receiver to his other ear. 'Yes, who is it?'

It was Peter Hammond, repressed excitement thickening his voice. 'They're out, Ben, I heard last night late . . . so I left it to this morning. But you and I need to meet.'

'You mean the Headey offer is off? Definitely?'

'Definitely. Caput! Finito! Over! Presumably Webcon will now accept a bid from Cameron instead – if he makes one. How are you fixed this morning? We'll need to get the Board together . . .'

Ben took a deep breath. 'Peter, I understand your excitement, but it's no good looking to me. I resigned because the Board didn't back me, remember? I'm a shareholder, so of course I'm interested, but Webcon has an acting chair. It's up to him.'

Inside Ben there was a rising tide of distaste for turning back the clock. He had adjusted to the loss of the family firm. But on the other end of the line Hammond was sounding dejected. 'Hanson's a good chap, Ben, but he was never more than a stop-gap. If this is handled badly, the firm could suffer. Cameron's people might then offload their stock, and God knows who would take it up.'

Ben hesitated. Webcon was more than a name, it was a workforce – and the shareholders.

'OK,' he said at last. 'See who you can get together, and I'll fit in.' But as he put down the phone on a relieved Hammond, he regretted giving way. If the Board reconvened, he would have to face Neville Carteret, Diana's brother, the man who had cast the vote that ousted him. And who knew what Neil Pyke would do?

* * *

'It's nice when we go on excursions, but, really, this is what cruising is,' Dolly said. 'Just lying back and doing sweet bugger all. And if it was only 11.30 and I could decently order a drink, that would be even better.'

'Drinking in the morning, Dolly? Why can't you be content with coffee like everyone else?'

Around them the sun-deck was full of somnolent passengers, laid out on loungers identical to the ones occupied by the sisters.

'I didn't come to France to drink coffee, Maggie. I can brew that at home.'

'I should hope you do. Alcohol before dinner-time. It's disgusting!'

'Dinner-time is 7.30, Maggie – 7.30 in the evening. This is lunch-time: that's what they call it in posh circles. Which is where we belong now, thanks to Ben Webster.'

'If it ever happens, Dolly. I don't understand all this share business. I'm just glad I had enough put by for this trip.'

'We're going to get money, Mags. Well, shares we can turn into money if we want to. But I'm going to hold on to mine, and so is Barbara.'

There was silence for a moment, and then she spoke again. 'Do you hold it against them . . . what happened? Us being split up? If we'd got what was rightfully ours, things might have been so different.'

'I know. And sometimes I do feel resentful. I know Billy's death wasn't their fault, but we never saw him grow up, Dolly. He never knew he had sisters who loved him.'

Again there was silence and then Dolly got to her feet. 'I'm going to have a drink, Maggie. If the sun's not over the yardarm by now, it damn well should be.'

The next moment she had made a beeline for the bar and, to Maggie's horror, started talking to the woman who thought she was Barbara Windsor. Maggie got to her feet and hurried over, but it was too late.

'Oh yes,' Dolly was saying. 'Dear Sid – and then of course there was Dirty Den . . .'

Maggie turned on her heel. She knew when she was beaten.

* * *

'The Headey offer is off, definitely off. Peter Hammond rang me this morning. So that explains the previous dip in the share price.'

'What does it all mean, exactly?' There was a faint note of anxiety in his sister's voice and Ben hurried to reassure her.

'Not a lot, financially. The firm is viable, as you know. Either the Board will appoint another chairman . . . or chairwoman, come to that . . . or there'll be a new offer from another quarter, which they may or may not accept.'

'And you? What will you do?'

'I don't want to go back to Webcon, Adele.'

'So you'll go in with Tom Finch?'

'I'm not sure. I have a meeting with him tomorrow, though, so we'll see.'

* * *

Barbara was summoning up her powers of concentration, readying herself to go into court, when Ian Harper erupted into the room. 'Wait till you see this! Breen's just given it to me and it's dynamite.'

Barbara tried to stay calm at the sight of her junior almost executing a war dance round the room, waving a paper above his head. 'All right, slow down. What is it?'

'Breen had them tracking Jed Hughes, putting his alibi through the wringer . . . and they've cracked it. He wasn't on a test drive at all!'

*   *   *

The sisters went into the restaurant for lunch, eschewing the snacks laid out in the lounge. 'Might as well have our money's worth,' Dolly said, picking up the menu. 'I fancy something fishy.'

Maggie snorted. 'Fishy, that's your middle name. If that woman comes over and you act up, our Dolly, I'm going to spill the beans. I've heard about the French police, and, family or not, I'm not winding up in a French jail for anyone. And that's not to mention what Barbara Windsor will do if she finds out.'

'There you go' Dolly said, her eyes widening. 'Exaggerating, making a mountain out of a molehill. I'm having a little harmless fun. And if Babs Windsor did hear, she'd laugh like a drain. She's a good sport, our Babs.'

'You'll be making out you're her best friend next. Well, I've given you a warning. Go ahead, but don't look to me when it boomerangs.'

'It says here there's butterfish again. I liked it the other day. Look at the menu, Maggie, and leave me to enjoy myself.'

*   *   *

The impulse to go to the Old Bailey came over Ben at 11 a. m. By 11.45 he was sitting at the back of Court No. 3. Barbara was on her feet. It was the first time he had ever seen her wigged and gowned, and she looked impressive. The man in the witness box was flashy, and trying to sound super-confident but his eyes were frightened.

'Mr Hughes, you have worked for Mr Skidelsky for some time, I believe?' The man was nodding. 'Could you address your answer to the judge, please.'

'Yes, for 15 years.' His voice was croaky, and he cleared his throat. 'She's got him scared,' Ben thought.

'For 15 years? So you were there when Mr Skidelsky bought the adjoining building and extended the showroom?'

'Yes.'

'What happened to the rest of the building, the part which was not incorporated into the showroom?'

'It was sealed off and rented out.'

'Not quite sealed off, but we'll come to that in a moment. During this conversion, did you meet the woman who was to take over the tenancy of the rest of the building?'

There was a pause and then a reluctant 'Yes.'

'And that was Julie Carter?'

'Yes.'

'You did meet her, you're agreeing that – and yet you told the police in your statement that you hardly knew her.'

'I said I knew her . . .'

'I have your statement here, Mr Hughes. "I never really knew her."'

'That's right.'

'I put it to you, Mr Hughes, that you knew Julie Carter very well indeed. That, in fact, you and she were lovers over a period of several months, a relationship that ended only when the defendant came into Julie's life.'

His head was down now and no answer was forthcoming as Barbara went into the attack. 'She's a fighter,' Ben thought, and felt a surge of pride.

'And that is not the only lie you told, Mr Hughes. You told the police that at the time of the murder you were out with a client on a test run of a car he might wish to buy. Is that what you said? . . . Mr Hughes, we're all anxious to hear what you have to say.'

There was no reply.

'I put it to you, Mr Hughes, that the "client" was none other than your long-time drinking companion, Bob Carlyle. A friend who was willing to lie to give you an alibi, but not so friendly that he would risk a charge of perjury. He has now withdrawn his statement. So, if you were not on a test drive on that afternoon, where were you?'

This time an answer was forthcoming.

'OK. I wasn't out on a test drive, but I wasn't at the salon, either. I hadn't spoken to Julie Carter for months before she died, and that's the God's truth.'

* * *

On his way home, Ben suddenly changed his mind and turned the wheel of the Bentley left, towards Notting Hill. The drama in the courtroom had been intense, and as far as he could see Barbara had scored a hit. The shifty salesman had been exposed as a liar. Might he also be exposed as a murderer?

As far as he knew the sale was going through, but the *For Sale* board still stood in the front garden

Ben pulled in at the opposite kerb and sat regarding the place where he would live, God willing. What had attracted him to the house was not its spaciousness or its location. It was the back garden, and what he thought of as the magic tree. It was a garden made for children. Would his children run and play there one day?

Into his mind came Diana's words when he had told her he wanted a child: 'Not yet, darling. There's acres and acres of time.' If they had got back together, that is how it would have been – endless deferring, until time ran out and their childless state became a *fait accompli*.

Ben waited for the pain of losing her to strike him, but it never came. What took its place was not painful, but it was startling nevertheless. He saw the courtroom in his mind's eye, the tension, the drama almost tangible, and through the haze the calm face beneath the wig. He told himself: 'I want to be with Barbara.'

* * *

One by one the other passengers had deserted the sky decks, and sought the warmth and jollity of the lounge. Now only Dolly and Maggie were left, side by side, reclining as the pale moon grew brighter in the darkening sky.

'Do you ever think life's funny?' Maggie asked.

'Funny peculiar or funny ha-ha?'

'Both, I suppose. Well, peculiar the most.'

'I'm not sure what you mean?' On the river bank, lights were beginning to go out in living-rooms and in bedrooms. The world was ready for sleep but still neither of the sisters stirred.

'Well, look at us. Right from the start we've had topsy-turvy lives – you adopted, me sent to Northfield.'

'Was it grim?'

'Sometimes. You just put your head down and got on with it. What was it like with your parents – the ones who took you?'

There was a long pause before the answer came. 'Patchy. It was patchy. At first, when Daddy was alive, it was good. Once I got over missing you and Billy, they made me feel really loved. As though I belonged there.' To Maggie's ears the 'Daddy' must have sounded strange, Dolly thought. They had had another Daddy once; could you have two?

But Maggie had moved on. 'What happened after he died?'

'My mother married again. A Mr Stainsby. He was the lodger, and then he just took over.' She could feel tears pricking her eyes. 'He made Mummy get rid of my dog.' It was Mr Stainsby who had caused all those years of abuse and heartache. She wanted to tell Maggie about Mr Stainsby's friend, who had taken in her beloved Lassie in return for pawing her for years, and then taking her virginity. About the pain of knowing you had ceased to matter, so that giving yourself to men for the price of a drink didn't seem such a big deal. If Eddie hadn't come along, she might have been dead in a backstreet abortionist's, or cast out of her profession when she grew too old to lure clients. Eddie had saved her from all that.

She wanted to tell Maggie – they were sisters, after all – but Maggie's life had been so different. Ordinary, Dolly thought. Blissfully ordinary.

'I envy you, Maggie,' she said suddenly. 'Your life's been calm as a mill pond.'

There was no answer, and she peered through the dusk to see if her sister had fallen asleep. But Maggie was staring down the moonlit river, and her eyes were wide open.

* * *

Barbara had rung Ben's mobile, but it was on answerphone, which meant he was either out somewhere nice, or driving. She didn't leave a message: there was no point. She showered and put on her pyjamas before pouring herself a glass of St Emilion, and carrying wine and case papers through to the living-room.

She needed to work hard on her questioning of Terry – pose questions that would show him as he really was. She had pushed Jed Hughes as far as she dared, but he had refused to reveal his whereabouts on the evening of the murder. Hopefully, the jury would see that as an admission of guilt. But until they had something definite against Jed Hughes, Terry's own evidence was all that lay between him and a verdict of 'guilty'. Hope was quivering inside her – but the impassioned 'That's the

God's truth' had sounded horribly sincere. She turned back to the papers in front of her.

Could she use the time element? The garage owner had testified that Terry was in a good mood when he had filled up at the garage. Ten minutes later he was entering the salon and six minutes after that he was exiting. What was it the prosecution had said?

'The defendant has stated that he ran from the salon immediately he saw the body. CCTV shows him entering at 5.35 p. m. Thirty seconds to finish his ascent, a minute . . . two at the maximum . . . to take in the scene, and then he's catapulting down the stairs and erupting into the street. Three minutes. But the CCTV shows him emerging at 5.41, six minutes later. What happened in that missing three minutes? I contend that he spent them trying to persuade Julie Carter to give him a second chance, and when she said no he took out his gun and shot her.'

She had to explain away those missing minutes, Barbara thought gloomily. Could you turn against your lover in a mere three minutes? According to Terry, he had spent them cradling Julie's lifeless body, and this was borne out by the blood on his clothing – but would that be good enough? The garage owner had sworn that Terry had been in high spirits on his way to the salon. No, there definitely wasn't enough time for a good mood to have evaporated and been replaced by a mood black enough to murder. And would he have been exchanging banter over a coffee while carrying a gun? Even if he had been angered by Julie when he got to the salon, he surely wouldn't have had a gun with him?

She was making feverish notes when the doorbell rang. It was 9.40 – who the hell was calling now? Surely not Diana again. She pressed the intercom button. Best to be cautious.

'Only me,' said the disembodied voice. 'I thought you might give a lonely man a drink.'

'Ben . . . of course. Come up.'

There was time to tighten the belt of her robe, check her hair in the hall mirror, and then take two deep breaths to steady her thudding heart.

Chapter Twenty One

TODAY TERRY BOWES WOULD DESCEND from the dock into the witness box. Somehow she then had to inspire him, make him believe acquittal was a real possibility. If she could do this . . . if he spoke out as he had spoken to her in the beginning . . . he might, he just might, persuade the jury that he was telling the truth.

The solicitor was trying to exude confidence but Barbara could see the beginnings of despair in his eyes. 'Look, Howard. However this turns out you can be proud of how you put the case together. I have little enough ammunition, but what I do have is down to you. If Terry gets off, he has you to thank. If he doesn't, you have nothing with which to reproach yourself.'

'Thanks, Barbara. And I know you'll make the most of what little we have. You've done brilliantly so far. The man I put on to Terry's case was good. Invalided out of the CID and keen as mustard. When we heard about the Cumbrian shooting, we thought "Bingo!", but it came to nothing. He was up there over a week, digging around. Still – onward and upward.' He looked at his watch. 'Time to go, I think.'

They went out into the corridor and made for the room where Terry would be waiting, both of them trying to exude a confidence they did not feel.

*   *   *

'It's your turn to pick,' Dolly said without enthusiasm. She was reading from the day's itinerary slipped under the cabin door before they woke. 'You can have a walking tour of Rouen, its cathedral and square – the Joan of Arc Square, the Clock Tower, and more. Unless "more" means wining and dining, I'm not stirred. Or you can go to Honfleur . . . just listen to that pronunciation, eat your heart out Edith Piaf . . . which has slate-covered houses and the largest church made out of wood in France. What do you think?'

'You can see houses anywhere, Dolly. But if we don't go, the others will all come back and tell us it was marvellous.'

'Let's just stay here and wallow. It's coming up to the Normandy beaches, and that'll be a strain. Of course, there's bound to be shops in Rouen . . .'

'We're staying put,' Maggie said hastily. 'Get in there and put your face on, and let's get some breakfast.'

*   *   *

It was Hamish Cameron on the other end of the line. 'Ben, we've got it! All the stock Headey's held.'

'Can I ask what you gave them?'

'Two per cent up on the quoted price. According to Headey's, they were loath to back out, but the current climate precludes the expansion they envisaged.'

'Which means you can now make a bid for Webcon, instead?'

'Yes. That's already agreed.' There was a pause before he spoke again. 'Providing, of course, that you are still on board.

We'll make our offer, and your Board can either accept it or can treat us as hostile and put our offer to the shareholders.'

* * *

'You've told us, Terry, how difficult your earlier life was, but in spite of these difficulties, which would have floored many of us, you managed to establish a business.'

'Yes. Well, I suppose it was a business . . .'

'You were a jobbing builder, and you advertised your services in the free newspaper.'

'Yes.'

'Stop mumbling,' Barbara thought, 'and hold your head up.'

'Tell the court what happened when Julie Carter saw that advert?'

'She rang up and asked for the names of two people I'd worked for.'

'Did you give her those names?'

'Yes.'

'Presumably they gave you satisfactory references because she called you again, didn't she?'

'Yes. She said to come round and give her a price, and if it was low enough I'd have the job. She wanted a room partitioning.' He was gaining confidence now that he was on his subject. 'Her salon was getting a good name and she needed more cubicles. "Rooms", she called them. Those red buildings are big, with high ceilings, and she wanted it done properly.'

'And you did it properly?'

'Well, she was happy . . . nicely finished, she said.'

'You grew friendly while you were working there. How did that make you feel?'

'I couldn't believe it at first. I thought she was just pleased with the work. And then – then we went out for a drink and after that . . .' His voice was thickening now, and he was struggling to speak.

'He loved her,' Barbara thought. 'Whether or not he killed her, he certainly loved her.'

*   *   *

Ben and Tom Finch left the chauffeured car on the road and walked up a rise, turning at the top. Finch drew an expansive hand across the scene. 'Before you lies some of the most beautiful countryside in England, soon to be the scene of the most expensive engineering project in British history: the high-speed rail link between London and the north of England. Estimated to cost a mind-blowing £17 billion, although experience suggests the true figure will amount to twice that. I want some of that money, Ben.'

'Seventeen billion to knock half an hour off the journey time from London to Birmingham?'

A small frown crossed Finch's face. 'You sound sceptical. The world is on the move, Webby. England can't get left behind. Time is money . . . wasted money.'

Ben was making rapid calculations. 'That's about half a billion pounds a saved minute, Tom.'

Now Finch smiled. 'You always were a bugger for maths. But the truth is that British railway lines were built in the 19th century. If they came across something beautiful or significant in those days, they went round it. We haven't time for that in the 21st century. To travel at up to 200 mph, a train needs to go in a straight line. So a great deal of new line will have to be laid.

'Yes, part of Buckinghamshire, one of Britain's most beautiful and unspoilt counties, will be scarred. Northamptonshire too, probably. But it's progress. It's what our forefathers did when they dug mines and built foundries. For the past year I've been buying up land on spec., because I had good vibes about the project. Now I'm told the Coalition government will announce in its favour in a few weeks' time. I'm set to make a killing, and I want you to oversee it for me. You're used to land acquisition and management, exactly the skills I need.'

Ben looked down at the green fields, neat hedges and roads winding as only English roads can wind. If what Finch said was true, a huge scar would be driven through the heart of England. Hundreds of houses would face compulsory demolition; others would be abandoned by occupiers who could not stand the disruption to some of the loveliest villages in England.

Sensing Ben's unease, Finch spoke again. 'It will reduce the north-south divide, Ben. You have to want that?'

'Yes, that would be good. But I can't see my role, or exactly where Pantheon would come in.'

'The line will generate development, and development needs land. If you hold that land, you can name your price. Do you know the difference between an acre of agricultural land in an area like this, and an acre with planning permission? It's nearly a million. A million pounds.'

'But you'd have to get planning permission first,' Ben said, 'and that isn't easy.'

Finch was smiling. 'Never easy, but always possible . . . if you have the right connections.'

* * *

'I want you now to cast your mind back to the summer before last: 2008. Where were you then?'

'I was here in London. I'd just got the van . . . the Ford. I was working in Tooting. It was a big job for me – I took a boy on. That was the May. May 2008.'

'Did you take any time off?'

'I had to take a week off to go to a TA training course. Didn't have an option, but it was bl . . . very hard work after that. There was a penalty clause in that job, so I had to go like the clappers.'

'There was no possibility that you were in Kendal? Kendal in Cumbria?'

He was shaking his head vehemently. 'Never. I've never been further north than Filey. I only went there once, but never to Cumbria. I didn't know exactly where it was until you told me.'

Out of the corner of her eye she could see counsel making a note. Surely he wasn't going to challenge on that? He'd told her the Kendal incident wasn't relevant. She was momentarily distracted but the judge's eye was on her, and she quickly recovered.

'I want to bring you now to the day in question. The day Julie was cruelly struck down.' In time she would have to ask him outright if he had killed Julie, but not yet. Not before she had shown him in a sympathetic light. 'Why did you go to the salon that day?'

'I'd landed a job. A good one. I knew she'd be pleased.' He paused for a moment, but she held back. 'She was really funny when she was pleased . . .' His voice was breaking – good. 'She would come over all excited and screw her face up, and . . .'

No doubt the prosecution would say he was acting, but if the jury had a heart they would surely recognise sincerity when they saw and heard it.

* * *

Outside, rain was lashing the river. The swans had vanished, no doubt in search of shelter. 'Miserable, isn't it?' Dolly said. They were sitting in the ship's lounge gazing morosely at uninspiring banks on either side. 'Might as well be at home,' Maggie said, and they both knew she was thinking that would have been the cheaper alternative. 'We could have a drink?' Dolly said hopefully.

Maggie's eyes shot skyward. 'At half-past ten in the morning?'

'Well, we can't just sit here as though we had corn growing, Dolly. We should have gone with the others to the open market. The crew were dishing out umbrellas.'

'I didn't come to France to sample the rain, Maggie. Rain is the same wherever you go, a bloody nuisance. Still, I've had an idea . . .'

She was half-way to the staircase when Maggie called after her. 'If it's anything to do with pretending either of us is something we're not, you'll have to do it on your own.'

* * *

'The offer they're proposing is less than Headey's original offer,' Hammond said.

Ben nodded. 'The market's gone down, Peter. We were land-rich rather than cash-rich, but what's land worth at the moment with nobody building? Besides, I don't think Hamish and Co. want to buy us out. When I say "us", I mean the firm, of course. They simply want in. Seats on the Board in proportion to the share they already have.'

'Which would mean a reconstitution of the Board to allow you to get rid of the . . . shall we say, undesirables?'

The call from Hammond had come just as Ben was parting company with Finch, and he had come straight to the pub to tell Hammond the extent of Cameron's offer; but it was the rail link that was in the forefront of his mind. He thought again of Finch on the hillside: 'Mega-bucks, Ben. And there for the taking.' Which was the truth, but not the whole truth.

Hammond clearing his throat brought him back to the present. 'Yes, Peter, I'm just thinking. It's quite a lot to take in. I think we should sleep on it, and I'll call you tomorrow.'

*   *   *

Inside the cabin all was calm. They were curled up on their beds, feet mercifully free of shoes, watching a film on the in-house television which a smiling young Filipino had conjured up for them. A tray lay on the bedspread, tea for Maggie and a gin and tonic for Dolly.

'Nice film,' Maggie said, trying not to think about drinking gin when you were hardly out of your nightie.

'Yes.' Dolly sounded a bit distracted, and Maggie looked at her questioningly. 'Oh, I was thinking about Tootsie, and wondering how he was getting on, that's all.'

'He'll be fine with Barbara. If you're feeling mopey, maybe we should have gone out, after all.'

'Nor on your life. They'll come back here like drowned rats,' Dolly said smugly.

'Don't be awful, our Dolly,' but Maggie couldn't resist a little smile as she said it.

'Are you following the film?'

'It's a bit complicated, but she's a bonny woman. Is she French?'

'Of course she's French . . . she's Juliette Binoche.'

'She could still be English pretending to be French. That's Judi Dench up there, and she's doing it.'

'Well, believe me she's French. He's English, although he doesn't look it.'

'I thought he looked foreign.'

'I think his father was Italian. He married that actress . . . big eyes . . . played a policewoman . . . Jill something.'

'I don't watch police things, so I can't help.'

'That's going to worry me all night. Jill . . . Jill . . . anyway, I expect it'll come to me.'

'Are they meaning she's putting something in the chocolate – you know . . . *something*?'

'No, I don't know. What do you mean?'

'Well, stuff to make them feel funny . . .'

'Like Viagra, d'you mean? Sometimes, Maggie, I wonder about your mind. No, she just woos them with chocolate. Makes them feel all romantic. Didn't your Jim ever buy you a box of chocolates? Well then, he wanted to butter you up and get his reward.'

'Don't be silly,' Maggie said.

'You're blushing, Maggie. Or you're having a hot flush – and it's a bit late for them.'

* * *

Howard Breen was waiting when Barbara emerged from the courtroom. 'Bad news, I'm afraid. Jed Hughes finally coughed under pressure, and admitted he was with a woman when Julie Carter was killed.'

'Why didn't he say that in court? If she'd confirmed his alibi, he'd've been off the hook.'

Breen smiled ruefully. 'It was Mona Skidelsky . . .'

For a moment Barbara was puzzled. 'Who? Oh, Skidelsky . . .'

'His boss's wife,' Breen said. 'No wonder he tried to keep quiet. Anyway, you've done your best. You showed your client to the best advantage.'

'But it won't be enough,' Barbara said. 'Not nearly enough.'

* * *

Conversation over dinner was more subdued than usual. The excursionists had indeed returned like drowned rats. 'The one good thing about going home to America will be to get some sunshine,' Mamie said. Maggie nodded. 'I bet you have nice weather over there. Not that we don't, and I wouldn't swap the British climate, but it must be nice to get a tan like that.'

At that moment the autograph hunter came into view, moving between tables. 'Who's she hunting now? Cary Grant?' Maggie hissed.

Dolly smiled serenely. 'Eat your nice ragout, Maggie, and think about the lecture.' After dinner they were to get a briefing on the following day's excursion to the D-Day beaches. On the opposite side of the table it was already being discussed.

'We took a beating that day.' That was the Yank with the John Wayne voice.

'So did we,' Dolly said. 'But someone told me there were hardly any French there. Which is funny, when it was their country we were liberating.'

'No, it was a US-British operation all right. Five beaches . . .'

'Utah, Omaha, Gold, Juno and Sword.' Dolly reeled off the names, and then added, 'My husband was keen on the war. He even had a book on it, that's how I remember.'

She was basking in her knowledge when they were interrupted. It was the autograph woman. Beneath the shelter of the table-cloth, Maggie's fingers sank into Dolly's thigh. 'Nearly home,' the woman said in a stage whisper. 'Nearly home, and I've never said a word.'

'And I'm grateful,' Dolly said. She tried but couldn't quite suppress a little yelp as Maggie's fingers sank home.

* * *

They went to Little Italy in Soho's Frith Street, and dined on calamari fritti and pappardelle.

'How did it go today?' Ben asked as they ate their squid.

'Pear-shaped. You know I was hopeful of getting something on Hughes?'

'The shifty salesman?'

'Yes. He was screwing his boss's wife, hence the lie, and the reluctance to tell. But he's not in the frame.' She wiped her mouth on her napkin. 'Let's talk about your day before I start weeping about mine.'

'The Cameron offer is in. It's fair enough, but it won't tempt the big institutions, so they're unlikely to get a takeover. Anyway, I don't think that's what Cameron wants. They simply want a share of the cake. Now they've got the Headey stake, it's enough.'

'With you in charge? Will you do it?'

'I don't know yet. And then there's the new house to sort and settle into. I need time to think.'

He wondered if he ought to tell her about his excursion with Finch, but decided against it. Finch's information about the rail link was still unofficial.

They changed the conversation then, and talked about the latest revelations about the Coalition government, before getting around to Maggie and Dolly and the cruise.

'I bet Aunt Dolly is living it up and dragging Aunt Maggie along with her. But poor Maggie, she won't know what's hit her. What if she comes back all dolled up? Dolly said on my card they were shopping.'

'Incidentally, what did you do with Tootsie tonight?'

'I fed him before I left . . . chicken as directed. It's prawns tomorrow, unless I can get some fillet steak.'

'You're kidding! It doesn't get fillet steak?'

'Only when there's an R in the month.'

Ben was reflecting what good company Barbara always was when he felt his phone vibrate. 'If you'll excuse me, I'll just look at this. It's probably Adele.'

But it wasn't Adele. The message was from Diana and it was stark.

'*I want you. I need you, Ben. I'm waiting. Don't let me down.*' He looked at it for a moment and then he pressed delete. He looked up and made a decision. 'I was offered another job today.'

When he had finished, Barbara sat back, looking thoughtful. 'Finch has a reputation for ruthlessness, Ben. But then you don't get to the top unless you do have a ruthless streak, and Pantheon is certainly at the forefront, all thanks to him. Will you go in with him?'

For the last few hours he had been wavering. Now, remembering what Finch's views were, he was sure.

'No, Barbara,' he said. 'Pantheon's not the place for me.'

Chapter Twenty Two

B EN WOKE EARLY WITH A feeling of optimism. He wasn't sure quite what the future held, but he was very sure now what he didn't want. He poached two eggs for his breakfast and wolfed them down with lashings of buttered toast. He was on to the Euston Road before he remembered that this was a big day for Barbara.

He looked at his watch, 8.45. Too late to ring her? Probably. Instead he texted *'Knock 'em dead kid'* and smiled at the thought of her reaction.

* * *

Barbara saw the message when she went to switch off her phone ready for court, and it had made her smile. Looking round her now, however, the smile faded. 'Look confident,' she had urged Terry before they went into court. In the dock he was doing his best to obey her instructions. She, it was, who was in danger of letting despair show through.

She looked at her co-counsel and saw her own gloom mirrored on his face.

* * *

Around them, the hotel lounge buzzed with largely female conversation. The hotel obviously catered not only for ladies who lunch, but those who have coffee beforehand. 'I suggested this place,' Peter Hammond said, 'because you never know who is lurking in our usual haunts, and we don't want talk of crisis meetings. There's trouble enough already.'

He was putting a copy of the *Daily Telegraph* down on the table, open at the financial pages. 'The City is getting restive,' he said. 'They've got wind of the Cameron interest, and now they're curious as to why it's not going ahead.'

'I know,' Ben said contritely. 'But it will happen, as far as I know.'

'Much longer, and the press will start to say there's something dodgy, Ben. We can't afford rumours, not with the industry in the state it's in. I know they want you back as part of the deal. You like Cameron, you've told me so before. Why are you hesitating? Is it anything I can help with?'

'No.' Ben shook his head. 'If anyone could help me, Peter, it would be you. But this is something I have to work out alone.'

The other man's eyes were still on him, questioning.

'You know how I came into this business: it was expected of me. Like grandfather, like father, like son. Nothing else was even considered. I always felt at a disadvantage because I didn't earn my place as you did. There must have been people who resented it, who thought I wasn't up to it.'

Hammond nodded. 'I'd be surprised if there weren't some like that Ben. When you were made chairman, and I'd only been there a couple of months, I thought, "This'll be a disaster." But it wasn't. You took Webcon by the scruff of the neck and you dragged it forward. Cameron and Co. want you because the firm is the better for your being there.'

'It's good of you to say that, Peter. But that's not the only complication. You know a little of what happened over my

211

grandmother's will. She left her considerable shares in Webcon to three people she'd never met – because part of Webcon was rightfully theirs. My grandfather had, in effect, stolen it. The half of Webcon that should have been theirs had belonged to their dead father.'

'One of them is Barbara Tulloch? And the others are the two old dears?'

'Yes. Barbara's father was the third child. He died some years ago, so she inherits in his place. But I've felt ever since as though Webcon doesn't belong to my family . . . not rightfully belong.'

* * *

Prosecuting counsel was into his stride now, and the jury were rapt. 'So here we have a woman who has shown him nothing but kindness, a resourceful woman who has established a business . . . not an easy thing to do nowadays . . .whose only crime is to be trusting and fall for a younger man who sees in her a chance to escape from the web of debt in which he finds himself. You have heard from witnesses how she indulged him, paid off his debts, showed him a lifestyle to which he could never have aspired on his own. You have heard how he boasted of her largesse. He was playing her for a fool, ladies and gentlemen.

'And then, when she begins to see the error of her ways, sees what a fool she is being, the whole situation changes. You have heard from Lady Darblay that Julie Carter was troubled that day.'

Barbara made a note to challenge the evidence of Julie's mood that day, and then gave counsel her undivided attention once more.

'The defendant said he went there that day because he had

some good news for his fiancée. He had landed a job. Surely she would have been ecstatic at the prospect of this drain on her resources being eased. But instead we're told she was tense.'

Barbara drew a line under her comment. He wasn't going to hang her client on the opinion of one witness if she could help it, even if that one witness was above reproach. But a woman in the jury box was looking ready to burst with indignation. There was one guilty verdict, for sure.

'I put it to you, ladies and gentlemen, that the purpose of the defendant's visit to the salon that day was to plead with Julie Carter not to turn off the tap, and when she refused he shot her . . .pumping five bullets into her body as she pleaded with him for her life.'

'You swine,' Barbara said under her breath. The man ought to be writing for Mills & Boon. No one knew what had happened in that room, but he had managed to create such a vivid picture that most jury members would now believe they did know.

*   *   *

The first stop on their itinerary was Bayeux. As usual Maggie had boned up on the facts. 'It was part of Gold Beach,' she announced. 'And they came in twice, the British troops. They came in the night and dished out cigarettes, and the next day they just walked in.'

'British troops?' Dolly was gazing out of the window. 'What's he doing here then?' The 'he' in question was Dwight Eisenhower, cast in bronze and towering over the entrance to the town.

'If you stopped pretending to be something you're not and listened, Dolly, you'd know more. She told us last night. Said it was all wrong him being there, and it should have been

Churchill. Well, it should, by rights. It was also the Durham Light Infantry. Some others, mind, but the Durham lads were there.' This last was said with pride.

After that it was the museum housing the Bayeux Tapestry. They walked around the glass case in which it was mounted, earphones at their ears and a constant commentary describing what was depicted.

'It's better than I expected,' Dolly said grudgingly. 'I mean, you can see what they're getting at. The lords look like lords and the peasants look like peasants.'

'And you can see the arrows . . . poor Harold with the arrow in his eye, and William the Conqueror just laying all before him.'

'It's funny to think of them lording it over us, isn't it? The Norman Conquest.'

'We've been wiping the floor with them ever since, Maggie, so I wouldn't fret over it. Now get a move on, we don't want to miss the bus.'

* * *

At last the prosecution's closing speech was coming to an end, and Barbara felt fatigue almost overwhelm her. She would have to shake it off, because it was her turn next. She turned her attention back to the prosecution.

'Ladies and gentlemen, I know you will deliver a just verdict. There can only be one such verdict – that the defendant did wantonly murder Julie Carter, for no other reason than that the lifestyle she had created for him was to be taken away. Defence counsel will try to persuade you otherwise, but I urge you to remember what you have heard in this court over the past days, and make sure that Terry Bowes pays the proper penalty for what was a heinous and inexcusable crime.'

* * *

Ben poured himself a drink when he got back to the flat, and then picked up the phone. Half of him wanted Finch's phone to be on answer, but could you turn down a job offer in a recorded message? In the end, it was a relief to hear the human voice on the other end.

'Tom? It's Ben Webster. How are you?'

'I'm fine, Webby. I'm in Zurich – and I hope you've got good news for me?'

'Sorry, Tom. It was unbelievably good of you to think of me, and I'm grateful . . .'

The voice that interrupted was a little testy. 'I didn't "think" of you, Ben. I was told by the very expensive headhunters I employed that you were the man. I don't operate the old boys' network and that crap. I wanted you because I was told you were an operator. If that's true, you'll take what is a fucking good opportunity . . .' The testiness had somehow transmuted into threat.

'I'm sorry, but I'm afraid I don't think Pantheon is for me . . .' Again no time to finish a sentence.

'Your loss, old boy. Keep in touch.' And the line was dead.

Ben waited for a feeling that he had burned his boats, but all he felt was relief.

* * *

'There's a woman's name up there,' Maggie said suddenly. 'Sister Dorothy A. Field.'

They were standing in front of the memorial arch at Bayeux's war cemetery, where the names of all the bodies that had never been recovered were listed. 'How could they not find a woman?' Maggie went on, doubtfully.

'Blown to bits, I shouldn't wonder. When she was trying to get up the beach. Those nurses must've landed just like the men,' Dolly said. 'I met one once. She said she had clean knickers and two lipsticks in her backpack.'

But Maggie had wandered on, and was muttering the names as she went. 'Baldwin, Dunphy, Kennedy, McDonald, Wildgoose . . .' On and on they rolled. 'What a waste,' she said at last. 'What a waste.'

Dolly sat down suddenly and fished in her bag for a hanky. 'I'm not upset,' she said when Maggie would have comforted her. 'It was a long time ago, and we can't bring them back.'

'They're still dying, Dolly, in Afghanistan, and all for nothing.'

'Well, this war wasn't for nothing,' Dolly said, getting to her feet. 'It's not much consolation, but it's some.'

They were walking away when Maggie halted and turned back.

'What are you doing?' Dolly said. Maggie's eyes were raised to the inscription that ran along the top of the memorial, and then she started fishing in her bag. 'She said something last night, at the lecture. Something about William the Conqueror. I wrote it down.' She was producing a piece of paper and smoothing it out. 'See up there.'

Dolly peered, but not for long. 'It's Latin,' she said. 'At least I think it's Latin.'

But Maggie was ready to translate, reading from her notes. 'Remember the tapestry, how William conquered England? Well, what that says up there is: "We, who were conquered by William, have now returned to liberate the land of the Conqueror."'

Dolly beamed. 'It's like I told you, Maggie. We bested them in the end.'

* * *

Barbara settled her wig more securely and began her closing speech as confidently as she could.

'Ladies and gentlemen, you have observed the defendant in the dock and in the witness box. Does he look like a man who could murder? You have heard from several witnesses how he and Julie Carter were in love. They had trust in one another. On that fateful day he was coming to tell Julie that her faith in him had been justified. He had landed a deal . . . a big deal for a business of his size. I expect he would have promised her dinner in celebration. But instead of being able to impart his good news and issue his invitation, he found her lifeless on the floor.

'Police witnesses have told you that her blood was found on his clothes. We don't deny that. What more natural, when he sees the woman he loves lying there, than that he should hold her . . . try to lift her up. Ask yourself – if he were the heartless assassin that the prosecution would have you believe, would there be blood on his clothes? No, ladies and gentlemen, he would have shot from afar, and then departed, gun in hand. No blood, no damning forensics.

'Which brings me to the gun itself. A gun used in a murder in another place, a location my client swears he has never visited, and where he could not have been on the night of that murder. A gun that has never been found. The prosecution is asking you to believe that there is no connection between the two crimes . . . that the gun used in Cumbria managed, of its own accord, to travel the length of England and wind up in my client's hand. I ask you, members of the jury, is that likely? There is no proof that he ever handled it.'

* * *

The graves stretched before them, neat and narrow. 'Boys,' Dolly said, regarding the headstones. 'Just boys.'

'There are 4,648 of them,' Maggie said, 'with 3,935 of them our boys, and 466 Germans.'

'You've been swotting again,' Dolly said, but she said it admiringly.

'Just to take back a foreign country.' Maggie sounded despairing.

'It was for more than that, Mags. They were fighting for their lives, for their freedom. For our freedom, come to that.'

'Do you think our Dad's buried in a place like this?'

'I don't know, but I do know we can find out. The War Graves Commission, it's called. They'll know, and if they don't we'll hire a detective. We'll find him, Maggie, don't you fret. Mam, too, I daresay. They must've kept records in the Blitz. We can go to their graves one day . . . and if you start me off crying, Maggie Riley, I'll go back to that ship and tell the whole bloody crew I'm Barbara Windsor.'

* * *

At least the jury were still paying attention, which was good after listening for hours and eating what was probably a stodgy lunch.

'I draw your attention to the photographs marked 46 and 47,' Barbara said firmly. 'They show the pattern of the bullets that thudded into Julie Carter's body. They are not so much random as haphazard. You have heard evidence from a Territorial Army weapons instructor that the accused was a crack shot. A man who could have killed with one well-placed bullet. Instead, the prosecution asks you to believe that he sprays bullets about, running the risk of none of them being fatal and of Julie Carter's being able to testify from a hospital bed exactly who her assailant had been.

'The prosecution claim that there are two possible explanations for this random shooting. First, that the defendant was deliberately seeking to conceal his identity by disguising his skill with a gun. I ask you, ladies and gentlemen, does the man in the dock seem capable of such deviousness?

'Which leads us to their other excuse: that he was in such a blind rage that day that he was incapable of taking aim. So mad with rage that he fired six shots and was only lucky that five of them hit the target. Let's examine that theory. The witness Edward Cousins has testified that at 5.20 p. m. the accused was in good spirits as he filled up his car. He made jokes. Twenty minutes later he was running from the salon because he had stumbled upon murder.'

The jury were paying attention now and she hurried on. 'Even if his mood had changed for some reason – a row with the deceased, say – is it likely he would have gone out that morning carrying a gun? Just in case he got angry with someone later? Just in case the woman who had befriended him, his lover and his future wife, should turn against him? Bought petrol and cracked jokes with a lethal weapon in his pocket, and murder on his mind? Does that seem reasonable to you, ladies and gentlemen?'

Out of the corner of her eye she saw a juror nodding in agreement. Perhaps she was winning after all.

* * *

There was silence in the bus on the way back to the ship instead of the usual chatter. 'Everyone's full,' Dolly whispered.

Maggie nodded. 'I felt sorry for the Yanks at that gun emplacement.' It had rained as they visited the huge gun – 'bigger than a street', she had called it. The guide had explained that it was the only gun the RAF hadn't managed to immobilise. It had been trained on Omaha Beach, the American beach, and the men landing there had been mown down.

'We'll be nice to them tonight,' Dolly said. 'Don't worry, this one night I'll behave meself.'

'Seeing's believing,' Maggie said, but she said it with a half-smile.

Chapter Twenty Three

NEXT MORNING TERRY BOWES LOOKED older than his years. The nails on the fingers twisting anxiously together were bitten to the quick. He was looking at Barbara now. 'I've had it, haven't I?'

'No.' She was as vehement as she could be. 'You can't give up. The judge is going to sum up the evidence, on both sides. It's vitally important that we both listen hard. I have to make sure that he doesn't misrepresent what was said. If he does, it would help with an appeal in the future. Not that we'll need an appeal if we get a proper verdict.

'Your job is to listen for anything that triggers off a memory – something you had forgotten, something that has just occurred to you. Anything, however insignificant it may seem. It's important that neither of us just sits back now.'

She was trying to banish the hopelessness from his eyes but she wasn't succeeding. She left him with a pat on the shoulder, and a glance at his solicitor to warn him to keep up the good work when she had gone. She tried to calm her own fears and marshal her thoughts, but the image that kept intruding was the image of Terry as he made the lonely ascent to the dock.

*   *   *

There were four of them around the table. Ben, Peter Hammond, Cyril Evans, the one Webcon director who had voted against the Headey offer, and Philip Purser, a man Ben had never met who Peter had told him was representing a major shareholder.

It was he who spoke first. 'We're worried about the state of relative flux that exists at the moment. I'm grateful to you for agreeing to this meeting, and I hope you'll feel that, in the present situation, a steady hand on the tiller is crucial.'

Ben nodded. The man was looking at him quizzically. 'A group headed by Hamish Cameron has taken up the Headey shares. I thought you knew this?'

'We want you to come back, Ben,' Cyril Evans said. 'Temporarily, at least, although you know how much I'd like to see you back in the driving seat permanently. Webcon prospered under your chairmanship . . . that's why it became a target. Now, with the recession biting, it's vital to restore confidence.'

'What's the matter with the chair you've got?' Ben said it truculently, part of him angry at this attempt to reinstate him in a seat they had summarily ousted him from. He resisted the impulse to say, 'Why not ask Neil Pyke?' Evans had played no part in that treason.

He cleared his throat. 'If I did come back, there would be snide talk in the City . . . clutching at straws, that sort of thing.'

'You underestimate yourself,' Cyril Evans said, and his tone was measured and somehow reassuring.

*   *   *

The judge was getting into his stride. 'The prosecution have set out a scenario, but that is all it is – their interpretation of the evidence. You must put your own construction on what you have heard. Some witnesses have told you that the defendant was a man of volatile temper. Others have described him as amiable. Where does the truth lie? Was he a happy man when he entered that building to find the woman he loved dead on the floor? Or was he a man hell-bent on preserving the easy way of life with which Julie Carter had provided him?

'Pay particular attention to timings. Was he in that salon for long enough to commit murder? If he didn't do it, why did he not avail himself of the plethora of telephones around him? Why did he put space between himself and the scene of the crime before he pulled out his phone and rang for help? Was it to rid himself of the weapon, and if so, how did he achieve that?'

He paused for a moment and gazed at the jury box. 'You need to weigh evidence very carefully. Witnesses who are convinced in their own minds that they are telling the truth will make convincing witnesses. But the evidence they give may be worthless because, in fact, what they believe to be the truth is not the truth. Ask yourself whether any witness has a reason to feel as they do, a reason that has nothing to do with the truth – personal animus, perhaps, or the reverse: a great liking for the subject of their testimony.'

'He's being fair,' Barbara thought, 'but will they think for themselves, or has the prosecution already made up their minds for them?'

* * *

'We've turned for home, Mags. Are you pleased?' The sisters were standing on the sky deck as the ship started back towards Paris.

'I'm always pleased to be going home, Dolly, but I've enjoyed this trip, I must admit. I'd have enjoyed it more if you'd behaved yourself.'

'I was lamb and salad last night. You've got to give me that.'

'One night, Dolly. One night! If my blood pressure's up when I get back home, I'll know who to blame. I'll hardly dare open the *Daily Mirror*. "I sailed with Barbara Windsor" – I can see the headlines.'

'Pish and tosh. That's what my Eddie would have said to that. He got sued dozens of times over his business. "It's all in the game, Dolly," he used to say. Anyway, I might tell her the truth before we leave, if that'll put your mind at rest.'

'No thank you. If there's going to be a scene I want to be back in County Durham when it happens. Now, what's on the schedule for today?'

* * *

Barbara shifted in her seat. It was getting to the crux now. The judge was looking round the court before turning his attention back to the jury. 'The prosecution would have you believe that the defendant was a scrounger, a cynical exploiter of a vulnerable woman. But you must consider the character of the victim. She had established a business in an industry that I am told is very competitive. Would she be easily deceived? That is for you to decide.'

'One for us,' Barbara thought, and did a mental high-five.

'Furthermore, according to the prosecution, the couple were arguing. One witness has spoken of rows over money, but the defence suggested that witness's evidence was less than impartial. Again, you must weigh up her evidence and decide how much weight to attach to it.'

Barbara felt herself relax. So far so good. But she had relaxed too soon.

'I turn now to the murder scene. According to the prosecution, the defendant was the only person with the opportunity to commit the crime. There is the CCTV camera guarding the door, showing quite clearly that Terence Bowes was the only person to enter it. The other doors were locked at the relevant time, and the police have testified that windows were either hermetically sealed or had safety locks. Nor is there forensic evidence of entry in that way.'

From under her lashes Barbara stole a glance at her opponent. He looked like the cat that had got the cream.

* * *

'I'm going to do some of my packing tonight,' Dolly said as they sat on the foredeck watching the river flow around them.

'The amount you brought, maybe you should start it now,' Maggie said scathingly.

'At least I've worn everything,' Dolly riposted. 'The only things you've worn I've had to force on you. Do you want another spritzer?'

'No, thank you, I do not. Sour. I'll have a cup of tea if you're getting up.'

'I'm not asking the steward for tea now, Mags. It wouldn't suit my persona. Stars don't drink tea.'

'Don't start that rubbish again, Dolly. My cheeks burned the other night . . . burned. How you've avoided jail all these years . . .'

'But you love me really, Mags.' Suddenly Dolly's voice thickened. 'You always did.'

* * *

The summing up was drawing to a close. Even discounting lunch, it had gone on for five hours. The judge had been fair but he had also been coldly analytical. If Barbara had ever thought she had a case, he had disabused her of the idea. She looked up as the remorseless voice went on.

'Society places a grievous responsibility upon a jury. You have heard the evidence given by both sides. Now you must discharge that responsibility by weighing the evidence and forming a conclusion. You must disregard any prejudice you may have against the defendant, and must equally disregard his youth and comparative inexperience. He is adult, and capable of murder. It is up to you to decide whether or not he is guilty of that crime. I have tried to set out the evidence as I see it without prejudice for or against either side. Now it is up to you. You may now retire and consider your verdict.'

There was a shuffling of feet and the court rose. Barbara flashed what she thought was a reassuring smile towards the dock, and began to gather up her papers as Terry Bowes vanished from view.

DCI Fisher was in the hall as she left the court. 'What do you think, Frank?'

'He's going down.'

'Don't be too sure.'

'I'm not enjoying it, Miss Tulloch. Like I told you, I don't think he's a villain.'

Barbara made a swift decision. 'Fancy a pint? I'll be out in 15 minutes.'

He thought for a moment. 'OK. The snug. Fifteen minutes.'

She did her best to raise Terry's spirits. 'Let's see what tomorrow brings,' was her parting shot. It was less than adequate in the circumstances. It took her two minutes to change and make her way to the pub.

She slipped into the booth and took the waiting G & T gratefully. 'Ta. Why are you so sure of the outcome?'

'The weight of evidence. Well, the absence of any counter-evidence. I mean, he was there, no one else was there, she died. That's the nub of it. Now that we've ruled out Jed Hughes – is there anyone he hasn't had it off with? – who else can you blame?'

'Did you ever consider the possibility of someone being hidden on the premises? From the night before, even? They could have done the deed and then left through the back door. The door at the end of that passage at the side of the stairs.'

He was shaking his head as she spoke. 'There are only two entrance/exits. One, the front door covered by the CCTV opposite; the other the back door at the far end of the passage. First, we've examined the CCTV from 6 p. m. the previous day and accounted for everyone who entered. They're all recorded on film as leaving. Then the back door: if they'd left by that exit, how would they have locked and bolted it from the inside? Because that's how we found it.'

'They could have had a key?'

'And shot the bolt home through the keyhole? Same thing's true of the door connecting with the sale-rooms. In theory, Hughes or anyone else could have had access to the key, but when we first asked for it they couldn't find it. That's how long it had been in disuse – they'd lost it. Believe me, if I could have found a loophole I'd have exploited it. I like to get my man, but as I said, not much joy unless you know you've nailed an out-and-out villain. Want another?'

'My turn,' Barbara said and rose to go to the bar.

'Your one chance in appeal is the gun,' the detective said when she returned. 'Those bullets. I'm satisfied in my mind that it did get back on to the market, and the accused bought it in London, but no one can be sure. We never really explained away that link with the murder in Kendal.

He paused. 'And you didn't get that from me.'

*　*　*

Barbara drank coffee with Howard Breen. 'What do you think?' he asked. And then, before she could answer, he shook his head. 'Hopeless?'

Barbara nodded. ''Fraid so. You did your best – in fact, you did wonderfully well, but no one, not even the best lawyer in the world, can make something out of nothing. The prosecution have CCTV, they have opportunity, they have forensics. What they didn't establish was motive. They suggested one – that she was getting ready to dump him – but they didn't prove it.'

'And you pretty effectively dispensed of it.'

'Only with the help of the people you turned up.' Barbara paused, wondering whether or not to tell. 'I've had a tip . . . a suggestion . . . that the weak link in the prosecution's case is the Cumbrian killing. Don't ask me who suggested it.'

Before she could finish he smiled. 'DCI Fisher? He hasn't looked as happy as he usually does when he's about to write "case satisfactorily completed". But, Barbara, we really plumbed that Cumbria case. I had a man up there for three days. It seems to have been a random killing. I think the murderer thought the old woman had cash in the house. She didn't, so he didn't bother with bric-à-brac. In fact, she had a hefty little nest-egg for a pensioner, but it was safe in the bank.

'We could prove Terry wasn't there – we talked to the TA. He was under supervision the whole time . . . had no chance of nipping up to Cumbria, so no connection with the crime. But you know guns travel, especially after fatal shootings.'

Barbara pushed away her cup and stood up. 'Let's hope we got through to them on the absence of motive. Better go and have another word with Terry. He must be going through hell down there.'

Chapter Twenty Four

BARBARA WAS UP BEFORE DAWN, unable to sleep. It was unlikely there would be a verdict today, but there was always the chance. In either event, the wait was unbearable, although an early verdict was usually for 'guilty'. Seven o'clock found her in a cab on her way to chambers. She alighted at Middle Temple Lane, the narrow, cobbled thoroughfare she had always seen as the entry to the land of the legals, leading to the leafy autumnal calm of Fountain Court. The assorted buildings bordering it spanned the ages, here Edwardian red brick, there elegant Restoration. Lawyers had learned their trade in these environs since medieval times.

She paused at Middle Temple Hall, remembering her first days here, new and untried but full of confidence. Ten years later, she was standing here terrified, all confidence fled. She shifted her bag on her shoulder and walked on. There was a legal hush about this place that suggested calm. She stood savouring it until her phone vibrated in her pocket. It was a text from Ben: '*Good luck, today. Everything crossed for you. Ring me when it's over.*'

She should have been elated to hear from him, heartened by his message. Instead she felt curiously flat. He was going to go to back to his wife – he might not know it yet, but it seemed to her inevitable. 'And I don't want him to,' she said aloud. 'I want him to want me.' Which was exactly the same as wanting snow in summer.

She turned on her heel and began to walk back to the hurly-burly of Fleet Street.

* * *

The American woman Maggie liked, Mamie, was at the break-fast table with her husband, and she made them feel welcome as they sat down. Of the woman Dolly was leading up the garden path there was no sign, so that was a blessing.

'Have you enjoyed the trip?' Mamie asked, sipping her juice. That was one thing Maggie had learned: Americans lived on juice.

'Yes,' she said. 'Yes, I have enjoyed it. At times.' Under the table Dolly, knowing exactly what was meant, gave her a sharp dig but Maggie's face never flickered

Mamie was fishing in her bag. 'Maybe you'll go further afield now you've got the travel bug. Come to us. You'll love Atlanta.'

Her husband was leaning forward. 'She means it,' he said. 'Mamie loves a houseful, and we have plenty of space. Ten bedrooms.'

'Fancy that!' Maggie said faintly. She would never go as far as Atlanta, if for no other reason than she'd have to ask Mamie and her husband back – and ten bedrooms was something Belgate didn't run to.

* * *

Around them, the Wolseley buzzed with conversation. 'So,'

Hamish Cameron said, looking round the table, 'crunch time. It's up to the Webcon Board now, but the purpose of this meeting is to talk about your personal situation.' He looked at the two men sitting either side of Ben. 'If we succeed, and I think you know we will, we want you to return as chairman of Webcon. We've done our homework. You have the confidence of the workforce . . .'

'So has Hanson,' Ben interjected.

'He has,' Hamish was nodding, 'but he doesn't embody the ethos of Webcon as a family firm. You are a Webster. There's still a certain cachet to a family firm, when it's well run.'

'Webcon hasn't been a family firm for decades. The entire family's shares put together form a fraction of the stock.'

'Agreed,' Hamish said. 'But to the public it's the name that matters, and to the institutions it's competence. You were competent, Ben, although you seem remarkably unwilling to accept the compliment.'

One of the other men, Steven Lord from a City institution, spoke now. 'Your lineage is less important to my people than your ability to hold Webcon together and make it prosper. You did that before, which led to Headey's desire to acquire the firm. We'd be foolish to lose you . . . unless of course you were unable to accept a new regime.'

'If I threw in my lot with a new regime there'd be no shilly-shallying. But I'd want Peter Hammond at my side.'

'No problem,' Hamish said firmly. 'Now, what's your answer?'

* * *

They had elected not to disembark at Les Andelys and visit Château Gaillard. Instead they stood on the lower deck and watched the brave-hearted go ashore. 'It's impressive,' Dolly said, 'but it looks more like a castle than a château.'

'It must have been something, years ago, perched up on a height like that. You can just see the knights riding up to capture the ladies . . . like that film. Vanessa Redgrave and Richard Harris.'

'*Camelot*,' Dolly said, and sighed. 'They don't make them like that any more . . . that bit at the end when he knights the little lad and sends him running to safety. I had to feel my way out of that cinema! Lovely!'

'My Jim liked that film too . . . and he was fussy.'

'They had an affair, you know.'

'Who did? Honestly, Dolly, the way you can dredge up scandal . . . who had an affair?'

'Vanessa Redgrave and the Italian fellow, the one who played thingummy . . . Lancelot.'

'He wasn't Italian, he was French.'

'He was playing French, Mags. There's a difference.'

'Like you play television stars? So that's where you picked up bad habits . . . going to the pictures.'

* * *

The call to return to court came at 4.30. Barbara's eyes met those of Howard Breen and found her own disappointment reflected there. It was too soon. Their best hope had been a stand-off between those jurors certain of his guilt and those unwilling to condemn if they had a scintilla of doubt. If there had been waverers, it had not taken long to overcome them, whereas for the unsures to have won over those sure of guilt would have taken days.

'It's bad, isn't it,' Terry said, as they walked towards him. It was not a question, it was a statement.

'Wait and see,' Barbara said and hated herself for the evasion.

'All rise.' They stood as the judge entered, settled his robes, and took his seat. The jury filed into their places, and the clerk to the court turned to face them.

'Will the foreman of the jury please rise.' A man was standing up, averting his gaze from the dock. So it was guilty.

'Have you reached a verdict on which you all agree?

'Yes.'

'On Count One, the murder of Julie Carter, do you find the defendant guilty or not guilty?'

'Guilty.' Two of the jurors, both women, looked close to tears. The rest had their eyes fixed on the judge. No one was looking at the man in the dock – except his counsel. 'God help him,' Barbara thought. Her own head was swimming. This wasn't fair. It simply wasn't fair. The odds had been stacked against Terry all his life, and when opportunity had opened up it had been snatched away from him.

There was no sound from the well of the court. They had received the verdict they had been expecting. There was no one to shriek protest, but no one to be triumphant either. 'He has only me,' Barbara thought, 'and I have let him down.'

* * *

Ben heard the news on the radio as he drove towards his flat, and his concern for Barbara blotted out his own concern about the 18-hour ultimatum Hamish had given him. Barbara had lost. She would be gutted. He himself had never believed in the man's innocence, but that didn't alter the fact that she did. She would need support.

When he pulled up outside the house he took out his phone and texted her. *'Heard the news. Bad luck but not your fault. Supper tonight? Ben.'*

* * *

'I wish she'd cut the cackle and get to the cheese,' Dolly whispered. Maggie shushed her sister. She wanted to hear every word of the tour director's advice about navigating the jungle that lay between the ship and Laburnum Terrace. As far as she could see, it was well organised. They had to put their bags outside the cabin in the morning with coloured stickers on them. The bags would reappear again at the Gare du Nord, and after that it would be up to her to keep an eye on them until they were back in civilisation.

'I'm dying for that cheese . . . I wonder if I can sneak a bit of it back for Tootsie?'

'Definitely not. Anyway, cheese is binding. You can't do that to the poor little dog.'

'He loves cheese. I get it from Selfridges food hall.'

Maggie groaned: you couldn't reason with someone who went to Selfridges to buy cheese for a dog. A sudden sadness came upon her at the thought. They were sisters but their lives were a million miles apart.

She had planned to tell Dolly about the rape and the search for her baby – but how could she do that now? Dolly would never understand. She would have to keep it to herself.

* * *

They met for an early supper. Barbara was putting a brave face on it, but she looked tired and Ben felt a sudden compassion for her. When she was seated and they had ordered, he laid his hand on her arm. 'You gave it your best shot.'

'It doesn't feel like that. I feel I let him down, Ben.' She shook her head wearily and looked around the restaurant. 'You feel as though life shouldn't just go on as though nothing has happened. An innocent man has gone to jail for life . . . at least 15 years . . . and no one cares. When I came out into the street outside the Old Bailey, I felt as though the traffic should've stopped.'

Ben nodded. 'I know. I felt like that when my parents died. But you won't always feel so bad. This is the first murder case where you've borne the major share of responsibility.'

'It's not that. I hope I'm more professional than that. When we start, what's the first thing we're told? Stand back. It's an essential part of the course, and it's drummed into you. Professional detachment. But this is different. I know, I know in my gut, that he didn't do it.'

He urged her to eat, then. 'Try to let it go for a while . . . although you may end by having to accept that he did do it. I'll help you all I can.'

* * *

The farewell cocktail party had been a whirl of chatter, the swapping of addresses and email addresses, and vows of eternal friendship. 'I don't expect any of them will make contact with us again,' Dolly said.

Maggie nodded. 'Ships that pass in the night.'

'Well, drink up, Mags. I don't know what's in these but I'm not far off singing.'

'One note, Dolly, one note – and that's the finish. I've put up with a lot but I draw the line at performances.'

'Not even a little one? I can do "Don't Rain on my Parade" better than Streisand.'

'You heard,' Maggie said ominously. She smiled then, but it was to hide the pain she felt. This afternoon she had realised that she could never be really honest with someone who had never had a hill to climb in her life. Still, it had made Dolly a joy to be with.

She reached out and patted her sister's arm. 'Come on, pet.

Let's go in to dinner, and make sure we get the best table in the house.'

* * *

Ben poured himself a stiff drink when he reached the flat, and stood with it at the window. Driving to the office had put a curb on his drinking, which was a bind. He should make more use of drivers. But today had been some day. Tomorrow he must decide whether or not his future lay with Webcon. Tonight, over dinner, he had deliberately blocked it out, in his desire to comfort Barbara, but he couldn't do that for ever. It worried him that Barbara was so hell-bent on proving Terry Bowes innocent. Sooner or later she too would have to face up to things.

He had felt reluctant to leave Barbara at the end of the evening, and had done so only at her gentle insistence that they both needed a good night's sleep. Had he sensed in her the same desire he felt? If so, she was being sensible, and he admired her for that.

'Do I feel something for her. . . something more than friendship? Or am I fooling myself?'

But the silent street gave back no answer.

Chapter Twenty Five

MAGGIE WAS AWAKE AT 4 A. M. when the ship glided to its berth on the Paris quayside. Paris by night – she had to admit it was a bit special. She turned from the window towards the bulk of Dolly asleep in her bed. Little Dolly – she always had been a good sleeper. In the dark she could make out the shape of their bags, ready packed by the door except, for the two which would take their toiler and night things in the morning. She turned back for one last look at the lights of Paris and then climbed into her bed in the hope of an hour more of sleep.

When she awoke Dolly was already up. 'Come on, sleepy-head. Home today to my little Tootsie. Barbara's putting him back in the house, and she said she'd get bread and milk for us. I've got stuff in the freezer for supper.'

On the way down to breakfast Maggie seized her sister's arm. 'Keep away from that woman, Dolly. Let's just get off this ship without any trouble.'

'Don't worry, Mags. I'll be good as gold even if she does come over, which I expect she will. You just close your eyes, and before long you'll be on Eurostar and half-way home. Although why I paid all that extra for First Class when all you get is a newspaper, a kiddy's meal and a free drink. I do not know.'

They were half-way through their bacon and eggs when Maggie's worst fears were realised. 'I've been good,' the woman said, 'so I know you'll sign this for me.' 'This' was a copy of the ship's itinerary.

'I will,' Dolly said, putting down her knife and fork, 'but I'm trusting you to protect me. If it gets out that I travel under a *nom de plume* I won't be able to go anywhere, so our paths will never cross again.'

The woman put her hand on her heart. 'I swear Miss Win . . . yes, well, I swear. You're a star, Miss . . . a star. I'll never forget this trip.'

'Silly moo,' Dolly said as she walked away. 'She wants to book an eye test as soon as she gets home.'

'You are a bit like Barbara Windsor,' Maggie said grudgingly. 'Except that she's got sense.'

* * *

Terry Bowes's face kept looming up, however hard Barbara tried not to think about him. Yesterday she had tried to turn his thoughts towards the appeal. 'I'll find grounds, you'll see. I won't give up.' Unprofessional to give hope where there might be none, but she couldn't help it.

Now she looked at herself in the bathroom mirror. Perhaps she wasn't cut out for the bar? 'This may be your come-uppance, my girl,' she told her reflection. There was a sudden whining at her feet and she looked down. 'That's how I feel too, Tootsie. But at least you're going home today, so one of us will be happy.'

Ben was meeting her at 10.30, together with the detective who had traced Maggie's baby for him. Perhaps he might bring fresh thought to the situation? Just talking about it with someone not involved . . . or not involved as yet . . . might help.

'I'm too close to it,' she thought. 'I care too much, so perhaps I'm missing something.' A tiny seed of hope blossomed. The truth was in there somewhere. If the facts were laid out before someone with a trained mind . . . She rinsed and brushed again, and then went off to get dressed and feed Tootsie.

* * *

Ben was ready in plenty of time. If Middlemiss could help Barbara, that would be a bonus. Even if all he did was convince her it was hopeless, that would be something. He was whistling under his breath when the phone rang. The voice on the other end was silky-soft.

'I hope you're having a lovely morning, Ben. Because if it isn't lovely that means I can't spoil it, which is the only reason I rang up.'

'Get to the point, Diana.'

'The point, beloved, is that I have just returned from a very satisfying session with my solicitor, who informs me that I can take you for almost every penny you possess. And I will. Every last fucking cent.'

'Is that all?'

'No, it's not bloody all . . .'

She was still talking when he put down the phone.

* * *

'I've read the reports in the papers so I've got the broad outline of the case,' said Ken Middlemiss. 'As I understand it, your client was in a relationship with an older woman. She had the money, he was struggling. According to the prosecution, she's ready to give him the heave-ho, so he walks in and shoots her.'

'That's partly true,' Barbara said reluctantly, 'but not the whole truth.' Ben sat silent beside her. 'They were in love. She was older but he was mature for his age, and streetwise, after his lousy childhood. And she looked younger than she was. The point is, they got on really well together. They were happy. He had no reason to kill her.'

'Leaving motive aside, then, the prosecution made much of the fact that no one else had the opportunity. The place was locked, one entrance covered by CCTV.'

'Yes, that was our biggest problem. But there has to be an answer. He didn't do it. Don't ask me how I know, I just do.'

Ben intervened then to explain the two doors and the dead end of the salesman Lothario; and Barbara took up the story, adding further detail.

'OK,' the detective said eventually. 'Here's what I suggest . . . that is, if you want me to come in on things?'

'I do.'

'OK. Then I think we need to look into the background of everyone involved in the case, especially the dead woman. Let me have a list – and I do mean everyone, including character witnesses. I'll take a look at that Cumbrian case and the matter of the other bullets.' They talked on over coffee and then came out into the street where Middlemiss made his farewells.

'Fancy a drink?' Ben asked when the detective was gone. Over gin and tonic he told her about his visit to Michael Martin, and the man's refusal to meet Maggie.

'How awful,' Barbara said when he had finished. 'How are you going to break it to her?'

'With difficulty, that's how. Still, let's not dwell on it now. What shall we do with the rest of the day? I feel like playing hookey, and you could do with a break.'

'I've got a suggestion,' Barbara said carefully. 'If you're up for it, that is.'

* * *

'It's nice to be home,' Dolly said as they paid off the cab and toiled up the path to the pink-and-white house. Maggie agreed, thinking longingly of her own home. Still, only two more days.

There was an ecstatic reunion in the hall as Tootsie went nearly as mad with delight as his owner, and then Dolly put her hand on the newel post. 'Let him out into the garden, Mags. He's probably bursting. I'm going straight upstairs to take my corset off. Half the pleasure of a holiday's letting it all hang out when you get back. After that we'll have a good cup of tea. That's the one thing that was missing on that ship, a proper cup of tea.'

Maggie elected to keep on her clothes. All the same she envied Dolly who came back in a comfy pink robe with a swathe of pink chiffon where her wig had been. 'That's better,' she said. 'And you've made the tea. Good girl!'

'Our Barbara's left all sorts in the fridge. Must have cost her a fortune.'

'She's a good girl, too. If we can get her safely married, I'll be satisfied.'

Dolly poured, and they sipped for a moment. Then, 'What will you remember most, Mags?'

There wasn't a moment's hesitation from Maggie. 'You making a show of yourself pretending to be Barbara Windsor.'

'I didn't start it, I only kept it up.'

'Kept it up. Telling her exactly what you and Sid James got up to, and how Dirty Den made a pass at her – at you. As if you ever got within arm's length of him. Honestly, our Dolly, you're . . .' She grasped for words.

'A proper little actress? That's what my Eddie used to say. But it's like I told you, Mags: you can be anyone you like when you're away from home.'

*   *   *

They reached the outskirts of St Albans by 12.30. 'Are we making a mistake?' Ben asked as they left the motorway.

It had seemed like a good idea, earlier. 'You never know, I might just be able to change his mind,' Barbara had said.

Now she said again: 'We have to try, for Aunt Maggie's sake. She's not only got a son, she's got a grand-daughter and two great-grandchildren. Do you ever feel this is getting too big? My family's mushrooming before my eyes.'

'I know.' Ben sounded contrite. 'I'm sorry.'

'Don't be. It wasn't your fault, Ben. If your grandfather was a bit of a crook, it can't be blamed on you. Besides . . .' She put a hand on his arm. 'I rather like unearthing all these family members. All the same, shall we turn chicken and head for home?'

'Or find a country pub with a fire and a fabulous menu?'

'Don't tempt me,' she said. 'Just keep on driving.'

They found a pub just outside St Albans. 'We'd better not intrude on his lunch,' Ben said as they settled at a table with glasses of Merlot and beef sandwiches. 'Let's give him till two o'clock. How do we handle it once we're there?'

'Don't make demands.' Barbara sounded authoritative. 'I remember that, when Grandpa first told me you'd made contact, I thought "What is he after?"'

'I gathered you felt like that,' Ben said drily. He was gleeful about the fact that Barbara was not preoccupied with Terry's appeal. That was good.

'Was I that obvious?'

'Horribly. But I soon forgave you. You were right to be vigilant for your grandfather.'

*   *   *

'Barbara's done us proud, all right. Wine, smoked salmon, cannelloni, a peach trifle, bacon and eggs for tomorrow . . .'

'And lovely bread. Feel that crust and soft inside.'

'She's a good girl, Mags. Well, she's got our genes so she's bound to be.'

'I'm not so sure,' Maggie said drily. 'Every family throws up a bad-un now and again.'

'And that's me. Over supper I'll tell you all about me and Kenneth Williams and what I said to Prince Charles at the Command Performance.'

'You'll wind up in jail, Dolly Brewis . . . or murdered. I can't say which.'

'Well, Maggie Brewis, if you pass that corkscrew I'll open this bottle, and we can drink to our next cruise. Or a life of crime. You can choose.'

* * *

They had gained admittance to the house easily enough, but Michael Martin's face was still unrelenting. 'Your mother didn't want to give you up. She was young, only 15, and without any support.' Barbara leaned forward. 'Her . . . look, she's my aunt, which means you're my cousin. My dad and your mother were brother and sister. There is another sister, Dolly, who's alive too. My Dad was a soldier; he died in Ireland.'

'I'm sorry,' the man said, but it was obvious he was still keeping his distance.

'The children's parents, your grandparents, were both killed in the war, and all three children were adopted. At least, my Dad and Aunt Dolly were adopted. Your mother, who was the eldest, grew up in a children's home. None of the three ever saw one another after that. 'Recently . . .' Barbara was ploughing on, 'recently, Ben, Mr Webster, heard the story, and sought out the three children to reunite them. That's when we first learned about you. So the question is, do you want to meet your aunts . . . and me . . . or not? It's entirely up to you.'

If she had hoped for an enthusiastic response she didn't get it. Michael Martin was shaking his head. 'I'm sorry,' he said at last. 'It's a lot to take in. Are there any more cousins?'

'No.' Ben answered this time. 'Barbara here is an only child, and your mother didn't have any more after you. Dolly has no children. But you'd like her and your mother . . .' he felt a pricking at his eyes. 'Your mother is someone I'm proud to know.'

'What about my father? Did he stand by her?'

'I'm afraid not. We don't know much about him . . . nothing, really. But if you meet your mother, she might be able to tell you more.'

As Barbara spoke, Ben felt a weight lifting. They were not going to discuss how conception had occurred, at least for the time being. Whether or not to tell of the rape should be Maggie's decision. He turned his attention back to Barbara.

'But you mentioned you had a child,' Barbara was saying.

'Yes, my daughter. And grandchildren, one of each. My wife died three years ago, so I'm alone here, but my daughter lives near. She's a good girl.' There was pride in his eyes now and it seemed to give him confidence.

'I need to think,' he said. 'And I need to talk to my family. Tell me how I can contact you, and we'll take it from there.'

Ben was fishing for a card when Martin spoke again. 'I can't make any promises,' he said.

* * *

The Stag and Ox was low-beamed and dark, and on the way home. They settled at a table by the fire and sipped Campari sodas. 'Well done,' Ben said. 'It's 60-40 Martin will agree to a meet. I hope so, for Maggie's sake. And today has done you good. It's stopped you thinking about the case.'

'I've enjoyed the day.' Barbara leaned forward to emphasise her words. 'I've really enjoyed it – but it hasn't stopped me thinking about Terry, Ben. I go round and round in circles. If he didn't do it, who did?'

'I'm going to go over the papers again tonight,' Ben said. 'There has to be something in there . . . and there's whatever Middlemiss unearths in Cumbria.'

'If he unearths anything.'

Ben was squinting down at his glass. 'I keep thinking about something . . . a line from a script – well a book, Sherlock Holmes, I think it may have been. Holmes said something like: "You rule out all the possibles, and then, even if you're left with what seems to be impossible, it has to be the answer."'

'Or was it Agatha Christie . . . Hercule Poirot? The trouble is, everything is impossible in this case. The possible is Terry, but I think that's impossible. It's impossible also that someone else got on to what is essentially a locked room, so is that your answer?'

'Maybe. But there's another possible: Lady Darblay.'

'That is impossible. Why would she want to kill a beautician? I'd be laughed out of court if I even suggested it.'

'What do you know about Julie's assistant? She seemed nice enough from what I've read in the report on her. She's like Lady Darblay, squeaky clean. Too clean?'

'Yes, Angela was a little too good to be true. And Lady Darblay does seem saintly. Devoted wife; besotted mother of a 12-year-old son; on more committees than you could shake a stick at. She's only once blown her cool . . . in public, that is.'

'Oh?'

'It was about a year and a half ago, maybe a little more.

She'd taken her son to an outfitter's before he went off to Eton. A photographer caught them coming out of the shop, and Lady Darblay attacked him. Trashed his camera, and left him to sob to one of the red-tops.'

'I remember now: Hamish Cameron told me something of that. What happened then?'

'Nothing. The photographer was obviously paid off, and the whole thing fizzled out. But they printed the photo, and in it you can see the rage in her face.'

'The boy's an only child?'

'Yes. And apparently hard come by. I think she lost babies beforehand.'

'I'm curious about what you told me about the locked door . . . a long passageway and then a door. The perfect setting for a getaway.'

'Agreed. But who got away? There was no one else in Julie's life. No family, few friends, no business rivals that I know of. The whole thing's an enigma, Ben.'

He leaned forward to pat her hand. 'Let's wait and see what Middlemiss turns up. He's good. Give him a chance.'

She relaxed back into her chair, and the convivial atmosphere of the bar, and Ben ordered a Pina Colada for her and coffee for himself. Tomorrow he must make decisions. Tonight was to be a night of freedom.

Chapter Twenty Six

THERE WAS NO PRESSING NEED to rush in to chambers. Barbara ought to have appreciated the extra time in bed, the leisurely bath instead of a two-minute shower, but she felt impelled to get up at the usual time. 'I'm becoming a creature of habit,' she thought. 'And I'm missing the dog.' The first signs of spinsterhood – it would be a cat next.

All the same, the sooner she got down to some real work on the appeal, the better. If there were grounds for appeal. She couldn't fault the judge, who had been meticulous and fair in his summing up. Though the prosecution, of course, had been hell-bent on conviction, there had been no dirty tricks. 'Without new evidence we're stymied,' she acknowledged.

Hopefully, Howard Breen would approve of Ken Middlemiss. If not, she would have to think of something else. He sounded as though he knew his job, and it was good that he was exploring the background of everyone involved. But what else could be revealed about Lady Darblay, whose life in the past years had been lived out in print?

In the end, she gave up worrying and instead thought about yesterday. 'I like being with Ben,' she thought. 'God help me, I like that almost better than anything else I can think of.'

*   *   *

Hamish Cameron was studying the menu as Ben slid into the seat opposite. The call to lunch had come at 9.15 – not so much an invitation as a summons. 'Good to see you again, Ben. You saw yesterday's papers?' Cameron was expecting an answer.

'I saw them,' Ben said, plunging in. 'I saw them, and I realise my havering is putting you in a difficult position.'

Cameron nodded. 'More importantly, it's putting Webcon in a difficult position. Any moment someone is going to come after the company, and when that bid's made my colleagues and I have to decide whether we sell our shares or stay with Webcon in the long term. We're not prepared to consider the latter option unless you're at the helm. We're not builders, Ben, we're venture capitalists. We need our money to work for us or we move it elsewhere.'

'I'm flattered but a little mystified. Why me?'

'Because, as I said, we're businessmen. We act strictly on the figures. During your tenure Webcon grew by 22 percentage points. The share price soared. Admittedly, this was all in a beneficent climate, but the price improved, nevertheless. A new chair would be an unknown quantity. Ergo, we need a yes or no from you, not alternative suggestions.'

Searching for the right words, Ben looked up as a tall couple, both fair and faintly regal, were escorted to a nearby table. Hamish followed his gaze. 'The Darblays. You don't often see them enjoying a meal together. They seem to live from one important function to another. And of course, he's at the UN a lot. Have you met them?'

'No,' Ben said, 'but I read about her evidence at that Bailey trial.'

'I bet there was gnashing of the Darblay teeth over that,'

Hamish said ruefully. 'They like to keep themselves to themselves.'

'You know them?'

'Slightly. The son was at Cheam with my boys. They're both besotted with the son. He's other-worldly, the father – you get the impression he's awaiting canonisation, or martyrdom, or both. Nice enough chap, but a bit unreal.'

'And the wife?'

'Always reminds me of Grace Kelly. Cool, unapproachable, but the hint of fire underneath. Blew that cool once in public, I think I told you, when paparazzi were attempting to photograph the boy. And talking of children, did I tell you my eldest's now a hockey blue?'

Ben smiled and simulated enormous interest as what amounted to showing the baby pictures ensued. So even tycoons had a soft spot. From time to time he glanced across at Lady Darblay. She was indeed beautiful, but had eyes only for the man opposite her. He dismissed the idea that she might have killed Julie because she was a rival for her husband's love as soon as it came into his mind: her husband looked as though sex with one woman would be as much as his libido could manage. 'He gives the impression of a medieval saint,' Ben thought.

Turning his attention back to his host, he drew a deep breath. 'Before we eat, Hamish, the answer's to your question is yes – and I hope neither of us lives to regret it.'

* * *

'We're whistling in the wind, Barbara. We have no grounds for appeal and we both know it. I just don't want to be the one to break it to the lad.'

'I know. Neither do I, although I will if I have to. But I

talked to an ex-detective yesterday, who comes recommended. He thinks it's worth taking another look at everything. I gave him a tentative go-ahead . . .' She mentally crossed her fingers at the lie – she had given a very definite go-ahead '. . . but if you don't like the idea . . .'

Howard Breen held up his hands. 'Please. I'll agree to anything that holds a scintilla of hope of a breakthrough. But we have to face it: all that stands between Terry Bowes and a long incarceration is the belief of his legal team that he didn't do it. And that's about as much use in the Court of Appeal as a chocolate fireguard!'

* * *

They had visited the local shops, and stocked up on perishables and dog food. Now they sat either side of the fire, sandwiches and wine in front of them.

'I never drank in daytime till you came along, Dolly,' Maggie said.

'Blame me – but I notice you don't say no. In fact, your little face lights up now when you hear the chink of glasses.'

'Get away. It is nice, though.'

'It's Chilean. Eddie was good with wine. Never read a book on it. With him it was all taste. "I either like it or I don't, Dolly," he used to say.'

'Have you got some photos?' Maggie asked.

'Dozens. Holidays mostly. I'll get them out later on. And next time you come down bring yours. I'd like to see your Jim.'

'You'd have liked him, I think. Mind, he was a straight talker. Called a spade a spade . . . a bloody shovel sometimes, if he needed to make a point.'

'We've missed a lot, Mags. Stuff we can't get back. All those years when we could have been together or kept in touch. Still, no use being bitter about it.'

'And it could have been worse.' She had expected an answer but Dolly was strangely silent.

*　*　*

As always when she visited her father, Barbara felt a sense of peace. Whatever fate had made their paths cross had been a good one. She had talked with her Aunt Dolly, and nothing definite had been said, but she got the feeling that adoption, in Dolly's case, had not been plain sailing. Whereas her grandfather had brought only love into her father's life, and later into hers.

'I'm waiting to hear all about your wild social life,' he said, as they sat on the little terrace outside the French windows in the mild autumn sunshine. 'I've followed your work in the newspapers. Very lurid reporting, but I hope you had a little time off?'

'Not much, Gramps. It's been a bit grim, to be truthful. Ben has been a brick, though. We've had suppers and things.'

'Suppers and things? I don't suppose you're going to tell me what the things were?'

'Nothing romantic, I promise. We've talked about the case . . . he's been very good with suggestions . . . and yesterday we went to talk to Aunt Maggie's child, who's a grey-haired man and quite grown up.'

'And nice, I hope?' The old man sounded anxious.

'Very nice, I should say. Of course you can't tell until you know him better. He has a child and grandchildren, so Maggie would be taking on quite something.'

'But of course he may not wish to become involved. Some adopted children don't want to know, I'm told.'

'True. He's only agreed to think it over, so far. But at least she'll know he's safe and had a happy life.'

'I've never forgiven myself for leaving her behind that day. And instead she had a life of servitude and then a barren marriage. And a child conceived in the cruellest way, whom she could only imagine growing up somewhere else. If only we could turn back the clock . . .'

'Well, we can't, and you're not to beat yourself up about it. You gave her baby brother a happy home, and I know she's grateful for that because she told me so.' Barbara tried to lighten the subject. 'I might adopt one day. Single women can nowadays. And I promise you, I'll take the whole family, even if there's ten of them.'

'I hope you have children of your own one day. And a loving marriage. I get the feeling there's a wistfulness behind your jokes. Am I right?'

'You're a witchdoctor, not a cleric. You see too much for your own good. Now I'm going to take that delicious meal I bought specially in M & S, and we are going to stuff ourselves rotten.'

* * *

'So you spent the whole day together?' Adele was beaming.

'Almost a day. But it was a nice day. She's good company.'

'You've noticed! Now pass me that oven-cloth and set the table.'

After that it was a blur of conversation around the family dinner-table. It was Friday night, and the children had a late pass because their favourite uncle was a guest. 'My sister is supremely happy,' Ben thought, watching them all. Harry, at the head of the table, was exuding warmth, listening intently to each child in turn, while Adele looked fondly on. From time to time they drew him into the conversation, but he knew that their family unit was complete without him.

That was what he had wanted with Diana – to be a family, but it had ended in tears and acrimony. The other night, in the enchanted garden, he had imagined how it could be, and how it never would be now. And then a wet nose was snuffling at his knee and a broad head was laid across it. 'I have Max,' he thought. 'I won't be alone in Edgerton Gardens.'

When he was ready to leave, he faced his sister. 'By the way, I'm going back to Webcon. I've agreed.'

Her eyes widened. 'Are you sure? Don't do it for my sake . . . for anyone's sake, for that matter.'

'No, I've thought it through, Del. I'm going to do my damnedest to bring Webcon through,'

* * *

Talking with her grandfather had disturbed Barbara, rather than comforting her as she had hoped. It wasn't anything he had said: as usual, he had been nothing but loving. But what he had said about his guilt over Maggie had reminded her of what a wasteland his own marriage had been. 'It doesn't always work out,' she told herself. Without the advent of little Billy, her father, into his life, her grandfather's existence would have been a barren one, dominated by his wife who was woman obsessed with having things her own way. A woman like Diana.

An overwhelming urge to phone Ben and tell him so consumed her, but she resisted it. It was his own business – and, anyway, he was probably off somewhere enjoying himself. He might even be with Diana, whatever he'd said about finality. The thought so appalled her that she downed her nightcap, and pulled the covers over her head.

Chapter Twenty Seven

THERE WAS A LETTER FROM Diana's solicitor in Ben's post. She wasn't wasting time. There were threats of proceedings, and warnings about the diversion of capital . . . as if he was going to send his money off-shore simply to thwart her. He put it aside to consider later, and concentrated on his breakfast but the food turned to ashes in his mouth. His marriage was over. A door had closed.

He tried to tell himself he felt relieved, but in truth he felt scared. What if he was alone for the rest of his life? He pictured sitting by the fireside in old age with only Max for comfort. Except he would lose Max, too in time. That prospect was so ghastly that it brought him to his feet and searching for his briefcase.

Tonight there would be a welcome-home party for the aunts at Adele's. There would be good food and talk, and Barbara would be there. At some stage he would have to take Maggie to one side and tell her he had found her son. It would be tricky, telling her the good news without raising too many hopes. The man had looked harmless, even pleasant, but what could you tell from a glance?

Please God he wouldn't refuse to meet her. Maggie had suffered enough.

* * *

The Old Bailey cells had been forbidding, but the room in which Barbara now waited for Terry Bowes was even grimmer. She had expected to find him in a degree of distress, but when he was ushered in she felt her breath catch in her throat. He had aged in the past week, and there was a pallor to him that had not been there before.

He tried to smile a greeting but the trembling of his lip forbade it. 'How are you?'

He shook his head. 'Like you might expect.'

She wanted to put out a hand and pat his arm but it wouldn't do. The figure of the watchful warder loomed large in the corner.

'I know it's not easy – that's why I came. I wanted you to know that Mr Breen and I are still working. We're not giving up.'

There was no flicker of response in his eyes. 'He's drugged,' she thought, at first outraged and then relieved. If something was taking the edge off his pain, that was good. 'We're preparing grounds for an appeal. I've got someone sifting through the evidence all over again. I want you to rack your brains for anything . . . the least little thing . . . that was out of place that day. Or the week before. Ever. Go over everything – things Julie said, especially the events of that afternoon.'

His head came up then and his eyes met hers. 'What's the point?' he said. 'What's the point?'

* * *

'I don't see why you're rushing back, Maggie. What's spoiling if you stay a bit longer?'

'I need to pay me rent. And I have a neighbour who relies on me. I've been away over two weeks, Dolly. I need to get back.'

'You want to think about buying when the money comes through. Renting's a mug's game, Eddie taught me that. "Be your own landlord," he used to say.'

'Somehow I can't really believe in this money they say's coming. It won't be actual cash, will it?'

'As good as. You can turn shares into cash through the broker. I'll take you to my accountant when the time comes. He'll see you right. And our Barbara's got her head screwed on, so you can always ask her.'

'"Our Barbara" – it sounds funny, doesn't it? I mean, I had no family and then, all of the sudden . . .'

'We've got family. Going to Adele's tonight . . . she feels like family really, putting herself out for us. And Ben – d'you think he's sweet on our Barbara?'

'No, but I think she might be sweet on him.'

'He couldn't do better. Our Billy would've been proud of her, I know that much.'

'It makes you think, though. If she did get wed, where would we stand?'

'What d'you mean?'

'Well, we're her close family. Her dad's sisters. We'd have to do it all . . . invites, everything.'

'She's got her grandpa, Dolly.'

'But he's not her flesh and blood, Mags. It's us that are that.'

* * *

Ben was half-way out of the door when the phone rang. He hovered . . . it might be Diana, in which case he'd rather not know.

In the end, though, he went back and lifted the receiver.

'Mr Webster? It's Michael Martin. I've been talking to my daughter, and she says I should give it a try.'

It was hard not to high-five space, but Ben tried to keep his voice even. 'I'm glad! If you're sure, that is? I will tell your mother, and then we simply need to see to the details. Talk to your family and get back to me with a date.'

*   *   *

'He should be here any moment. I thought you ought to see him, and get his measure. I like him. I hope you will, too.'

'I don't have to like him, Barbara.' Howard Breen sounded desperate. 'If he can get us both off the hook, that'll do me.'

A moment later Ken Middlemiss was ushered in. Howard motioned the newcomer to a chair, and rang to order coffee. 'Now, tell me what you've been doing for us.'

'I've been going over all the old ground, and checking everyone's background again,' Middlemiss said. 'I checked out the showroom people first because that looked a bit promising: was something going on between Miss Carter and one of them? I'm taking a toothcomb to the man who we know had the affair with Julie. With the others, it's a no-go. The proprietor is a nice Jewish boy, lovely wife, besotted with his kids, spends every minute he can at home or in the synagogue. That leaves three salesman, and a cleaner. She's female; one of the men is Jed Hughes; one is gay; and the other's a sixty-something alcoholic.

'What clinches it for me is that both her salon assistants say that Terry brought Julie to work each morning and collected her each night – so where was the opportunity for hanky-panky? If there was any, it pre-dated Terry. That's another thing we're checking on now. Which brings me to one of the salon assistants, Angela O'Brien.' Middlemiss looked down at the notebook he had taken from his pocket.

'As she told the court, she'd spent her whole career working for Julie Carter. Went from school for work experience, proved herself useful, so Miss Carter saw her through her apprenticeship and then took her on as an assistant. As far as I can make out, she worshipped her boss. Her private life is clean, boyfriend a young electrician.'

'So you don't see her involved in the murder in any way?' Barbara asked.

'No.' The shake of his head was emphatic. 'She's not the answer. She was more than willing to co-operate. She likes young Bowes, insists the two of them were happy together. Besides, she was caught on CCTV leaving the premises, and 25 minutes later she's shopping in Sainsbury's – she gave the police her till receipt. I can try their CCTV, if you think it's necessary?'

'No.' Solicitor and barrister spoke in unison, and then Howard went on: 'So who else was in that building around the relevant time . . . who that we know of, that is?'

'I looked at the other assistant, Lena Savage. But, as she said in court, she went straight to a dress fitting and didn't leave there till after six. There's three people to testify to that.'

'Anyone else?' Howard Breen said, sounding defeated.

'Lady Darblay,' Middlemiss offered. 'I approached her and got turned down. Her ladyship doesn't think she has anything more to offer.'

'So that's it then?'

'Not necessarily. I still want to take a look at her background. There's an ancient retainer, who had been Lady Darblays' own nanny, and came out of retirement to care for the boy. She's recently retired again, so I'm going to have a go there. Not that I'm expecting to turn up anything, but in these cases you have to check everything, every blade of grass. I'll be looking at the defendant just as closely, I can tell you.'

When the detective had taken his leave, counsel and solicitor looked at one another. 'He'll do,' Breen said, with relief.

* * *

Barbara was at Adele's when Ben arrived. 'You two look cosy,' he teased. They were sitting on either side of a log fire, looking more like sisters than women who a year earlier had not known of one another's existence. Ben took the drink Harry offered and sat down. 'No aunts?'

'Not as yet,' Adele said. 'Barbara says you want to take Maggie off for a chat? She says you got a call from Michael Martin today.' He had rung Barbara as soon as he put the phone down, and she had almost wept with relief. Now he grinned at her.

'Yes. Probably better to get it over at once, then we can all relax.'

'Who's going to head off Aunt Dolly?' Barbara was speaking in tones of mock-terror, but it was a genuine problem.

'Don't you think Maggie might have told her about the baby by now?' Adele asked.

But before Ben could answer there was the sound of voices in the hall, and Harry was ushering in the two women. There was a flurry of coat-taking, and drinks poured, and general welcome, and then Ben took Maggie by the arm. 'I'm borrowing you for a few minutes,' he said smoothly, and led her across the hall to what Adele called the sewing room but which was actually his sister's bolthole when family life became too much.

'Sit down. I wanted to tell you this tonight so that you have time to think about it while you're still here.'

Maggie looked startled. 'I'm going home tomorrow, Ben. I need to go back. I have bills to pay and things to see to. I'll come back again – I'm used to the journey – but I can't stop any longer now.'

'OK. I'll come straight to the point. I think we've found your son, and he wants to meet you.'

Maggie looked down at her hands, and when she spoke her words were totally incongruous. 'We came here in a hire car. Terrible extravagance, she's a terror, our Dolly. Always has been.'

Ben was lost for words. There was a long silence and then, as if his words had just sunk in, she said, 'Is he all right?'

'As far as I can tell. He's a father, Maggie, and he has a daughter and two grandchildren.'

'Grandchildren? Well. I suppose he would by now. What does he . . .?' She faltered.

'He looks very nice, if that's what you mean, solid and respectable, grey-haired, and, as far as I could see, happy.'

'You haven't told him . . . everything?'

'No. He only knows that he was born when you were very young and that you never wanted to give him up.'

'What has it cost, all this? I must pay you – you can't be out of pocket on my account.'

'Time enough for that later. For now, you need to think about all this, and let me know what you want me to do. I take it you do want to meet him?'

There was a long pause, but when Maggie spoke her voice was strong. 'You know I do. But I'm afraid, Ben. I'm really afraid.'

* * *

Conversation around the table flowed. Maggie was quiet, but Dolly, cute as a box of monkeys, Ben thought, obviously knew something was up. To cover her sister's silence she played valiantly, describing what happened on the cruise ship, and on their excursions ashore. 'So it was a nice peaceful trip,' she concluded.

Her words brought Maggie suddenly to life. 'Peaceful? She's not telling you the half of it. There was this woman thought our Dolly was Barbara Windsor, off *EastEnders*.'

'You're joking,' Adele said, eyes alight with merriment.

'I wish I was. I was mortified. What does madam do? Plays up to it, that's what. Tells them all about her carry-on with Sid James . . . says what she thought of Dirty Den . . . she was loving it, I tell you. I only hope it doesn't make the papers.'

'You never did?' Barbara said. 'Aunt Dolly!'

'It was harmless. You should've seen her face when I told her the beer they drank at the Vic was double-strength lager. "We're all rolling about by the end of the episode," I said, and her jaw dropped. Silly moo.'

'Well, I still say she could've got herself arrested,' Maggie said stoutly.

Dolly shook her head. 'For all I know, Babs Windsor pretends to be me sometimes, as an alias – oh, you can pull a face, Maggie, but how do you know what anyone does when they're in foreign parts? It's like I told you: you can be anyone you like when you're away from home.'

There was general laughter and Ben felt himself relax. Somehow the atmosphere had lightened. 'It's going to be all right,' Ben thought, and looked across at Barbara for confirmation.

* * *

'What a lovely night,' Dolly said. They had divested themselves of shoes and party dresses, and were sharing a mug of Ovaltine before bed.

'I suppose you want to know why Ben took me off like that,' Maggie said suddenly.

'Not if it's none of my business.'

'He wanted to tell me he's found my son.'

'Son!' For once Dolly was taken aback.

'I had a son when I was 15. I was raped, Dolly, so I never knew the father. They took the baby off me, not that I could have kept him. I was on a train. It was the end of the war. There were men on there celebrating going home. That's when it happened,'

Dolly had put down her cup and now she crossed to kneel at her sister's side. 'Oh, Mags, and here was me thinking you'd always had it easy, a happy marriage and all that. I wish you'd told me before.'

But the big sister was leaning on the little one now as tears trickled slowly down her cheeks.

'I've waited for this, Dolly. All his life, all my life I've waited, and hoped to find him. But now Ben has, I'm so afraid.'

Chapter Twenty Eight

Ben was awake before dawn, and watched the night sky lighten. In an hour or two the car would arrive to whisk him to Farringdon Street for his first day back at Webcon.

Events had moved swiftly since he had agreed to go back. Hanson had stepped down, and the press had been informed of Ben's return. It had prompted some lurid headlines: 'Ousted chairman returns to save ailing firm'. Webcon wasn't ailing, but a few more headlines like that and it might be.

He rang Barbara while his coffee percolated. 'Hi, how are you this morning?' She assured him she was fine, but he could tell she was a little surprised at such an early call. 'I just wanted to know what you thought about last night.'

'It was lovely . . . and so kind of Adele to have her house invaded.'

'She loved it. She's taken to the aunts, and to you.'

'Well, I'm glad. It's mutual.'

'You're seeing your client this morning, aren't you? If you want a listening ear later, on I'm available.'

'That might be helpful. I could do some pasta tonight? And good luck for your first day today.'

'Pasta it is. See you around seven.'

Denise Robertson

When he put down the phone and returned to the coffee, Ben was humming softly under his breath.

*   *   *

'Maggie?' Dolly tapped on the door, holding the tray awkwardly in one hand.

'Come in.' Dolly opened the door and advanced towards the bed. 'I left you sleeping, so I've brought you a tray. Sit up and I'll pour for you.'

It had been three o'clock before they went to bed. Amid tears and sometimes laughter, Maggie had laid bare her life: Northfield, the years in service, the rape, and the loss of her baby, and then Jim. They had cried together when she told of their stillborn baby, and laughed together over Jim's idiosyncrasies. 'He sounds lovely, Maggie.'

'He was, Dolly. He was.' And on that note they had kissed goodnight and gone to their beds.

Now, when toast and tea had been dispensed, Dolly took a deep breath.

'I haven't been honest with you either, Mags, not altogether. I was ashamed. But I've been up all night thinking about it, and if I can't tell my own sister, it's a shame. It's true I was adopted by nice people, especially him. If I called him "Daddy", he would smile. But he died – in the snow, in 1947. As I told you, Mum's new husband, Stainsby, didn't like me. I had this dog, Lassie. I loved her, Mags. She filled the space where you and our Billy had been. Mr Stainsby gave her away – it was that, or have her put down. The man who took her said I could come and see her every day. But there was a price to pay.'

Maggie began to shake her head as if aware of the horror to come.

264

* * *

Apart from acknowledging English when he got into the car, Ben was silent on his way to Farringdon Street. 'Good to have your back, sir!' The doorman was beaming.

'Thank you, Fleming.' There were smiling faces all around as Ben made his way to his office. If only Madge had been there as usual, coffee and instructions at the ready. Instead it was Emma Clunes, who had stood in for Madge on the very few days off she had taken.

'I hope you're going to keep me right, Emma. I've got a lot of catching up to do.'

'I'll try, Mr Ben. Everyone's thrilled you've come back. Would you like some coffee?'

'Please. And can you tell Mr Hammond . . .'

But Peter Hammond was already striding through the door, a huge file in his hands. 'I thought you'd like sight of all the current projects. And, by the way, it's a bloody relief to see you here. The share price has risen by one and a half on the strength of your appointment. We're hoping for further improvement after you've issued a statement.'

Ben winced inwardly. He had stepped back into Webcon and he could feel its mesh closing around him with every passing minute.

As the morning went on, he missed Madge. She had fussed over him like a mother, but there had been a brusqueness about her that made him get down to work. He wanted to work now in order to block out his worries, but it was hard actually to make a start. He walked to the window to look down on Farringdon Street below. Traffic was inching forward in both directions, towards and away from King's Cross and the Euston Road. He was seized with an impulse to leave, drive somewhere, pick up Barbara, and just get the hell out of London. But in real life there was no such easy getaway.

He turned as Emma brought in more coffee. 'Thank you,' he said. 'Now can you find me the Connaught Building file? I think that's the first thing to tackle.'

* * *

It was 11 o'clock now, and still the sisters sat on in the bedroom.

'Did you ever see your . . . your adoptive mother again when you were older?' Maggie asked at last.

Dolly shook her head. 'I might have gone back, in the beginning. I would have if Stainsby hadn't been there. But I knew he'd wanted me out, and I suppose I never forgave him for Lassie. Or for what happened because of that. After a while, after all the men and the abortions . . . well, I couldn't go back, could I? I was damaged goods. A prostitute.'

'Oh, Dolly. I'm so sorry. I should have fought harder to keep us together . . .'

'You were a kid, Mags – what, eight? What could a little kid do even now, when there's the welfare state? Nothing. Back then, you wouldn't have had a prayer.'

They sat in silence for a moment and then Dolly spoke again.

'Who do you blame, Mags? The Websters for cheating us? Or Hitler and the war?'

'It's life, Dolly. If I blame anyone or anything, I blame life. You win, you lose. I did have Jim, and you found Eddie in the end. Even if . . .'

'Even if he did pay for me in the beginning? Well, all the time, if you count marrying me. Yes, I was lucky and so were you. Our Billy did all right, too. And we found one another, at the end of it.'

'And you couldn't blame Ben for any of it. Or his sister. They've done their best to put things right.'

Dolly stood up. 'I'll make some coffee . . . and then we'd better get a move on if you're going to catch that train.'

* * *

Ken Middlemiss opened the file in front of him, looked at it for a minute, and then looked up, first at Howard Breen and then at Barbara.

'I knew Julie Carter left no will, so I wanted to find out exactly who would benefit from her death. You made a point in your submission that the defendant would lose, not profit, from her death, and it was a valid point. But the prosecution had tried to suggest that Terry Bowes believed there was a will of which he was a beneficiary, so he thought he would profit, which was just as damaging. So who does inherit? As you'd already discovered, Mr Breen, it's an elderly, disabled aunt who had no contact with her niece. She's not capable of murder, even if she was so inclined.'

'We checked her out, too, and as you say, not in the running. Nor did she have offspring.'

The detective was continuing. 'Once I'd ruled out the profit motive, I looked at the other possibilities. If Bowes didn't kill her, who did? We've ruled out her staff; you'd checked out pretty thoroughly the idea of a rival for Terry's affections, which was a non-starter; and so was the idea of her having another lover while she was with Terry.

'Could it have been a rival beautician? Unlikely. There are plenty of women foolish enough to spend money defying age, and a rival would have found it easier to get new clients than bump off the competition. Did someone want the lease on the property? There have been no such enquiries, and in the current climate properties are two a penny in London. So was she killed to settle a score?'

'A revenge killing,' Barbara said. 'That's an interesting idea.'

'Or to shut her up.' Middlemiss folded his hands together. 'My money is on the last two – but which?'

'What could she possibly have known that was worth someone killing her for?' the solicitor offered. 'She had a good head for business, but she was hardly that high a flier. And she wasn't involved with anything shady – we checked.'

'I agree with you.' Middlemiss was shuffling papers. 'But I've gone thoroughly into her history, up to the time when she set up the salon. She was born in Middlesbrough in 1972. Father unknown, mother died when she was 19. No siblings, went to a comprehensive, then got a YOPS job . . .'

'Yops?' Breen and Barbara spoke together.

'Youth Opportunities Scheme. It was the government's way of getting kids trained for a job. Actually, by the time she joined it was known as the Youth Training Scheme but everyone still called it YOPS. She was then 16, and got a job in a salon as a dogsbody, where she showed an aptitude . . . and she was a bonny kid, which helped. Anyway, she qualified, worked her way up, and eventually took a job in salons on cruise ships. After that she opened her own salon.'

'How did she pay for it?' Barbara asked. 'I know it was on a lease but that wouldn't be cheap, and then she'd have to buy all the equipment.'

'True. I can only estimate, but my guess is that she'd have needed precious near £50 grand. Perhaps more.'

'Cruise ships pay quite sparsely, I'm told,' Breen said, 'but with tips from rich people, I suppose a determined saver could do it in time. She was on the ships for a few years.'

'And she'd be kept in that time, so no expenses,' Barbara offered.

'It's still a hell of a sum to have got hold of . . . or it was then,' the detective said thoughtfully.

* * *

Maggie stood obediently beside the luggage in King's Cross while Dolly went in search of a trolley. The great echoing hall was the same structure that she had struggled through that night, 65 years ago. It didn't seem possible. She couldn't remember much about getting off the train or through the station. She had felt dirty, she could remember that. She had asked someone where the taxis were because Lady De Vere Wentworth had told her she must do that, and had given her the fare.

Then, when she got to Eaton Square, Mr Charles, the butler, had taken care of her. She hadn't said anything – what words could she have found to describe what had happened? He had looked at her a little strangely but she had looked him straight in the eye and smiled – like an actress. She had been proud of that. He had made her some tea, and offered her bread and cheese too, but she couldn't eat, aware as she was of her under-clothes soaked with urine because, in her fear, she had wet herself. When at last she had escaped to her cold upstairs room, the wetness had tuned out to be blood. And now there was a man somewhere, her son. He had been a lovely baby, however he had been conceived

'Here you are!' Dolly said, pushing forward the trolley. 'Let's get your cases on it. I've brought you some magazines.' Her arms were full of newspapers and glossy covers. 'I've checked the platform. It's 4, and they're boarding now.'

Inside Maggie, as the train made its way north, serenity blos-somed. She had Dolly to take care of her, and all would be well. She would pay her rent tomorrow, see to her other jobs, and then she could think about coming back to London to face her son. If, indeed, she would be welcome.

The train had entered the County of Durham, now. Outside the window, Darlington station was almost deserted except for alighting passengers. Soon there would be fields interspersed with mining villages, thrown up by coal-owners for the men who toiled in their mines. Maggie smiled to herself, remembering Jim on his hobby horse: 'They stabled their horses better than they did their workers, Maggie. Narrow streets, outside privies, little children sent down the hole hardly weaned.' She had demurred at that. 'They were 11 or 12, Jim. That's not hardly weaned,' and he had stuck out his chin and said, 'They'd've sent them down their in nappies if they could've got away with it.' She had teased him about being a radical and he had said, 'Yes, and proud of it.' All a long time ago.

She looked from the window again, this time on her right, half expecting to see Durham, its castle and cathedral floodlit by night. Time to get her things together. 'I feel peaceful,' she thought. And then they were in the station, and it was time to hurry to the door before the train started up again and carried her off to Newcastle.

* * *

They settled in Barbara's sitting-room, wine in a chiller before them, Middlemiss's file on Barbara's lap.

'You look tired,' Ben said.

'Do I?' She sounded as though his remark had been a rebuke, putting up a hand to wipe under her eye, and tuck her hair back behind her ear.

'Tired but nice,' he said by the way of making amends, and then cursed himself. Nice! What a bloody silly word to use.

'Well,' Barbara said, suddenly authoritative, 'your man is certainly getting on with it. He's got a rundown on everyone's background now and he's back up to Cumbria tomorrow.'

'Even the ice-cold Lady Darblay?' Ben asked. 'I thought she said no to him?'

'She did, but he interviewed the old nanny instead. I have a feeling he may have misrepresented himself a bit . . . not that the nanny said anything damaging. Both Darblays are saints, she would die for them, and the boy is the world's best. It seems she stayed with them until he went off to school. It was quite moving . . . Middlemiss had her on tape – there's the transcript. The old nanny had obviously dedicated her life to Lady Darblay's family, who were called Wyndham, and then went with her after the marriage. She lives in a sort of grace-and-favour flat now, and the Darblays pay her rent.'

Ben was looking down at the printed page. 'No wonder the child is so precious to Lady Darblay. It says here she had multiple miscarriages before he was born.'

'Yes. And she was nearly 40 by the time she had him, so her chances of conceiving would be diminishing fast.'

'According to the old nanny, Lord Darblay was the one desperate for offspring. It says here, "He was so keen on having a family. She wanted to please him."'

'That's a bit chilling, isn't it? "She wanted to please him." Although if you loved someone, you would want to do that, wouldn't you?'

Ben nodded, but he was remembering Diana. She had known he wanted a child, but it hadn't mattered to her at all. He waited for the usual stab of pain, but it didn't come, and he turned his attention back to the page.

'His Lordship wasn't keen enough to be around for the actual birth, apparently. It says, "She was like a little girl when she brought the baby back to London. Sir Stephen . . .' He paused. 'Sir?'

'He was "Sir" then – the peerage only came in 2004, gift of

Michael Howard,' Barbara supplied.

'I see. "Sir Stephen came back from New York a few days later. I've never seen a couple so happy." New York – I suppose he was at the UN. After that, her interview it seems to be a long paean of praise to the Darblays, all three of them. So nothing there.'

'Let's take a break,' Barbara said. 'I've made a risotto. I thought you might be hungry.'

At the dinner-table they ate and Barbara sipped wine. Ben drank water, aware of the Bentley at the kerb. At last he looked at his watch. 'I'm loath to go, but you need a good night's sleep. May I take the file with me? I'd like to go over it again.'

'Please do. I made copies at chambers.'

At the door he bent to kiss her cheek. He had done it before but somehow this felt different. Very different.

* * *

'Only you and me now, Tootsie,' Dolly said. The dog put his head on one side and stared back at her, until his eye flicked sideways to the jar of dog treats beside her chair. 'Have you been a good boy?' The dog's eyes were fixed on her face, but she could see he was itching to turn to the jar again. 'Well, perhaps one . . . But we did have fun, Toots. Your mummy was a famous star for a week. She even signed an autograph. Isn't that wicked? You should've seen your Aunty Maggie's face. There you are – one more, and then it's time for bed.'

* * *

Ben parked outside the Edgerton Gardens house and switched off the engine. Tonight had been confusing. 'I didn't want to leave,' he thought suddenly, remembering the kiss. It was such an unexpected thought that it drove him out of the car. He mustn't be stupid, and mistake need for want. He needed warmth in his life right now . . . the comfort of a fellow spirit. Barbara gave him all that. But was he being fair?

He crossed the street and pushed open the gate, looking apprehensively at the windows of the adjoining houses. Most of them were dark, but there were no curious faces at the few lit ones. He moved down the side of the house, and into the garden. Against the night sky the tree . . . the enchanted tree . . . stood out, a swirl of branches, now nearly bare, reaching out like hands. This garden would be heaven for children. 'There's a hole in my life,' he acknowledged. 'I must be careful not to hurt anyone by being desperate to fill it. Especially not Barbara.'

But when he had kissed her cheek on the doorstep, he had wanted to kiss her mouth, to slip his tongue between her teeth, and then carry her, a weight in his arms, up to her bed.

Chapter Twenty Nine

MAGGIE FELT A REAL SENSE of relief as she paid her bills and tucked receipts into her purse. There had been relief, too, when she returned last night and found her home unviolated. You read about terrible things nowadays – homes stripped bare by thieves, or foreign squatters breaking in to change the locks and laugh at you from behind your own nets. She made a mental note to steep her nets next week: they were less than brilliant white, and that wouldn't do.

She walked through Belgate, feeling safe, glad to be back where she belonged. And yet she had known nothing of pit life when she came there. Jim had been the youngest-ever deputy in Belgate's history. 'He'll be an under-manager one day,' his mother had said proudly, but it had never happened. Too active in the union, that had been the reason. When he was on back-shift, she had lain awake, listening for his footfall in the street, the creak of the gate, the thud as his pit-boots hit the floor, and then the splashing as he washed off the grime of the pit. Now, all that was gone. She shifted her bag to her other hand and turned for home.

She called on her neighbours on either side to say she was back and they could stand down their watch, then she returned to her house and closed the door. Her own home. Lovely as Dolly's house was, all peaches and cream, it couldn't compare with this, her kingdom.

*   *   *

Ben was about to pick up the phone when there was a knock at his office door. It opened before he could call 'Come in,' and he looked up to see Neville Carteret, still a director and therefore entitled to unannounced access, advancing towards his desk.

'Don't get up, Ben. I won't take up too much of your time. I just wanted to say I think you've been a shit to Diana.'

Ben had always disliked Diana's brother. It was Carteret who had cast the vote that had rocked Webcon, and ensured the Headey bid. Now he took a deep breath. 'Thank you for telling me, Neville. And now, if you've quite finished . . .'

The other man had paled except for a red spot of colour on each cheek. 'Oh, you can dismiss it as much as you like, but we both know you led her up the garden path, promising reconciliation, raising her hopes . . .'

'Get out!' Ben said, rising to his seat. 'And take your foolish ramblings with you. If I led your sister up the garden path, it was she who taught me how.'

*   *   *

Dolly had stripped the bed in the room Maggie had used, added in towels and any other whites she could find, and set the washer churning. The daily woman had swept and polished and dusted, and the house was restored to its former glory. Now Dolly looked at the clock: 2.15. Even if she had an early night, there were at least eight hours to fill.

She settled on the sofa, Tootsie at her side, and leafed, for the third time, through the morning paper. If they'd still been on the ship, she'd've been sipping *vino* on the sun deck with Maggie at her side, or, if it was raining, they'd have been close together in the cabin, watching a film. That *Chocolat* had been good, even if it was French. Who knows, they might even have been toiling up a cobbled street with a madwoman talking 19 to the dozen about the subject of the expedition. On balance she had enjoyed the van Gogh visit the most. The gloom in which he had lived hadn't prevented him from understanding happiness. She didn't know much about painting but she knew the joy of living when she saw it, and it was there in his work.

On an impulse, she riffled through the CDs till she found 'Vincent'. She had bought it because she liked the tune and the lyrics. She had known, vaguely, that it was about Vincent van Gogh. That hadn't meant anything to her then, but it did now. She put her hand on the dog's soft flank and gave herself up to the music. As it ended she fished a hanky from her bag and wiped her eyes.

'Your mum's an old softie, Tootsie,' she told the dog, who had cocked an ear at the sound of sniffles. 'But she looks like Barbara Windsor, so it's not all bad.'

*   *   *

Barbara had pleaded fatigue, to avoid going in to chambers. There would be new briefs on her desk – but how could she get down to another case with this one still unfinished, at least as far as she was concerned? Besides, she couldn't bear the thought of her senior's sanctimonious face. '*You brought this on yourself, Barbara*,' she mimicked. '*I told you to go for mitigation.*' Could she have coerced Terry Bowes into changing his plea? If she had, he might be facing a much shorter sentence than the one that awaited him. All the more reason to find grounds for appeal. She twisted her hair into a ponytail, made herself a strong coffee and got down to another read-through of the mountain of files with *Bowes v. Regina* on them.

* * *

'So you see if we book up now, we'll get it cheaper and a better cabin. I fancy forward this time. What about you?'

Maggie shifted the phone to her other ear. 'Well, I've hardly thought about it, Dolly, to be truthful.'

'But you did enjoy it. Don't say you didn't, our Mags, because it was written on your face.'

'That was shock, Dolly. Holy terror at what you would do next. When I opened the paper this morning I thought, it'll be there: "Woman Masquerades as TV Star." If I set foot on another ship, there'll have to be none of that hanky-panky.'

'You always were a stick-in-the-mud, Maggie.'

'There you go again, Dolly, romancing. You can't possibly remember what I was like. You were a bairn.'

But they both fell silent then, knowing they did remember, especially the pain of separation.

* * *

They had come to view Ben's new house, collecting the keys as they went.

'You'll be happy here,' Barbara said, as they walked from room to room.

'Yes, I think I will. It's big, but it doesn't feel remote.'

They paused at an upstairs window. 'The garden is full of possibilities,' Barbara said. 'I've never asked before: are you a gardener?'

'No, but I can learn. I have a lot of learning to do, I think.'

'You'll need a gardener,' Barbara mused. The lawn was covered with fallen leaves, neglected for so long that they had darkened and solidified into a carpet.

'I don't know . . . I quite fancy tilling the soil.'

She was laughing now. 'City boy,' she said mockingly, but her tone was kindly.

'I hope I'm in by Christmas.'

'Of course you will be. It's weeks and weeks away.'

They stood for a while in companionable silence, and then turned to go downstairs.

'How are you getting on with Webcon?' Barbara asked as they walked back to the car.

'Don't talk about that now. Talk about something else.'

'What are you suggesting?'

'Anything you like. Just no mention of Webcon, and not a whisper about *Bowes v. Regina.*'

'Agreed. Get in the car, and we're off!'

They decided against a pub or a restaurant, and went back to Barbara's flat where she whistled up a very palatable seafood pasta.

'You're not a bad cook,' he said, wiping his mouth with his napkin as he spoke.

'Well thank you kindly, sir. Anything to oblige.' She had meant to kiss his cheek, but suddenly his mouth was on hers, hungry and questing. She felt his tongue touch her teeth and drew back.

'Ben?'

'I'm sorry. I thought . . .' His arms were around her and she felt them disengage.

'Don't think,' she said simply, and locked her mouth on his again. His hands were moving, touching her breast, her thigh, and they were sliding to the floor.

She stayed him. 'Not here,' she said and led him towards her bed.

Chapter Thirty

IT WAS STRANGE TO WAKE in her bed and feel the bulk of Ben there beside her. Barbara lay for a moment, gazing at his sleeping face. Last night their need for one another had been insatiable, but was it born out of simple lust or something more? 'I must be sure,' she thought. 'For both our sakes, I must be sure.'

Ben stirred, and opened his eyes. 'Are you real?' he said sleepily. 'I thought I only dreamed you.'

He turned then, taking her in his arms, and she felt his body hardening against her. 'Later,' she said, laughing. 'Later. We have work to do.'

She kissed him on the forehead and got out of bed.

* * *

Maggie bought apples in the fruiterers. She didn't much care for them, but they were supposed to be good for you. 'What's this about your going off to foreign parts?' the fruiterer said as he rang up the till.

'I went on a cruise,' Maggie said. 'With my sister.'

'Sister? I never knew you had family.'

'Oh yes. I have a sister. And a niece. They're down south but I visit sometimes.' She couldn't keep a note of pride out of her voice – but she must be careful. It didn't do to tell everyone your business.

On the way back, she paused at the Welfare park. The seat had beads of dew on it . . . or perhaps rain . . . and she brushed them away before she sat down. Since yesterday she couldn't help thinking about the past. She had woken in the night, remembering how Jim would love her, something she hadn't done for years.

She was roused from reminiscence by a sudden and quite terrifying thought. Once she and her baby, now a man, had met each other, she would have to own him – tell all of Belgate that she, the barren widow, was in fact a mother. It was at once a horrific and an uplifting thought.

* * *

'I am bored, Toots.' It was only 11 o'clock, and Dolly had already done everything that needed doing and some things that didn't. The dog yawned and rolled on to his back. Dolly obliged by tickling his tum, but then got to her feet. Why did she feel like this – bored out of her mind? 'I was all right before,' she thought. Before she had family and knew what it was not to be alone.

She looked at the telephone. She could ring Maggie, but that wasn't really a solution. She couldn't spend the rest of her life ringing County Durham. She looked down at the dog. 'On your feet, Toots. We're going upstairs to do some chucking out.'

* * *

'OK,' Ben said, as Barbara set the tray on the coffee table and

resumed her seat. 'We go through every report and every statement line by line, make a note of anything in the least interesting, and then discuss what we've found. Where shall we start?'

'With Julie,' Barbara said firmly. 'She's at the centre of everything. And one thing is puzzling me, since I talked to Ken
Middlemiss.'

'What?' Ben put down the file and looked at her.

'How *did* Julie get the money to set up her salon? We agreed
she might have saved it while working on the cruise ships, but
. . . I wonder. OK, she ran her business efficiently, but nothing
about her strikes me as indicating she was hugely ambitious.
She got the salon, but she was quite happy for it to tick along
with two assistants. I mean, it wasn't big time. So quite how
she'd have summoned up the drive to save every red cent
towards this end escapes me. My guess is she was more likely
to blow her earnings, and her tips, at every port of call.'

Ben was nodding, but she could see he was thinking about
something else. 'Which leads to the fact that I can't make fit.
Why was Lady Darblay patronising a Grade 2 salon? I'd've
expected to see her in somewhere classier – Harrods, or somewhere like that.'

'Yes,' Barbara sounded a little unsure. 'We women are
strange creatures, though. We cleave to certain therapists, and
if they give us that X factor we'll seek them out wherever they
are. So I can't be as sure as you, but it's worth some thought.'

They went on to Lady Darblay then.

'We've been through the possible motives she might have for
murder, Ben, and none of them holds water. Julie manifestly
wasn't her rival for Lord Darblay's affections. That's all Lady
Darblay cared about . . . her marriage.'

'And her boy. There was the time she blew her cool . . . when
was that?' Ben asked suddenly.

Barbara turned a page, and looked up, surprised.

'Three months before the Kendal murder.'

'Pass me the Darblay file.'

Barbara gave it to him. 'You've been through it three times.'

'And I may be chasing the wildest of geese, but there's one phrase here, in the nanny's interview . . . she says, "When she brought the baby back to London" – *back to London*? I'd've thought it would have been born in a London clinic, that place where the royals go to give birth.'

'It may have been a slip of the tongue . . . or faulty transcription,' Barbara said, but Ben had taken out his phone and was punching in numbers.

'Ken? Can you check where the Darblay baby's birth was registered . . . where it was born, I mean?' He listened for a moment. 'That'd be great. And while you're on, could you also check whether or not the Darblays were ever passengers on one of the cruise ships Julie Carter worked on.'

'What are you thinking?' Barbara said, suddenly serious. 'About the boy? Adoption?'

'I don't know, Barbara. Maybe I'm just clutching at straws.'

* * *

Dolly lifted a hand and summoned a waitress. 'Could I have some hot water. Thank you.' She smiled benignly in what she hoped was true Barbara Windsor fashion.

While she waited for her teapot to be refreshed, she glanced around the other tables. Everyone was engrossed in gossip. No one else was alone. And no one was looking at her. It had been different on the ship. She had enjoyed the fact that someone couldn't take their eyes off her. She had to make Maggie go again – and why wait till next year? They could afford it, whether or not the promised money had come through. 'I might as well spend it,' she thought. 'And who else have I got to spend it on but Maggie?' Suddenly she felt wistful. Maggie had a child somewhere – Maggie's genes going on. And none of hers.

'There you are, madam, piping hot!'

Dolly smiled her thanks and blinked back some stupid moisture from her eyes. 'I need something to occupy me,' she thought. Clearing out her wardrobe that morning hadn't taken her five minutes. Perhaps she could be an extra somewhere? *EastEnders* . . . no, they wouldn't want her on there, looking like one of the stars. But she could be a stand-in for Barbara Windsor. Except that Barbara had now left the Queen Vic.

'The story of my life,' Dolly thought as she poured. It would have to be another cruise.

* * *

In a deliberate attempt not to sit staring at the phone waiting for Middlemiss to ring back, they had got out the file on Jed Hughes. 'What a sleazeball,' Ben said. 'There's a page and a half here just listing his extra-marital adventures.'

Barbara frowned. 'But to me that suggests that he wouldn't bother trying to reclaim a woman he'd lost, or be mad enough to shoot her if she spurned him. He'd simply move on and find another sucker.'

'I suppose you're right. On the other hand, Casanovas often have one woman who matters to them. They say Sinatra never got over Ava Gardner . . .loved her till the day he died.'

'Granted but Jed Hughes as Ol' Blue Eyes Mark Two takes some stretch of the imagination. Let's go back to the other therapists.'

* * *

'Dolly?'

Dolly moved the phone to her other ear, startled. 'Maggie? You never ring me! Are you all right?'

'Yes. I'm fine. Have you heard from anyone?'

'By "anyone" d'you mean Ben?'

'No. Well, I did wonder . . .'

'No, pet, I haven't heard from either of them. They'll ring eventually, don't fret. I hope they're off somewhere enjoying themselves.'

There was silence for a moment, and then, 'Do you think they might . . .'

'What? Have sex?'

'Our Dolly!'

'Well, I'd like to think they might, but I doubt it.'

'I was meaning might they ring tonight?' Suddenly Maggie's voice was stern. 'You're getting carried away again, Dolly. Still it makes a change from cruises. Where are we going this time . . . Vladivostock?'

* * *

They were relaxing now, their heads too fuddled with facts and theories to function. But today had been good. Ben had enjoyed wrestling with Barbara's case, but nothing they had turned up so far was strong enough to stand up in court. Even if the Darblay baby had been adopted, and Julie Carter its birth mother, surely Lady Darblay would then have been grateful to Julie? Except that a public acknowledgement of her inability to produce offspring would have dented her so-perfect image. Was that a powerful enough motive? And if the baby had been adopted, how had it worked? How could Lady Darblay have known Julie was pregnant?

There was also the effect on the child, of course. Perhaps that was a strong enough motive – to protect the child from revelations? He looked at the clock: 10 to 11; perhaps it was time to go.

As if she had read his mind, Barbara spoke. 'Do you want to go? There was silence for a moment, and then she said, 'You can stay if you want to.' And then she was in his arms, and he felt a wave of tenderness for her. 'I want her,' he thought, 'but I want to give and not to take.' Afterwards, when they lay, limbs entwined, flesh on flesh, he found he was smiling. 'So this is love,' he thought, and put his lips gently against her cheek.

Chapter Thirty One

THE CALL CAME AT 5 to 10. 'Ben, you are on to something!' For once Middlemiss sounded excited. 'The Darblay child's birth was registered in Kendal, Cumbria! The documents bear the address of Hollymere Nursing Home in Kendal, and list the Darblays as parents. The obstetrician was a Mr Hirst-Bowen – hyphenated. According to the hotelier here, he was a posh old geezer . . .'

'Was?' Ben interjected.

'Was. Died in 2004. Hollymere ceased to be a maternity home then, and now it treats geriatrics. But when it was a maternity unit it was pricey. Very pricey, apparently.'

'Well done. I'm not sure how far this will get us but it must mean something.' Ben was about to put down the phone when another thought occurred to him. 'One more thing: was Hollymere perhaps the place where the other murder victim worked, the midwife who was shot with the same gun?'

'Not sure, but easily checked. I'll get back to you. And by the way, you were right about the cruise ship, too. The Darblays made two voyages on the *Carinthia*, in 1996 and '97. Julie Carter was working aboard the *Carinthia* from '94 to '97.'

When the detective had rung off, Ben dialled Barbara's

number, and told her the news. 'So we just might have made a breakthrough! Are you free at lunchtime?'

* * *

Barbara had been sitting at a desk littered with documents, feeling helpless. Whichever way she looked, she could see nothing she could use to get an appeal. And then Ben had rung, and suddenly there was a chink of light. A link – and also a piece that didn't fit. Why would a woman, metropolitan to her fingertips, go to the other side of the country to give birth? It was not as though Lady Darblay had any links with Cumbria. Her every detail was in the dossier in front of Barbara, and the Lake District did not figure in it. She had no family there.

For a moment, Barbara contemplated confronting her: 'Lady Darblay, why did you go to the other side of England to have your baby when London has some of the best maternity units in Europe?' But that would get her precisely nowhere. The face would remain lovely and inscrutable, and the perfect lips would utter some plausible explanation that everyone, including the Appeal Court judges, would believe. All the same, it was a beginning. A fragile thread that, gently tugged, might turn into a rope to hang someone with.

Barbara picked up the phone to pass on the good news to Howard Breen, and tried not to get too excited over the fact that in two hours' time she would be seeing Ben.

* * *

Maggie was just sinking into her chair for a nice cup of tea when the phone rang.

'Margaret?' She knew it was Ben Webster. He was the only one who called her by her proper name. 'Is everything all right?'

At the end of the line he was chuckling gently. 'Don't get alarmed. It's not bad news.'

'Yes. I'm all right, just tell me . . .'

'Your son has spoken to his family, and wants to meet you as soon as possible. So I've fixed it for Friday.'

When Maggie put down the phone she was trembling, slopping the tea all over when she tried to pour a cup. All those years of wanting this moment – and now it had come she wasn't sure how she felt. It would have been different if he had still been a child. But this was a man. He might have ideas, prejudices, habits she would hate.

As for him, he would subconsciously be expecting a young girl, a teenager. She looked across to the sideboard mirror. 'I'm an old woman,' she told her reflection. 'I'm bound to disappoint him.'

* * *

'I've thought of everything,' Barbara said. 'Adoption. Even surrogacy. But Jean Darblay was the one who had the baby – you can't get round that. Besides, even if the boy was adopted, why would that lead her to murder? The public are sympathetic to that sort of thing nowadays.'

'What if the boy doesn't know? She might want to protect him.'

'That's hardly a motive for murder, Ben. Besides I'm almost sure there's a rule that says children have to be told that they're adopted. It was made law a few years ago. I'll check when I get back to the office, but I'm pretty sure there'd be a social worker making sure that the rules were obeyed.'

'What if there were two babies born?' Ben put down his knife and fork. 'Two babies – one Darblay's, one Julie Carter's. The Darblay baby dies, so she takes Julie's.'

'Just like that?' Barbara's tone conveyed amusement.

'OK, it's far-fetched, I know, but what if Julie didn't want her baby? If there was effectively no father, or the father was a married man . . .'

'Lord Darblay?' Now Barbara was interested. 'So the two women put their heads together, and decided to pass his son off as the union of the marriage and not the affair?'

They sat for a moment, exhilaration subsiding. 'You can't imagine it, can you?'

'Him having an affair?' Ben said, at last. 'Not really, but then we're all human.'

'But that still leaves the big question: why did Lady Darblay leave London to have her baby? She could hardly have expected it to be stillborn, and a convenient substitute baby to be handy.'

'I've asked Ken Middlemiss to check whether or not the Kendal victim – who had been a midwife, remember – worked at Hollymere. If she did, then the answer's there in that home. We just have to dig until we find it.'

They parted in the street outside the restaurant, Barbara turning down Ben's offer of a lift because she wanted to walk and clear her head. Ben was half-way into the driving seat when his phone rang.

'You were right, Ben: Beryl Rutherford did work at Hollymere. She retired from there when the place closed.'

Ben sat for a moment after the call ended, digesting the latest development. This was obviously important – the clincher, even. There were too many coincidences to be anything else but significant.

* * *

Now that he had acquainted himself with current operations, Ben was feeling more at ease in the office. Considering the state of the construction industry at the moment, Webcon was holding its own. But only just – there was no room for error. They still had good cash reserves, but land that had been valued in tens of millions before the start of the recession had been down-valued because no one wanted to buy, and that would be the situation until things picked up and people had the confidence to start building again.

He was about to ring Peter Hammond and congratulate him on the figures, but something was nibbling at the edges of his consciousness. Something to do with Maggie. Or Dolly. Something one of them had said. Or was he imagining it because Maggie and her son were in the forefront of his mind? That was probably it.

He had picked up the phone and was half-way through dialling Peter's extension when Adele's dinner party popped up into his mind. They had all been sitting round the table, laughing and chatting about the cruise. It was something said then, and Dolly had said it – said the thing that had been nagging at him all morning! He downed the remains of his coffee and reached for the phone.

'Barbara? I think I've got something. I'm coming over as soon as I'm finished at the office.'

* * *

'I don't mind telling you I'm scared, Dolly. You will come with me?'

'Try keeping me away. He's family, Mags. My nephew, our Barbara's cousin. You bet we'll be there. And you say he's arranged this with his family?'

'Yes. Apparently that's why he didn't agree straight away.'

'So what's happening, then? Is Ben fixing it all?'

'Yes. He says he'll talk to Barbara, and they'll arrange it all.' There was a pause. 'He wants me to come down and meet him on Friday.'

'Come tomorrow. I was going to suggest it anyway. I'll meet you off the train.'

'I'm not sure I can come that quickly . . .'

'Maggie, if you mention your neighbour or paying your rent, I'm going to come up there and do you some damage. I'm going out of my mind with boredom here. If you want someone to worry about, worry about me. Just not until you've packed your bag and got on the bloody train.'

* * *

'Not a word till we're sitting down!'

Ben obeyed her, although Barbara could see that he was bursting to impart his new theory. She poured two drinks, and handed one to him. 'Right. Fire away.'

'It's been bugging me all day, something Dolly said that I knew was significant. And then this afternoon it came to me.'

'What? Spit it out.'

'It was at the dinner table that night at Adele's. Maggie was telling us about the cruise, and Dolly pretending to be Barbara Windsor . . . well, not pretending, but letting people think she was. Maggie was saying how terrible it had been, and really disapproving, and Dolly got defiant – and then she said it.'

'Said what, Ben. I'll strangle you in a minute.'

'She said, "You can be anyone you like when you're away from home."'

Barbara was looking puzzled. 'So?'

'Away from home you can pretend to be anyone you choose, or . . . .'

'Or . . .' Barbara spoke slowly, 'someone else can pretend to be you. So maybe the woman who booked into Hollymere as Jean Darblay wasn't Jean Darblay. It was Julie Carter.'

There was a moment of silence, and then she said. 'My God!'

'It was surrogacy,' Ben said, 'but surrogacy done in a very clever way. To all intents and purposes, that boy is the natural child of the Darblays. No need to ask permission, go through the courts – no one need know except the woman who actually bore the child. In London they'd never have got away with it – someone would have recognised Julie, or, rather, known that she wasn't Lady Darblay. In Cumbria, and dropping the title, she was just one more woman.'

Barbara was still puzzled. 'But why would Lady Darblay wait 12 years to kill Julie? I can understand the desire to get rid of the only witnesses, but why wait so long?'

'I don't think she did want to get rid of Julie. I think what happened is that when that picture of the boy hit the papers . . . remember the fracas with the paparazzi? . . . Beryl Rutherford saw it and remembered her patient. Only the woman in the newspaper photo, the mother of the boy, wasn't her patient. I think that then she probably made contact with Lady Darblay . . . even asked her for money. And that meant she had to be silenced.'

'You're saying Lady Darblay killed twice?'

'The two murders with the same gun have to be linked. When she'd killed once, it would be easier to kill again, and put an end to the risk once and for all. The reason the gun hasn't been found is because she's still got it.'

'But why wait over a year to kill Julie too?'

'My guess is she didn't mean to kill her . . . not at first. She may even have been grateful to her. And I don't think Julie meant to expose her, but she was bound to have asked about the boy. And once doubt had entered Lady Darblay's mind she had to make sure, hence her visits to the salon – did Julie perhaps show too much interest in him? Or did Jean Darblay decide to clear the decks, just in case?

'We need to find out whether she deliberately asked for the last appointment of that day – did she know Julie's lover was coming, and take advantage of that to transfer the blame to him? We won't know until they question her. Perhaps she just kept visiting the salon, the gun always in her handbag, waiting for the optimum moment.'

'Yes . . .' Barbara said slowly.

'What's worrying you?'

'I'm wondering how two women so far apart in every way did something as intimate as share a baby. Think about it. From the moment that ship docked, they would have gone their separate ways.'

Ben was nodding. 'I wondered about that, too. We can only conjecture, of course, but here's how I see it. The Darblay woman is cool . . . cold even. My guess is that she was determined to have a baby, and she thought out a plan. All she needed was the right woman to bear a child for her.'

'And she saw Julie on the ship . . .'

'Exactly. And she chose her because they were the same type: blond, tall, good-looking. So the baby was certain to resemble her, at least superficially. I'll bet Julie told of her ambition to own a salon while they were having those intimate treatment moments, and ever so gently Darblay would have said: "There might be a way you could raise the money."'

'But how did she get pregnant?'

'Who knows? Insemination by donor, maybe . . . and wasn't there a film where a woman collected her husband's sperm after sex and transferred it to another woman?'

'I remember . . . but the other woman was dead.'

'Was she? Maybe Lady Darblay picked out a blond donor just as she picked out Julie, then. The point is, the birth was no accident. It was planned to the last detail.'

'You've cracked it.' Barbara put down the drink, and launched herself at him. 'You clever, clever man!'

Chapter Thirty Two

THIS MORNING IT WAS LESS strange to wake with Ben there beside her. She kissed him gently, and he stirred and opened his eyes. 'Hello you,' he said sleepily.

'Do you always sleep so late?' she teased.

'Who said anything about sleep?' And then he was above her, and inside her, and she let the last of her fears slip away. 'I think I love you,' she said, when it was over and all they wanted to do was lie there, at peace.

'Good,' he said. 'You're a sensible woman.'

Later, over eggs and toast, he asked, 'What do we do now? Go to the police?'

'I thought that at first, but what have we got? Conjecture. Some supportive details. But who's going to believe that the Darblays would be involved in anything so bizarre?'

'I've been thinking about that,' Ben said. 'For a normal person to take a life there has to be a powerful motive, and I'm not sure that the disclosure of the fact that your son does not share your genes is motive enough.'

'So what are you saying?' Barbara's eyes were wide with disappointment.

'I don't think simply its becoming public knowledge would

be enough, and I have difficulty in believing that Lord Darblay would lend himself to murder, anyway. The man has a UN peace award, for God's sake. I think the impelling motive for her is that he doesn't know. That's what she's afraid of – that he will discover she's deceived him, and the boy isn't his.'

'But how could she have done it?'

'Easily enough. He was always out of the country – he was even away at the time of the boy's birth. All she had to do was tell him the good news at the beginning, and then appear to be pregnant. Medieval queens did it when they were barren . . . feigned pregnancy, and had a peasant's baby smuggled in when the time came. My guess is that she gave him a date a little later than Julie's real due date, for he'd surely have tried to be at home for his child's birth. But then she rings him in New York, or wherever he was, and says, 'Darling, guess what? It's arrived early.'

'My God, she thought it through.'

'So what do we do?'

'Lady Darblay killed the Rutherford woman because she was blackmailing her, I'm sure of that,' Barbara said slowly. 'So we should ring Lady Darblay, and say that we know that, and we want a cut. Say we know she's a murderer. So we fix up a meeting . . .'

'And then what?'

'If she's innocent, she'll ring Scotland Yard straight away. If she doesn't, if she turns up at the meeting-place, then the police will believe us, and once they start looking – well, the boy's DNA will match Julie's, for a start.'

'So which of us will make the call?'

'Neither of us. She knows my voice from court, and you're too male and too posh. How would you have discovered what happened in an obscure nursing home?'

'Then who?'

'We need a woman, an older woman . . . someone who might have worked at that clinic, or been a friend and confidante of Beryl Rutherford.'

* * *

Dolly had been contemplating another boring day when the phone had rung. 'Aunt Dolly? It's Barbara. Is it OK if Ben and I come over? We have something to ask you.'

Dolly had almost gushed a welcome, but when she put down the phone doubts occurred. Why would two busy people want to visit her in the morning? Something must have happened. Fear seized her. Maggie – it must be Maggie, and she really couldn't bear to lose her now. Not when she had just found her.

It was a relief when they laughed her fears away in the doorway. 'Don't look so worried, Aunty, no one's died. We've come to ask a favour, that's all.'

She insisted on making coffee before they talked, which was not only good manners but also allowed her to quell her flutters. 'Now,' she said, when they were seated, 'whatever it is you want, it's yours.'

Her eyes widened as Barbara outlined the case. 'We need proof that Lady Darblay is implicated, Aunt Dolly. We want you to phone her pretending to be someone who knows the truth. A blackmailer, if you like. If we're wrong and she's innocent, she'll go straight to the police. If she doesn't, and if she turns up at a rendezvous, then that's proof she has something to hide. The police will take it from there.'

'And you want me to make that call?'

'We need someone mature, someone who might have been a friend of the Kendal midwife. I'm too young, I think, and anyway she knows my voice, so we wondered . . .'

'There'd be no danger,' Ben interjected. 'You wouldn't need

to go anywhere near her, or say who you are. And we'd give you a script.'

'Will you do it?' Barbara asked.

'Try and stop me,' was Dolly's answer. 'It sounds right up my street.'

*   *   *

Her packed cases were by the door, the water was turned off, milk cancelled, key left with neighbour in case of fire. It had been too easy, Maggie thought, looking round the room. She'd be back in a few days, but she'd cleared out the perishables, just in case. Nothing worse than coming home to something stinking in the fridge. She looked down at her hands. Ages ago she'd read something in a magazine . . . if you could pinch together the skin on the back of your hand you were old. Young hands were plump, too plump to let the skin be pinched.

Suddenly and sharply she remembered the last time she had held her baby. She had kissed him one last time, and then tucked *Milly Molly Mandy* inside his shawl because it was the only thing she had to give him. And now he was a grown man. Grey, they'd said, with a family.

For a second Maggie wavered. Then she stood up, reached for her handbag, and made for the door.

*   *   *

'OK,' Ben said, trying to sound confident about a plan that seemed madder by the minute. 'You've gone through the script, and we've blown it up so you can read it easily. It's important to stick to it, Aunt Dolly, because she may try to trick you.'

Dolly was nodding understanding.

'You'll sit here at my desk, and I'll dial the number and I'll hand you the phone. She must believe you're on your own.'

'What if she does 1471?'

'The number's blocked. Anyway, it's my office number. Don't worry. Keep it as brief as you can. If she throws a trick question at you, just repeat the bit about meeting tomorrow. It's possible she may ring straight off, and that's OK. If she doesn't, you ring off when you've said what's written there. Barbara and I are just next door, listening on the speaker-phone. We'll come in if necessary, so don't be scared.'

'I'm not scared, Ben. Let's get on with it. And Barbara, stop looking worked up. It's not becoming.'

'If you're sure . . .' He walked behind her and began to dial the number. Barbara leaned to kiss her aunt and whisper, 'Thank you.' And then the number was ringing out, and it was time to hand the phone to Dolly.

In the outer office they sat on either side of the desk as the ringing ceased and a woman's voice said, '734 8297'. 'It's her,' Barbara mouthed. So far so good.

'Is that Lady Darblay?' came Dolly's voice

'Yes. Who is this?'

'You don't know me, Lady Darblay, but I was a friend of Beryl Rutherford's.'

At the other end of the line there was silence. Ben prayed for Dolly to keep her mouth shut.

After a while Lady Darblay spoke. 'I don't know anyone of that name.'

They hadn't anticipated that response. Dolly was on her own now. Barbara signalled with her eyes to the door, but before Ben could move Dolly was speaking, her tone silky-smooth.

'Oh, I think you do, and I think you know why I'm ringing.'

'She's going off script,' Barbara mouthed. Ben nodded, tense.

'I don't know why you're ringing . . .' This was it, the moment when Lady Darblay would either ring off or talk turkey. '. . . so please tell me.'

'We need to meet. Face to face.' Dolly was back on script – good. But again there was an agonising silence.

'Hold on, Dolly,' Ben breathed – but as he whispered, Dolly spoke again.

'I'm getting tired of this. Be on the steps of the National Gallery at ten o'clock tomorrow morning. Come alone.' Back on script, good!

'How will I know you?'

'I'll know you, your Ladyship, don't worry. But I'll be wearing a green coat. And you'd better bring money with you.'

'She's making it up now,' Barbara said, agitation showing on her face. 'She's going to blow it.'

But the bait was being swallowed. They had not mentioned money because it seemed amateurish, but seemed to be working.

'How much?'

'I'm not greedy. Shall we say £3,000? From your point of view it's worth it, because as far as I'm concerned it ends there.'

There was a click as Dolly put down the receiver, and both Ben and Barbara let out their breath in a gasp of relief.

'You were marvellous, Aunt Dolly,' Barbara said when they were back in the room.

'Even if you didn't stick to the script,' Ben added.

'Was it all right?' Dolly looked unabashed, eyes shining, head erect.

'Helen Mirren couldn't have done better.'

'I've been thinking,' Dolly continued. 'I've got a green coat, and I . . .'

'No!' came simultaneously from both their lips.

'Pity,' Dolly said. 'I could do with a bit of excitement.'

* * *

Barbara decided against going back to chambers, after she had seen Dolly home from Ben's office in a taxi. If she did, she would have to tell Henry what she had done, and she could almost hear the sneer: 'Well, well, we have a Perry Mason among us.' Barristers were supposed to stick to their brief, not seek to influence it. But to hell with that! A man's liberty was at stake and, even more important, so was justice.

Instead she went to see Howard Breen, and filled him in on the day's events. 'So now we wait and see?' he said when he had got over his astonishment.

'Yes. We wait and see, but I'm going to tell Detective Inspector Fisher about it. Unless, of course, Lady Darblay's already been in touch with the police, in which case we're back to square one.'

But the lady had not contacted Frank Fisher. 'What do you think?' Barbara asked anxiously, when she had told him her tale.

'I think it's . . . interesting.'

'Worth following up? So you'll be on the steps of the National Gallery at ten tomorrow?'

'Oh yes, we'll be there. But I hope you won't be. Leave it to the police from here on in.'

* * *

Dolly and Maggie had gossiped and reminisced throughout the evening. Now, both tired out, they sipped Ovaltine laced with whisky.

'How do you feel about tomorrow, Mags? I'm glad you're meeting your son here. When Ben rang tonight, I was going to suggest it, but he was way ahead of me. Better than a hotel, he said – more homely.'

Maggie looked around her at the magnolia walls. It wasn't her idea of homely, but it was lovely nevertheless and, above all, it was family territory.

'I don't know how I feel, Dolly, if I'm truthful. I mean, you can't prepare yourself for something like this. Meeting your flesh and blood after 60 years – more than 60 years. Not that you were prepared for what you did this morning, I shouldn't wonder. Still you always did have nerve for anything.'

'I loved it, Mags. I felt a bit giddy at first – you know, light-headed. But then I thought, "I can do this," and by the time I'd finished I felt almost as though I was a real blackmailer after me pound of flesh. I would love to be there tomorrow morning, just to see what happens.'

'You're doing no such thing! But I hope Lady Darblay does turn up, for our Barbara's sake. She's taking this very seriously. She's a lovely young woman. Our Billy would've been proud of her.'

For a moment they were both misty-eyed, and then Dolly got to her feet. 'Come on, Maggie, we're getting really sloppy now. It must be the Ovaltine. Besides, one way and another, it's going to be a hell of a day tomorrow.'

*   *   *

'I ought to go home and let you get some sleep,' Ben said but he did not stir from the sofa.

'Yes,' Barbara was nodding but she too made no move. At last Ben moved across the space between them and put his arms around her.

'I don't know what's happening any more than you do, Barbara. I only . . .' Suddenly she realised he was shaking with laughter, and she pulled away to look into his face.

'What's so funny?'

'Nothing really. It's just that I rang Adele this afternoon to bring her up to speed, about the case and about the situation at Webcon. And mentioned that you and I . . .'

'You didn't!'

'Not that, but I did tell her that I had considerably warm feelings towards you.'

'What did she say?'

He was laughing as he answered. 'She said . . . she actually shouted . . . "There is a God!"'

Chapter Thirty Three

BEN AND BARBARA SPOKE VERY little at the breakfast table, each tense at the thought of what hung on this day's events.

'Everything is fixed for tonight. Ken Middlemiss is bringing Michael Martin and daughter over. I gather they're coming together.'

'His daughter? I expect he wants moral support. What must be going through his mind? "Will I hate her on sight? Will she hate me?" Sometimes adopted children resent the mother who let them go.'

'I think I disabused Michael Martin of any idea that Maggie willingly let him go. He was taken from her by people who thought they knew best. Half the harm in the world is done by people who act for the very best reasons.'

They were silent then, for the other event of the day and all that depended on it seemed too huge to discuss over toast and marmalade.

* * *

Dolly had carried in a breakfast tray. Now she planted it in Maggie's lap and climbed into the bed beside her. There was no response, not even when she poured out two cups of tea.

'Come on, Mags. It's not that bad. Suppose you don't take to one another? There's nothing spoiling. You didn't have him before; you might not have him after.'

'But things have changed, Dolly. Before, I had this dream of him. Of finding him. I even looked for him, paid out a fortune. But I could always tell myself, "One day. One day." Well, it's here, the one day. If it doesn't work out. there'll be nothing afterwards. No dream, no one day, nothing.'

'Now just stop it, Maggie. Thinking like that'll get you nowhere. Think of it this way. We've been through hell and high water, you and I, in the past 65 years, and we've survived. And we'll survive this, if we have to. But if we don't – if it all goes pear-shaped – well, I like excitement. I thought I had the life I wanted, shopping, dusting a bit, watching *Countdown* in the afternoon and *Midsomer Murders* at night. But that wasn't living, Maggie. This is living, and yes, it's sometimes shitty, but one way and another it's being alive.

'Now drink up your tea, and let's get ready for that phone call from our Barbara. Unless you want us to jump in a cab, and go and see what happens at the National Gallery for ourselves.'

* * *

By mutual agreement Ben and Barbara travelled by Tube. 'We'd never get rid of the car,' Ben said. 'Not anywhere near.' Besides, they shared an unspoken desire to be lost among the crowd on this occasion.

Frank Fisher had made it very clear that he didn't want them there. 'But I've got to be there,' Barbara had told Ben in the small hours of the morning when sleep was evading them both. Now as they were pushed and jostled by the crowds at Charing Cross station, their hands met and twined. 'Can't afford to get separated now,' Ben said.

When they left the station they crossed over and walked down Craven Street, avoiding Trafalgar Square. 'If we bumped straight into her it would be fatal. She'll probably come by taxi, but we can't be sure of that.'

They slipped through Craven Passage and then up Northumberland Avenue, but as they reached the end and the square lay before them, Barbara took fright. 'Should we be doing this? If we blew it I'd never forgive myself.'

Ben nodded. 'I know, but we'll be careful.'

Across the way, Nelson stared down Whitehall; there were parents lifting children on to bronze lions; a man pointing a camera at one of the plinths, and stepping back to get a better shot. It was a bog-standard London morning – and yet a man's fate hung on a set of steps on the far side of the square. He tucked Barbara's arm into his. 'Pretend you only have eyes for me. People turn away from lovers, it embarrasses them.'

A moment later they were in Trafalgar Square and mingling with the tourists, all the while edging closer to their goal. They passed the lions and halted by a fountain. Ben swung Barbara against the rim and positioned himself in front of her. 'I can see,' he said, 'I'll tell you if she appears.' It was five to ten.

They stayed like that for the next ten minutes, sometimes appearing to chat, once kissing – 'Just for dramatic effect,' Ben said. 'I had to force myself to do it.' But all he got in return was a weak little smile.

'Look!' He couldn't bear to see her so tense. 'If it doesn't work we'll try again.' He scanned the approaches to the steps but there was no purposeful figure in view, at least not the one he wanted to see.

'It's no good,' Barbara said, moving to free herself. 'She won't come now.'

Ben scanned the road once more and then lifted his eyes to

the huge doorway at the top of the steps. A figure was emerging.

'She's there!' he said, on a gush of relief. 'She was inside all the time.'

* * *

Terry was waiting in the room when Barbara and Howard Breen entered. He looked haggard and scared.

'It's good news, Terry,' Barbara said quickly.

'Well, it seems like good news,' the solicitor said, ever cautions. They sat down opposite Terry. 'I think we've found out who did kill Julie,' Barbara said. 'It's not definite yet, and I can't give names, but I'm pretty confident. If I'm right, we should know by next week.'

'Next week?' The anguish in Terry's tone was almost tangible.

'I'm afraid these things take time,' Breen said, 'but we may get you out on bail before long. After that there'll have to be a hearing to overturn your conviction . . .'

'But I didn't kill her.'

'I know,' Barbara said soothingly. 'But as it stands now, you did – it's a matter of record. We have to overturn that, and we will.'

'It was her, wasn't it?' he said suddenly. 'Lady Darblay?'

'What makes you say that?'

'She was the only other one there. I told them so right at the beginning, but they didn't listen. Who'd listen to me or take my word against hers?'

There was such bitterness in his tone that Barbara's heart sank. Whatever happened now, the damage was done.

'He's taking it badly,' Howard Breen said as they walked back to the car. 'And who can blame him? Still, he should be grateful to you. If he walks free next week, he'll have you to thank.'

'I still feel I've let him down. I should have suspected her sooner . . . it isn't fair.'

'It seldom is, Barbara. It's called the justice system, but the scales are weighted, I'm afraid.'

* * *

They had tried small talk, so as to avoid thinking about the day's real dramas, but it wasn't working. At last Maggie said, 'If you mention the word "cruise" again, Dolly, I won't be responsible for my actions. I don't fancy *A European Odyssey*, well, not at this moment, and as for *Timeless Japan* . . .'

They never got to know her opinion of the Japanese excursion, for the phone rang at that moment and Dolly leaped to answer it.

'Yes . . . Never! . . . Would you believe it? . . .'

Maggie waited patiently until at last Dolly put down the phone. 'They've got her. She turned up, bold as brass. The police were waiting and they carted her off. She went quietly, apparently, but the detective phoned our Barbara and told her that the gun was in Lady Darblay's bag. In her handbag – so what do you make of that? And to think I might've been there.'

'You're daft enough. Thank Heaven our Barbara saw sense.'

'And Ben . . . he was really protective. He'll make a lovely husband.'

'You're at it again Dolly – romancing. You did a good job for them, but now come back down to earth.'

'All right, is this down to earth enough? I've put two bottles of bubbly in the fridge, and got some vol-au-vents out of the freezer. It's not every day you meet a nephew for the first time . . .'

She broke off at the sight of her sister's face. 'It's going to be all right, Maggie. I promise you, it's going to be all right.'

* * *

Ben didn't feel in the mood for work. It seemed mundane in view of the morning. Nevertheless, there were things he had to do there, and his attention had been diverted for too long. He was deep in columns of figures when the phone rang.

'It's Mrs Webster,' the receptionist said questioningly.

Ben hesitated but it couldn't be shirked.

'Put her through . . . Diana?'

'Have you come to your senses yet, Ben? I've given you time to think.' So that was the line: he was to be forgiven and welcomed back, the penitent sinner.

'Yes, Diana. I think you could fairly say I've come to my senses.'

'Good. Well, the sooner you come home the better.'

'I won't be coming home. It isn't home, and, thinking back, it never has been. Now, as they say in Hollywood, your people will hear from my people. Goodbye.'

He could hear Diana's outrage as he put down the phone.

* * *

Dolly could see them through the window, getting out of two cars, the detective shepherding them up the path. Suddenly she panicked. Should she say 'your mother' or 'my sister', or stick to 'Mrs Riley'? It was Ben who saved the day, gently separating Michael Martin from the others and shepherding him towards the dining-room. 'She's in here,' he said, and pushed open the door.

Dolly turned back towards the younger woman, who was staring at her father's retreating back with apprehension on her face. Dolly held out her hand. 'You must be . . .?'

'Jennifer,' the woman said. 'Jen for short.'

'Well, Jen, I'm your great-aunt, which is no mean feat as I'm only 39.'

The woman's expression lifted, and her eyes smiled. 'You're wearing well,' she said. 'I hope it's in our genes.'

* * *

For a moment there was silence in the room as mother and son stared at one another. Ben stood, uncertain whether to retreat or effect an introduction. At last Maggie spoke, and Ben was proud of the way she controlled her voice. 'I've waited a long time for this, but I've never once stopped loving you.'

The man was advancing towards her now, and Ben felt a pricking behind his eyes. Time to get lost, and leave mother and son together.

* * *

Barbara had watched her aunt and the girl, and relaxed as they appeared to laugh and talk a little, but now Aunt Dolly was looking tearful. 'It's getting to her,' Barbara thought, and came forward. 'Do you want to see to some coffee, Aunt Dolly?' she said firmly. 'I'll look after . . .?'

'It's Jennifer,' Dolly said, obviously relieved.

'Hello, Jennifer. I'm Barbara and, if I've got it right, I'm your father's cousin. Anyway, we're related. Let's sit down, and see if we can unravel it all.'

Ben felt strange as he came back into the living-room. So much emotion was contained within this little house, both behind him in the dining-room and here. He watched as Barbara took Dolly's place on the sofa, and, after a moment, followed Dolly to the kitchen.

'I'm not crying,' she said defiantly as he entered to find her dabbing her eyes. 'There's nothing to cry about. It's going to be lovely.'

'Come here,' he said firmly, and folded his arms around her when she obeyed.

* * *

'So the three children were split up. Aunt Dolly and my father were both adopted, though to different homes. Aunt Maggie, your grandmother, went to a children's institution. When she was 14 she went into service, with a titled family. But they didn't take very good care of her. She . . .' Barbara hesitated. How did you disguise rape? 'She was taken advantage of, and your father was born when she was only 15.'

'Did she want him?' Jennifer's eyes were anguished.

'She wanted him very much, but she was just a child herself, and wasn't given any choice about keeping him. She gave him up because there was nothing else she could do.'

'I wondered.' Jennifer's eyes were moist. 'I didn't know about it until I was a teenager, and then Mum told me that Gran and Grandpa had adopted Dad as a tiny baby.'

'Aunt Maggie looked for him,' Barbara said. 'As soon as she had some money, she employed a detective, but he didn't find anything. And then Ben . . . Ben Webster . . . found out about it, and he managed to trace your father.'

'Dad said no at first. He came to tell me and he said, "I've turned them down, Jen." I think he did it for me, because didn't know how I'd take to it all.'

'It is a bit overwhelming.' Barbara was smiling but her words were heartfelt. 'It happened to me some months ago, so I know what it's like. But that's a long story.'

'I could tell he really wanted it . . . to meet his mother, I mean. So I said. "Go for it, Dad."'

'I'm so glad. You'll like Aunt Maggie . . . well, Grandma to you.'

'Laura, that's my daughter, she's quite excited about having another granny. A great-granny, as well.'

'You've told her?' Barbara couldn't help her surprise.

'Yes. She took it very well, better than me at first. They grow up quickly nowadays, don't they? She's 13 going on 40. Dad adores her and she him. If it makes him happy, she'll be OK with it. So will I. Her brother, he's nine . . . well, he just took it in his stride. But that's our Peter all over.'

* * *

Inside Dolly, contentment, at first a little bubble, was blossoming. She put out a hand and stroked Tootsie, freed now from the bedroom. A few months ago all she had had was a dog, and the slow progress of the years to look forward to. Now in this house she had a sister and a niece and a nephew and a great-niece. Family – who would probably turn out to be a bloody nuisance, but would never bore her.

And there would be a wedding to plan for soon – a blind man could see that, whatever Maggie might say. 'I'll wear eau-de-nil,' she thought. Then there would be Mam and Dad's resting-places to be found, and more cruises to take . . . Maggie was a pushover when it came to an argument.

'It's going to be all right, Toots,' she whispered, and smiled benignly all round.

* * *

'They've been in there an age,' Barbara said as she carried the coffee pot back to the kitchen, where Ben was boiling the kettle again.

'They've got 64 years to get through, Barbara. You can't do that in five minutes.'

They were back in the sitting-room and everyone was chatting amicably when Maggie and her son emerged. They weren't touching, but the body language was mutually protective. 'Sit here,' Ben said, vacating the sofa.

But Michael was crossing to his daughter's side and holding out his hand. She smiled, and bent to the bag beside her on the floor. What emerged was a cloth-wrapped bundle. 'They gave me this,' he said, unwrapping and holding up what lay inside.

'It's the *Milly Molly Mandy*.' Dolly clapped her hand to her mouth. 'It's the *Milly Molly Mandy*, down all these years!'

* * *

'Well, it did for me, Ben – him producing that book. You knew she put it in his shawl before they took him away? It was the only thing she had to give him.'

They were alone in the car, speeding towards Notting Hill. 'Don't,' Ben said. 'I'm just as full up as you. All that separation, all that pain – and all my family's fault.'

'No,' Barbara said firmly. 'Not really anyone's fault, except life. Your grandfather didn't plan to abandon them and then get rich. He did what he thought was right for his family at a tough time . . . what anyone might have done. If he'd known that one day there'd be enough money for everyone, he'd have kept those kids. In which case, if I'd been born part of the Webcon empire, I'd have been brought up alongside you and probably would have hated your guts.'

'I think your reasoning's a bit spurious, but I like it.' The car was coming to a halt now and the new house lay before them.

'Do you mind unlit gardens?'

'I adore unlit gardens . . . in the right company.'

In the cold darkness the garden was mysterious, but the branches of the enchanted tree stood dark and intricate against the paler night sky. 'I can see children in this garden,' Ben said, 'nine or ten, I think.'

'Only six . . . if they're mine, that is.'

'Oh, they're definitely yours. We can negotiate numbers later.' And then she was in his arms, and around them bushes rustled approval. 'It's been a hell of a day,' she said, when they paused for breath. 'But satisfying. Definitely satisfying.'

If you've enjoyed this book and would like to find out more about Denise and her novels, why not join the **Denise Robertson Book Club.** Members will receive special offers, early notification of new titles, information on author events and lots more. Membership is free and there is no commitment to buy.

To join, simply send your name and address to **info@deniserobertsonbooks.co.uk** or post your details to The Denise Robertson Book Club, PO Box 58514, Barnes, London SW13 3AE

Other novels by Denise Robertson

All Denise's novels are available from good bookshops price £7.99 Alternatively you can order direct from the publisher with FREE postage and packing by calling the credit card hotline 01903 828503 and quoting DR10TP1.